Born in London ... and English father, Anita spent her childhood moving between the two countries. She met her husband when she was eighteen and they laid down roots in sunny Dorset to raise their four children. With the children now grown and flying the nest, and the family expanding, Anita divides her time between tracing her ancestral roots across Ireland, England and Scandinavia, and writing in her nature filled garden with her cats.

For more information on Anita, on her writing and books, read her blog on anitagriffiths.blogspot.com, follow her on Instagram anitaegriffiths and Twitter @anitaegriffiths and join her on Facebook @anita.e.griffiths (Anita Griffiths Writer)

**By Anita Griffiths**

*The Cobbled Streets saga*

### **Cobbled Streets & Teenage Dreams**

### **Close Your Eyes**

### **Beyond the Ironing Board**

### **The Box**

### **Anam Cara**

*Short Story Collection*

### **Zara**

# Anam Cara

**Anita Griffiths**

ISBN  9798833158401

Cover design by Carina E Photography

and Inkpots & Paper

For Simon,

Mo Anam Cara

xxx

Dedicated to Jackie,

My beautiful, brave sister-in-law.

xxx

# Chapter One

*'It all started with a Christmas wedding in July. Because that's where all good stories start, don't they?'* I muttered the words under my breath as I typed. I was perched on the edge of the office sofa, my bulging tote bag at my feet and a mug of cold coffee on the low table in front of me. I always perch on the sofa – we all do. It's a glorious piece of furniture; wide and long, with a shaped back and upholstered in a deep claret velvet. It deserves to be sat on properly. Maybe I will one day. Kick off my shoes, sit back and sink into it. But not today.

"What are you up to?" Linda peered over my hunched shoulders at the laptop balanced on my knees.

"I'm doing the blog."

"Oh, but isn't that Annabelle's job?"

I nodded, running a hand through my tangle of auburn curls. "Yes, only she's off sick with concussion and a broken arm."

"How on earth did that happen? And do you want a fresh cup?" She pulled a face as she picked the mug up. "This is stone cold, Bree!"

I laughed. "Yes, I know. I was on my way to the kitchen to get a fresh one but then Annabelle phoned and…"

"What *did* happen?"

"She fell out of her apple tree. Landed awkwardly, as you do."

"My God, she never does things by halves, does she!" Linda perched next to me. (Yes, *perched*.) "I'm not sure she'll thank you for doing her job, though. I mean, she's quite protective of her blog, isn't she?"

"I know, but …"

"And you have enough on your plate right now." She patted my knee, standing up again. "Seriously Bree, do yourself a favour and leave it. The blog can wait."

I gave her a resigned nod, trying to hide my frustration at her advice. Linda is head of admin and mother figure to all the staff, and her word is usually gospel, but on this occasion, I chose to ignore her. She's right of course; I *have* got enough on my plate, but I hate leaving deadlines to the last minute. Yes, the blog is Annabelle's responsibility but the whole department is mine and I thrive on running a tight ship.

I landed the job of *Wedding and Events Coordinator*, at this beautiful Tudor manor, completely by chance some three years ago. The twins had started sixth form and Patrick had left for university, in Exeter. He was only a two-hour drive from our home in the pretty Dorset village of Corfe Castle but not seeing him every day completely threw me. I suddenly felt superfluous. I needed to be doing something more than two afternoons a week at the doctors' surgery. More than cooking and cleaning an already spotless house. And the big five-o was looming fast, filling me with an unfamiliar sense of panic. Age had never bothered me before, until Patrick was gone.

"You need a proper job," my best friend, Julia, had said. "None of this helping out at the surgery just because your neighbour happens to be the GP. You need something to really sink your teeth into. And I know somebody who knows somebody at Athelhampton House, and their wedding coordinator has just left."

"But I know nothing about weddings!"

"So?" she snorted. "You know how to talk to people, and you know how to organise stuff. Sorted. You'll be fantastic!"

And she was right. I sailed through the interview and threw myself into my new role, one hundred percent. It was exactly what I needed. Geoff, however, had been less than thrilled. My husband likes his ordered life, his ordered home. He didn't like me going out to work and he particularly didn't like that I was developing a new circle of friends. *My* friends, not ours. I can see his point, really, I can. He's always been a bit jealous of new people in my life – not that he has anything to worry about, but I know it's a struggle for him. I put it down to him being an only child with an overprotective mother. She doted on him completely – and I mean, *completely.* It doesn't take a genius to see that my in-law's marriage is not a happy one. Not like ours. And she compensated for that lack of love from her husband by pouring all of hers into Geoff. And he expects that same devotion from me. I won't lie; it's been a test of strength sometimes and I have often felt like a mum of four children, not three, but on the whole, we work well together. We're a team.

He could see the job at Athelhampton House made me happy, took my mind off missing Patrick, and he mellowed with time. In return, I keep my work social life to a minimum, which isn't that hard, to be fair. We're all married with families. However, Julia, my lovely best friend of twenty-three years, divorced and remarried, can also be demanding sometimes, wanting my attention but I am a dab hand at juggling, dividing myself up between them all. I don't complain – far from it – I consider myself blessed. Lucky.

I'm lying of course; I *do* complain. Not often but come on, I defy any mother to say family life is a constant bed of roses.

The office door opened and Len, our security guard, ushered in a man I didn't recognise. Late thirties, tall, thin – but not scrawny – dressed in jeans and a worn t-shirt, with a camera bag strapped across his chest and a holdall in his hand. The photographer we'd hired – not quite what I was expecting.

I smoothed down the skirt of my tailored summer dress as I stood up and pulled a natty little cardigan over my bare shoulders. Raising a hand of thanks to Len, I smiled at the man in front of me. He gave me the briefest of smiles in return; the type that doesn't even reach your eyes.

"Hi, I'm Niall Feenan. You must be Annabelle." He took my offered hand and shook it. He seemed irritated. Even that unmistakable Irish lilt couldn't disguise it. I love accents, especially Irish ones, so I chose to ignore his apparent bad mood.

"Hello, Niall. I'm sorry but Annabelle isn't here today, so you'll be working just with me. I'm Bree."

"As in, the cheese? How are you spelling that?" The corner of his mouth twitched but the rest of his face remained dead pan.

"As in, short for Brianna."

"Ah." He regarded me for a moment. "But you prefer Bree? I suppose that's more American; I'm guessing your accent *is* American?"

I nodded; the smile still fixed on my face. "It is. But my grandparents were Irish."

"Really?" He inclined his head then glanced at his watch. He may as well have come right out and said, '*not interested in what you have to say*'. Flustered but determined not to let it show, I quickly shut my laptop and picked up my bag.

"I'm so sorry, I didn't realise the time. Is it nine already?"

"Only just. I got here early. I was told to wait in the reception hall for Annabelle, but I think your security guard got fed up with me just hanging around."

I was about to object to his judgment of Len but thought better of it.

"Right. I'm sorry, I was a bit distracted. Shall we?" I gestured to the door and led the way back down to the hall. "Have you been to Athelhampton House before?" He shook his head. "Oh, you're in for a treat, then."

I have a well-rehearsed spiel used for prospective couples that I thought I'd impart on Niall but something about the noncommittal grunt he emitted, put me off. As if I wasn't nervous enough already about today – not that he could possibly know that, but his bristliness wasn't helping one bit.

It's a huge project I've undertaken; huge for me, anyway. I've spent the past year diligently attending evening classes twice a week, in web design and business management. Initially, it was just something to do that could be useful, but its primary function was to, once again, fill the void made by my children leaving home. The twins – Sean and Kitty – had aced their A-levels and landed places at their first choices of university, in Bath and London. And although I was beyond sad to see Sean go, it was Kitty that had left the greatest hole. She was turning into a wonderfully caring, funny,

5

young lady and our relationship had shifted from mother-daughter to the closest of friends.

"You can never be friends with your children," Geoff's elderly aunt had said. "Not if you want to remain in control."

I begged to differ but just smiled and listened, choosing to ignore yet another of Aunt Maud's outdated pearls of wisdom.

When the day came for the twins to leave, the wrench was unbearable. The silence afterwards, even more so. The ache in my chest made me panic; I wasn't sure if I was going to collapse and vomit or just drown in my tears. I'd never experienced pain like it and I couldn't see how to move forward. I felt totally bereft and the slightest thing set me off; the mug tree laden with clean mugs, the washing bin barely half full, the food shopping a fraction of what it used to be. I had damp tissues permanently stuffed up my sleeve for those first few weeks – months, even. I longed for the chaos, the constant noise, the bickering, the infectious laughter, the loud music and even louder TV. I yearned for the hugs and chatter, the demands to know what's for dinner, the groans at early morning alarms and the mad dash to catch the school bus. Most of all, I longed to be a full-time mum; to be needed.

"I need you", Geoff had said when I tried to explain, through watery sobs, how I was feeling. I know he'll always need me but it's not the same.

It had been Kitty's idea for the evening classes.

"I can see you as an independent wedding co-ordinator. Weddings are big business now; why tie yourself down to just one venue when you have so much expertise to offer?

Besides, if you have your own business up and running by the time I graduate, you can help me set up mine!"

I wasn't so sure about leaving the safety of Athelhampton House, wasn't as confident in my abilities as Kitty was but I did like the idea of learning a skill that could help the children in the future. And despite my misgivings, I actually did really well. I worried that I'd be that old cliché mum who is completely baffled by technology but no, I '*excelled*', as my tutor said. And now, I am putting everything I've learnt, into practice. Persuading my boss, Martyn, to give me free run to design a new website had been remarkably easy. I had intended to redesign the online wedding brochure, but he was so enthused that he asked me to take charge of a new website, to include the house and gardens overall. Already a busy tourist attraction, he felt it could do with a boost, a revamp, and he put all his faith in my abilities.

"What have I let myself in for?" had become my most uttered phrase of late, as my confidence dwindled.

"But Mum, you *know* what you're doing, you *know* what you want to achieve, so just believe in yourself," had become Kitty's most used reply to my crisis of confidence calls. "Start with your winter wedding brochure. You love Christmas. Be inspired!"

I'd spent hours scouring other wedding venue websites, borrowing ideas I thought could work in the Tudor manor house, while Annabelle searched for a local photographer to work with. Niall Feenan's portfolio stood out by a mile compared to the rest, and I gave her the green light to hire him. They had exchanged a few emails and he had seemed friendly enough but now I was regretting not having spoken to him in person first. His easy-going, no-nonsense chat online was one thing; in real life, his charm was distinctly lacking.

"The Great Hall," I announced. "This is where we hold the ceremony, then move on to the Coach House for the reception. If it's a bigger wedding, they can have the ceremony in the Long Hall, which is part of the Coach House, so I want to cover both options."

We stood in silence for a moment, admiring the room; the dark panelling dramatically offset by the pale stone walls above it. Flames flickered in the impressive stone fireplace at the far end of the room. I know it seems daft lighting a fire in the height of summer but even on the hottest day, this room has a chill in the air. Besides, it adds to the atmosphere.

We had spent the previous afternoon decorating it for a winter wedding; '*we*' being myself and a small team from a local event stylist. They're new to the game and part of my grand scheme to revamp things. Exciting and nerve-wracking at the same time but I needn't have worried; we worked together so well. They took onboard all my ideas and executed them perfectly.

A net of twinkling fairy lights hung over the panelling surrounding the fireplace, bringing that part of the room to life. In front of the fireplace, an elegant centrepiece of white and red roses dominated the dark oak table where the register is usually signed. A twelve-foot artificial Christmas tree stood by the window, laden with oversized baubles, velvet bows, glass beads and a string of soft white lights weaving through the boughs. We had placed rows of chairs, five deep, on either side of the room, and lined the aisle with heavy duty brass lanterns. There was only so much we could do with the room so as not to detract from its gothic beauty, but I was really pleased with the finished effect.

I waited for his approval but when it wasn't forthcoming, I asked for it anyway.

"What do you think?"

He inclined his head. "It's stunning," he said quietly. "You've done a good job."

I felt ridiculously pleased. I got the impression he doesn't give praise lightly. Funny how quickly you can assess somebody's character, isn't it?

"Thank you! I just love Christmas, don't you? I wish I could go crazy, do the whole magical grotto kind of thing but we have standards. It has to be classy. Understated."

"And it is. I love the fairy lights; they'll work well in the photos."

I nodded, pleased. "I got the idea from a venue in York. It's an old barn and they have a curtain of lights hanging from the far wall, just where the bride and groom stand to take their vows. It looks incredible, so romantic."

"Do you mean The Normans?"

I stared at him in surprise. "Yes! You know it?"

"I've been there. A friend's wedding. And yes, it was beautiful. Lighting is key for these kinds of venues."

I listened to him intently, my smile growing. I couldn't believe he'd been to the venue I've styled most of my ideas on. What are the chances?

I watched him sizing up the space, visualising the best angles, checking for natural light from the leaded stained-glass windows. It struck me how much he looked like a nineties Jon Bon Jovi. Not a bad look.

Turning, he caught my expression and looked away abruptly. I've often been told I have a very transparent face, like an open book, and he'd just seen the teenager in me, swooning over a rock star. Oh well, it's not like the day was going particularly well anyway. I pretended it hadn't happened and carried on talking – an old tactic I've used plenty of times over the years.

"I would've loved a Christmas wedding. I would've had the full works; reams of thick tinsel, hundreds of baubles, fairy lights everywhere, a *huge* tree – bigger than this one. A snow machine!" I laughed at my own suggestion. He shot me a look and shook his head.

"You've just crossed the line from classy to tacky."

"That's the story of my life," I sighed. "I never get it quite right."

He straightened from his crouched position, watching me. "I was joking."

I waved a dismissive hand. "I know. I'm just … never mind. So, no snow machine for the picture shoot?"

He laughed lightly, shaking his head, unpacking a lens from his case. "Have you been married long?"

"Yes," I nodded. "Twenty-two years. Ours was a summer wedding. A big marquee at my in-law's country house. Pimm's on the terrace, that kind of thing. Very British. Very proper. You?"

"I got married last year."

"Ooh, where?"

"Dorchester registry office. And a pub lunch afterwards." He watched my face drop. "Not quite a Pimm's reception." The derision in his voice was unmistakable. I could feel my cheeks burn – not unusual for a red-head – stunned by his sudden rudeness. He picked up his discarded holdall.

"You said the house opens up to visitors from midday, right?" He glanced at his watch again. "Shall we make a start?"

"Yes, of course," I nodded. "I have a list of things I want included." I pulled a file from my bag but stopped short when I saw his raised hand.

"I have a copy. Annabelle emailed it to me."

"Right, yes, she did. Shall I ... leave you to get set up? Coffee? Tea?" I could feel my forced smile wavering, waiting for his reply. He barely nodded.

"Coffee, please. One sugar."

The rest of the day followed in the same vein. He would be indifferent – sullen – and then he'd say something encouraging or complimentary about my plans for the website, but when I responded and chatted back, he withdrew and practically ignored me. It was exhausting! His mood reminded me so much of my boys when they hit puberty. I thought the days of walking on eggshells were long gone; apparently not.

As I sat behind the wheel of my car at the end of the day, I watched him carefully put his equipment in the boot of his clapped-out Fiat, then slam the door shut, making the car shake. I honestly thought it was going to fall apart in cartoon fashion. Sensing I was watching him, he turned and gave me a curt nod. I raised my hand and forced a smile.

"See you tomorrow!" I know he heard but he chose to ignore me. He revved up his engine and without a backward glance, was off down the country road heading for

Dorchester. I sat back in my seat, closing my eyes. I don't know why it bothered me so much. I suppose I'm just used to people being nice to me and vice versa. I hate an atmosphere. I think deep down, I just need to be liked. And when I'm not, it crushes my confidence so easily.

Ed Sheeran blasted out when I turned the ignition and I tapped along to *Shape of You*, as I watched the roof of my convertible slowly come down, folding effortlessly into a neat pile behind the back seat headrests. I smiled up at the afternoon sun, taking in a lungful of warm air filled with the heady perfume from the oriental lilies that grow in large stone pots, dotted around the car park.

I love my car, it's my pride and joy. Geoff bought it for me shortly after Patrick left for university. It seems an extravagant 'pick me up' but I really appreciated it. Still do. It helps that no other mum in Corfe Castle has a yellow Volkswagen Beetle Cabriolet convertible – I do like to be different.

The drive home is definitely the highlight of my day, especially during the summer months. Athelhampton House lies sixteen miles from Corfe Castle, nestled in lush countryside on the edge of the Piddle valley. Very rural, very picturesque. Initially, when I first started the job, I took the back route in a bid to avoid traffic but after the fourth time of reversing along a winding country road to let oncoming lorries and tractors pass, I opted for the safer, slower route. Either way, the scenery is beautiful, soul restoring. I never take it for granted, and I've been here a long time. Twenty-four years – nearly half my life. I feel more British than American, although, in fact, I'm all Irish.

I was on my way to Dublin, to visit the birthplace of my grandparents, via England. I'd planned a short stop here to visit Dorset; more specifically, Corfe Castle. As a child I was a huge fan of the *Famous Five* books and when I discovered that Kirrin Island was based on Corfe Castle, I made it my mission to visit. I hadn't intended on staying long. Or meeting the man of my dreams. Or settling down where my childhood heroes were created by Enid Blyton.

The commute takes half an hour on a good day. I would say it's my time to unwind but there's very little stress in my job, so it's more my time to reflect. Clear my head. Just enjoy the journey. It's very green – as you'd expect for Dorset.

Verges stuffed with tall grasses, wild yarrow and hogweed, soon give way to neatly planted edges, filled with cheerful bedding, as the market town of Wareham draws nearer. It's where the children went to secondary school and I still find myself expecting to catch a glimpse of them, or their friends, ambling down the road to the bus stop.

Wareham's a beautiful town; small and pretty, with the River Frome running through it. We spent many happy hours down by the stone bridge, feeding the ducks and eating ice creams, when the children were younger. Or taking one of the hire boats down the river, shouting greetings to the curious cows watching our noisy journey from the safety of their field.

Those trips inevitably ended with one of the children in tears – usually Sean – as they bickered over the oars or the seat at the back of the boat. Sean wasn't a cry baby as such, but he did struggle with being the 'middle' child, despite being Kitty's twin. Patrick was the leader, the head boy, the voice of authority. Kitty was the bossy one, the one who strived to do everything better than the others, and then let them know she had achieved it. Neither meant any harm; it's just the natural order of siblings, I suppose. But they've all grown into wonderful young adults; all very close, all very caring. I worried that they'd drift apart once uni life took over but no, they keep in close contact with each other. In fact, Patrick has spent more time visiting Sean in Bath than he has visiting us. He rarely comes home. Very rarely. I try not to let it bother me. I don't want to be that mum who demands a visit, but it does hurt. He phones me though and sends a message most days. Just a *'Hi, I'm fine, how are you, Mum?'* And that's good enough for me. I know he's busy with his studies, especially now that he'll be starting his fourth year, doing a Masters in Geology.

Once out of Wareham, and after a usual stop-off to pick up some groceries from the local Sainsbury's, the wild verges take precedence once again. Coconut-scented yellow gorse fluoresces along the final stretch to our village, wedged between two hills and dominated by the castle ruins. The jackdaws that screeched in every *Famous Five* story, nest in the ruins and surrounding trees. I love the sound they make. I could sit and watch them for hours, as they strut about the grounds, then break into an ungainly, hobbledy run before taking to the sky, squawking loudly. I know *hobbledy* isn't a word, but it should be; if only to describe how a jackdaw runs.

There are two roads in Corfe Castle: East Street and West Street. East Street runs through the village and on to Swanage and the coast. West Street runs off the Square and up to the common. It's the quiet road, with delightful chocolate box cottages of stone. Some have thatched roofs, others have slate. The front gardens – if you can call the tiny strips of grass a garden – billow with flowers of all colours and sizes; anything that will grow is welcomed to enhance the beauty and charm. Roses and ivy cling to walls, self-seeded poppies sprout by doorsteps, and swallows claim space under eaves. Every inch is used by nature. It is teeming with life.

Our cottage is the prettiest on West Street. I know I'm biased but I'm also right. It's a detached seventeenth century rubble stone and thatched roofed cottage, oozing character and history. We fell in love with it instantly and have lived here for our entire married life. I can't imagine living anywhere else, I really can't. I know four bedrooms seems excessive now that they've all gone but they'll be back. Maybe not for long but it will always be their home. Besides, I've invested so much time in doing it up, getting it exactly how I want it. And the garden is my haven. It's where I start and end the day, especially during the summer months, watching the butterflies flit through the crowded borders, and bees burrow into foxglove blooms.

The best bit about coming home – aside from all the beauty that I harp on about endlessly – is the greeting I get from Pip, my beloved Jack Russell. You wouldn't believe she's eleven years old, the way she jumps up and down and spins on the spot in her excitement. She's a joy. She's my best friend; yes, even more so than Julia.

Work clothes off, comfy jeans and trainers on, and we head straight out for the common, my mind longing for the cup of coffee in the garden that'll be my reward once we're back from Pip's walk. It's the simple things in life; nothing can beat it.

# Chapter Two

"And then he had the cheek to say he'd need to start straight away tomorrow, with no interruptions because we had wasted too much time today with our *'preliminary chat'*," I angrily did air quotes. "Can you believe it! Such a rude man! I've got no time for people like that."

Geoff and I were in the kitchen, clearing away after dinner. I hadn't wasted much time telling him all about my disastrous day.

"And yet, you've spent the past forty minutes talking about nothing else but the rude man. Should I be worried?" he replied. I gasped in mock horror and threw the tea towel I'd been using, at his head. He ducked effortlessly, laughing at my abysmal aim.

"Of course you should be worried! Have I not just explained what a catch he is?"

He chuckled but I saw a flicker of jealousy cross his face. It was only fleeting; however, I knew it was time to change the subject. "More wine? *Line of Duty* before bed?" I took our glasses through to the front room.

"So, after tomorrow, is that it?"

I frowned. "What do you mean?"

"The photographer. How long will it take?"

"He's booked for two weeks, Geoff!"

His eyes narrowed. "Two weeks? Why so long?"

"I told you why. Didn't you listen?" I laughed lightly. "Never mind that now; shall we watch an episode? Have we got time for two? I've had enough of thinking about work." I snuggled up to him on the sofa, nestling under his outstretched arm. I didn't want to admit to him that I was

17

really quite nervous about working with Niall. And the fact that he had other commitments so could only fit in a few hours here and there over the next two weeks, didn't help either. I would've much rather got it all over and done within a few long days, but Annabelle hadn't run the scheduling by me before booking him. Then again, his was the best portfolio so I would just have to grin and bear it.

Geoff groaned when the alarm went off the next morning. I'm always up first – years of children waking at the ungodly hour of five a.m. – but even I lingered longer than usual under the duvet.

"Why do we keep doing this to ourselves?" he muttered. "We said *one* episode, not four!"

That's the trouble with watching things on catch-up. There's no such thing as a cliff hanger anymore; you just click on to the next episode. And *Line of Duty* draws you in and ends each episode with you needing to watch more. And regret it the next day when the alarm goes off.

"Early night tonight," he said, stretching as he headed for the bathroom.

"We can't!" I called after him. "I'm out with Julia and you're off to see Matthew." I heard him swear under his breath, resigned to another late night. "Julia might crash here tonight," I added, wincing at his expletive.

It's not that he minds Julia, not at all, but she can be quite loud and loves to chat, especially first thing in the morning. Geoff has never been a morning person; he would often disappear to work early when the children were younger, to avoid their morning chatter. In his mind, an early drive to work rather than suffer breakfast with them, was the lesser of the two evils. I didn't mind. It meant I could let them enjoy their morning routine without worrying about keeping the noise down. All that's changed now but Geoff is still not a morning person, and he prefers to disappear early rather than feel obliged to walk Pip with me before work.

I sat in the car park at work, leaning on the steering wheel and smiling inanely as I watched a fluffy, juvenile robin hop along the ivy clad wall, in pursuit of its parent rooting around in the foliage for insects. The fluffball finally caught up with said parent and was rewarded with a mouthful of food. He showed his appreciation by flapping his downy wings, opening his beak for more. More morsels, more wing flapping, more hopping along the wall in tandem. I could watch this all day.

Athelhampton House shone proudly in the early morning sun, its buff stone walls glowing. When it comes to stone, I consider myself a bit of an expert – after all, it is the family trade. I'm kidding – I had to ask Geoff and he *is* the expert.

The manor house, built in the late fifteenth century, and later restored in eighteen-ninety-one, is constructed from ashlar – large, rectangular blocks of limestone with squared edges – and Ham Hill stone for the dressings round the windows. Ham Hill stone is also used for features throughout the gardens; there are twenty-nine acres of gardens, both formal and informal, stuffed with an abundance of plants, trees, fountains and obelisks, all beautifully offset by the River Piddle which runs round the boundary.

With features such as the Great Hall and its stained-glass window, it makes for the perfect wedding venue, steeped in history and romantic charm. I really am living every American's dream, working in a lovingly preserved Tudor manor house, bursting with history, and raising a family in an idyllic village, home to a romantic castle ruin.

And that's basically the spiel I would've given Niall Feenan, if he'd been bothered enough to listen.

I was getting out of the car when Niall arrived. He pulled up next to me. I noticed his jeans and t-shirt had been replaced with a smarter pair of chinos and a cotton shirt. His whole demeanour was less unkempt. He smiled.

"I'm sorry about yesterday, Brianna. I realise I was rude and grouchy. In my defence, I hadn't slept in four nights, and I really don't do well with a lack of sleep."

I blinked, taken aback by the change in him. Even his voice was different, his pitch lower, tone softer, accentuating that wonderful, southern accent.

"Why haven't you slept?" I asked.

"My daughter, Layla, is teething. And the Calpol we've been spoon feeding her religiously, only kicked in last night." He held out his hand to shake mine. "I hope we can start again? I would appreciate that."

I took his hand, laughing, feeling unusually shy. "Of course we can. And don't worry; I've been there, done that. I had twins, so double whammy with the teething! You *will* survive it. You *will* get over it. And she will grow into a beautiful, bubbly little girl, rather than the red-faced, screaming monster you're seeing right now."

"She'd better! Actually, she's been a model child until now. It's not her fault, I know, but it's so wearing."

"That's usually the way. Wait until you've had three."

"*Three!* Well, you deserve a medal. And now I feel so bad being grouchy about *one* child."

The way he smiled at me, for some reason, made me blush. I quickly stuck my head back in the car, busying myself with an imaginary mess in my bag. He was still smiling when I straightened up again. He nodded towards the house.

"So, go on then – tell me the history of this place."

I shook my head, suddenly reminded of how insignificant he'd made me feel the day before. And my face being the mirror that it is, told him exactly that. A flash of remorse darkened his eyes but undeterred, he continued.

"I know it's a Grade One listed building. And it's very haunted. See, I did my homework!"

Unable to help myself, I laughed. "But did you know it's haunted by a monkey?"

His eyes widened. "No!"

"Family pet, apparently. Sorry, I can only give you half marks for your homework effort," I teased. "And did you know the original film of *Sleuth*, with Michael Caine and Lawrence Olivier, was filmed here?"

He shook his head. "No, I didn't. I've not seen the film although obviously, I've heard of it."

"I've not seen it either, but my husband has. He raves about it." It felt good to be talking. He seemed like a completely different person. Amazing what a good night's sleep can do.

"What does he do, your husband?"

"He's a company director of a branch of quarries, locally."

"Oh."

"Basically, his father and uncle founded the company years ago and gave their sons jobs as soon as they were old enough."

"I see. So, quite well off then."

"And I'm guessing you don't like money."

"Oh no, the opposite; I wish I had more of it. But I tend to not like the people who have it in abundance. Present company excluded, of course." He did a mock bow, making me chuckle.

"We're not *that* well off. The company is probably worth a fortune, but we don't see much of it." I tried not to sound like I was defending myself. He looked pointedly at the Radley tote bag hanging from my arm, then at my car, which at that precise moment, was caught by the sun and gleamed expensively. He raised his eyebrows, a knowing smile aching to erupt across his face.

"Okay," I laughed, "we see a fair bit of it." I started walking towards the house, indicating for him to walk with me. "If I'm honest, that was half his appeal. I come from nothing, so marrying into money wasn't a bad move. Is that too shocking?"

"Not really, but somehow, I don't think that's true. You strike me as far too genuine to be that devious."

"You're right," I nodded, "I have no excuse; we're loaded and we're probably the type of people you despise. Quite rightly. I think we're disgusting." For once I managed to keep a dead pan face. He looked mortified.

"Now, hang on, that's not what I meant at all!"

"I know, I'm just teasing! Now, tell me about Layla. How old is she?"

The day couldn't have been more different than the previous one. We got on so well. I felt quite guilty about the way I'd bad-mouthed him to Geoff. He was nothing but polite and funny, and incredibly professional in his work. We chatted amiably about our children, about his wife, Lizzie, and about Geoff. He was like the brother I never had. In fact, he reminded me of my best friend in college, Dean.

Dean and I were inseparable for the years of our studies, and then for the years that followed until, aged twenty-six, I headed off on my adventures to England and Ireland. Dean was going to come with me but only three months before our departure, he'd met and fallen head over heels in love with James. I was a bit in love with James too, so I couldn't blame him, but I did regret him not coming with me. He would've loved Dorset, although I suspect he would have got restless after a while and headed off for London instead. We still keep in touch. And he's still with James. So, everything worked out for the best in the end. But I do miss male friendship. I've never found it here. Maybe it's because I met Geoff so soon after arriving, and making other friendships went out of the window a bit. Especially male ones.

"It went amazingly well!" I replied to Geoff's inquiry of how my day had gone. He asked with that fake sincerity, that simpering tone people use when you've been ill; *'and how are you feeling today'*, knowing that the answer is going to be a negative one. Geoff poked his head round the bathroom door, pulling his tie undone.

"Really? How come?"

I turned from the mirror, mascara brush in hand, and kissed his cheek. "I don't know, he just seemed to change overnight. Huge relief! How was your day?"

He grunted, nodding. "Fine. The usual. What time is Julia here?"

"In about half an hour. There's lasagne defrosting in the fridge, so just whack it in the microwave for a few minutes." I turned back to the mirror, deliberately avoiding the dejected face he was pulling. Initially, I had felt so guilty about going out and leaving him to his own devices; I think he knew and played on it quite a bit. But to be fair, I have only been going out regularly with Julia since the twins left, whereas Geoff has been having a weekly night out with Matthew for years. Every Friday, without fail. I did suggest once that he stay in and spend it with the family – there was a film on that the children wanted him to watch with them – but he was what can only be described as, apologetically adamant. *'Blame Julia'*, had been his reasoning.

Julia and Matthew, Geoff's cousin and business partner, were once married. That's how I met Geoff. Julia was working at the Knoll House Hotel in Studland, where I was staying when I first arrived. I'd chosen it because it's the hotel that Enid Blyton used to stay in every year on her holidays in Dorset. It seemed the obvious choice for me. Anyway, Julia was the receptionist there and we hit it off instantly. She and Matthew hadn't been married long and were still in the honeymoon period, all very lovey-dovey. It was infectious. I was invited to one of the family Sunday lunches and that's where I met Geoff. He was such a typical Brit and more uncannily, such a grown-up version of my childhood crush, Julian. Yes, I know, Julian is the slightly obnoxious one of the *Famous Five*, but I loved him. It wasn't difficult falling in love with Geoff either. He's still a bit of a Julian but he's mellowed with age.

Anyway, Julia and Matthew's marriage ended very acrimoniously eight years ago. Matthew had met somebody else. It was as simple as that, except Julia hadn't seen it coming at all. She still thought they were blissfully happy. When she discovered that Tamzin had two young children and that had been part of the appeal, she was beyond devastated. She and Matthew had ached for children – obsessively so – until after a third miscarriage, they agreed to stop trying and start living instead.

Understandably, Julia didn't let Matthew leave without giving him a piece of her mind. All the frustration and boxed away grief came flooding out. Unfortunately, she didn't let it rest there.  She sought out Tamzin and turned up on her doorstep, venting her anger. Her behaviour was such that the rest of the family, instead of taking pity on her and shunning Matthew, took pity on Matthew and turned their backs on Julia. They welcomed Tamzin, turning a blind eye to the circumstances behind their union. I couldn't join them; I was appalled at Matthew's behaviour. Appalled at what Julia had been driven to. And then karma happened.

After less than a year, Tamzin met somebody else. Matthew hadn't seen it coming. He thought they were blissfully happy. After a month of heavy drinking and another month to sober up, Matthew came crawling back to Julia, full of remorse at what he'd thrown away. Julia didn't exactly laugh in his face, but she made it clear how she felt. She moved on with her life, met a lovely man named Curtis, and they're now happily married and living across the bay, in nearby Poole.

Matthew never recovered. Single, sorry for himself and very lonely, he's a shadow of the charismatic man he once was. And poor Geoff feels dutybound to bolster him, to keep him company, to rebuild his ego. It's a very slow process; I don't envy him at all.

"See you later; we'll be back some time after ten I should think." I planted a kiss on Geoff's cheek, giving him a little twirl so that he could appreciate my new dress.

"You look lovely," he said, wiping coral Charlotte Tilbury lipstick from his face. "I'll aim to be back at the same time, then. Have fun, ladies." He extended his smile to Julia, nodding approval at her strappy dress; a red version of my navy one. "Did you two shop together, by any chance?"

"Yes!" we chorused, laughing at the ridiculous question. We always shop together, as he well knows.

I hadn't been to Dorchester for a night out in ages, although my evening classes were there, and I do like to shop there every now and then. Julia and I tend to favour Poole or Swanage, or sometimes Weymouth, for our nights out together. Closer to home. There's a different kind of buzz in Dorchester; for a start, it's not a coastal town. It's lively but not as loud. I prefer it, if I'm honest.

We had a lovely pasta meal at Zizzi's in Brewery Square – they do an amazing dish with lots of peppers – then went on to Tom Brown's on the High Street. You could hear the live music all the way down the street, the bass thumping out through the old windows. It's a great pub, full of character. Again, I hadn't been there in ages, but Julia's colleague had raved about a particular band that plays there, so we'd arranged a meet-up.

The heat hit us as Julia pushed the door open. The pub was heaving. We scoured the sea of faces for Maxine and Claire but to no avail.

"I'll phone her," Julia said, then took my hand and pulled me to the other side of the pub. I spotted a hand waving at us above the mass of heads, like a beacon guiding a ship through mist.

"You made it!" Maxine shouted, hugging us. "I tried to get as close as I could."

To be fair, had she got any closer, we would be sitting on the band's laps. Before I took my seat, I glanced over at the lead singer and caught my breath.

"What?" Julia asked, following my gaze. I leant towards her, and half shouted in her ear.

"It's him!"

"Who?"

"*Niall*!"

"Where? *Who*?"

Just as I was not so subtly pointing at him, the song came to an end, and he caught my eye. He looked as surprised as I did, then grinned. He spoke into his mic.

"Look lively, lads, my boss just walked through the door." Then he held a hand up to me. "Evening, Brianna."

Suddenly all eyes were on me, and a cheer went up. Some even clapped. I sat down abruptly next to Julia, willing my crimson face to cool down. It did not. Maxine stared at me in utter disbelief.

"You *know* him?" She didn't expect an answer, it was more of an accusation; a '*how dare you know the guy I have a crush on*'. Maxine's lovely though, like a younger version of Julia, and her cousin, Claire, is a younger version of me. Funny how opposites attract, not just in relationships but in friendships too.

"Well, you didn't tell me *that* about him," Julia said.

"What, that he's a singer? I had no idea!"

"No, I meant, you didn't tell me how good looking he is." Maxine nodded in agreement, still eyeing me suspiciously.

"I hadn't noticed," I shrugged. Julia snorted.

"Oh, come off it, Bree! Even married women notice things like that. Besides, it's pretty hard to miss." On cue, we all turned to look at him. It made sense now, the whole Bon Jovi look. The artistic temperament.

There's four in the band; two guitarists, a bassist and a drummer. Niall plays lead guitar and sings. He has a good voice. I didn't recognise any of the songs.

"No, it's all their own stuff," Maxine said. "They're called Stray Dogs."

After a while, the band took a break and Niall headed straight over to us. I think Maxine stopped breathing.

"Hello! I did not expect to see you here," he said to me.

"Yes, snap! What a surprise. I had no idea you're in a band."

"Well, why would you?"

"It was Maxine who suggested it; she's seen you here before." I quickly introduced her and the others to him. He shook their hands, thanking Maxine for bringing us along. She pulled out her phone and asked if she could take a photo of us all. He smiled – such a broad, open smile – and offered to do the honours. He pulled a chair up next to

28

Claire and we all leaned in to him, bright smiles that lingered long after he'd finished taking photos.

I had expected Maxine to chat to him, but she seemed dumbstruck. So, it was up to me, and after our great day together, it wasn't so hard.

"So, photography is just your day job," I said.

"No, photography *is* my job; this is my hobby." He took a glug of beer that somebody put in front of him and put his thumb up by way of thanks. I suspect he often gets given pints by the punters.

"A pretty good hobby! You sound great, Niall."

"Thanks."

"You're a bit like Jason Mraz," I continued. He grimaced.

"Ah. I was going more for Imagine Dragons – if you know who they are."

"Of course I do! I have teenagers. I know things." We both laughed. The drummer called him, he made his apologies and left us staring after him.

"So, tell me again that you haven't noticed how lovely he is," Julia insisted. I shook my head in mock despair.

"Alright, he's lovely. But ladies, get over it – he's married and a dad. A pretty devoted one at that."

We didn't chat much; we were far too busy watching the band. Niall was mesmerising. I wasn't alone in thinking it; he seemed to have the whole pub hanging on his every word.

Once they'd finished playing and packed away, Niall came over to our table. He rested a hand on my shoulder.

"See you tomorrow, Brianna. Night, ladies, thank you for coming." He graced us all with that smile again, then held a hand up in farewell to punters as he passed by their tables.

29

"Tomorrow?" Julia mouthed. I waved a dismissive hand at her and watched him walk out the door. We all watched him.

"He's got to get home to help with Layla. She's teething," I said, with an authority that suggested I know him well and for a lot longer than forty-eight hours. Forty-eight hours – is that all? It's crazy how quickly we can connect with people, and they become part of our daily lives, as if they've always been there.

Not long after, we parted company with Maxine and Claire, and headed back to my car, linking arms, Julia a little unsteady on her feet. It was my turn to be the designated driver. Neither of us drink much when we go out together, but I think Julia had been trying to keep up with Maxine.

"What did he mean, '*see you tomorrow*'?"

I tightened my grip of her arm as she slipped on the cobbles.

"Oh, there's a wedding at the house tomorrow and he's coming to take a few photos of the Coach House, before the guests arrive."

"I see." There was something about that, '*I see*' – her whole tone – that annoyed me a little. Why is it as soon as there's a good-looking guy on the scene, everybody assumes you fancy them? It's so juvenile.

"I don't fancy him, Julia."

"I didn't say you did. But now that you mention it..." she smiled.

"Shut up and get in the car," I laughed, silently cursing myself for falling into her trap.

Luckily, it was soon forgotten about. She kept dozing off, so conversation was sparse. Ed Sheeran filled the silence, as he always does in my car.

Back home, I poured us both a glass of wine and stuck on an episode of *Friends*, as is our tradition after a night out. We kicked off our shoes and curled up on the sofa, and it wasn't long before Julia was sound asleep.

"Morning!" I put a mug of tea on Geoff's bedside chest and tapped his shoulder. He grunted and rolled onto the other side of the bed. "Geoff, I'm off. See you later." That got his attention. He rolled back and opened bleary eyes.

"Off where?"

"Work."

He sat up. "What time is it?"

"Just gone nine. What time did you get in? I didn't hear you come home."

"After one. I deliberately didn't wake you. Sorry." He pulled a face.

"How is Matthew?"

"Same old. I don't think he'll ever change now."

"Maybe don't mention that to Julia. She's still asleep. Can you make her breakfast when she wakes up, before she drives back home?"

He nodded. "Of course. What time are you back?"

"Lunch time, maybe sooner." I pulled back the curtains and headed for the door.

"Pub lunch when you're done? Or a picnic?" he suggested.

"Lovely. You choose. See you later."

I poked my head round the door of Kitty's room. Julia was still fast asleep. Downstairs, Pip was also fast asleep, stretched out on the front room floor in a patch of sunshine. It's her favourite spot after our morning walk, then she moves to the kitchen as the sun moves round to the back of the house. She's a sun worshipper, like me, and our kitchen is south facing, which means uninterrupted sunshine for most of the day.

I love our kitchen; it's the room I spent most time on to get it just right. It's the heart of the home, as my nana always said, and it deserves attention to detail. When we bought the cottage, there were three reception rooms and a smallish kitchen downstairs. We had the kitchen and back reception room knocked through, giving us a space that stretched the breadth of the house, overlooking the garden, with patio doors opening wide to let the sun in and children out. The larger of the front rooms became our family room and the smaller one, just off from the generously sized hall, was commandeered by Geoff, initially as an office but quickly became his bolt hole from noisy children.

Geoff's family were appalled at our choice of home, although its beauty didn't go unnoticed. They'd expected us to opt for something grander, something more akin to their houses, something more in keeping with Geoff's position. It wasn't what we wanted. Geoff's description of his childhood home was brief: *too big, too cold. Soulless.* Not the sort of home we hankered for to raise our family in. I wanted cosy, I wanted warmth, I wanted space for the children to play, to explore, to express creativity. The kitchen became their art studio, their music room, their space for weaving train tracks, their place to build a cosy den under the table.

"No dining room? Where will you host dinner parties?" had been the family's first question as they eyed the large, rustic table of worn pine, taking centre stage in our airy country kitchen. An old upright piano and solid pine Welsh dresser complimented the array of cream and pine cupboards and old cast iron Aga; everything bathed in perpetual sunlight, which warmed the flagstone floor. Flagstone from Geoff's quarry, no less.

"Here!" I smiled, undeterred. "Why have a room that is rarely used when it's so much cosier in the kitchen."

Geoff's father raised sanctimonious eyebrows, his uncle gave me a look of disdain (one he has perfected well, over the years), his grandmother tutted loudly and shook her head. However, his mother, Jessica, smiled and quietly touched my arm – I took that as a sign of approval. I'd spotted that unmistakable look of envy but also of relief. That's when I knew I had won her over; I was good enough for her son.

Geoff had confessed to me once that he loved his mother unconditionally, respected his father as much as he feared him, and hated their home with a passion. It had been a daunting, lonely place to grow up as an only child, with rooms reserved for entertaining and show. No space for train tracks. No floors welcoming muddy wellies, fresh from playing outside. No tolerance for music-making – or noise of any kind, for that matter.

As it happens, we have hosted many successful dinner parties in our kitchen and even my stuffy father-in-law relented eventually, and enjoyed himself, leaning back in one of our imperfectly perfect kitchen chairs. He even accepted that Pip always joins in with family meals; I saw him reach under the table once, to pet her and offer her a chunk of cheese. The sight of him laughing at one of Sean's

33

terrible juvenile jokes and patting his leg affectionately as they sat side by side to eat, filled me with joy. It filled Geoff with regret.

Niall was already there, leaning against his car, when I arrived at Athelhampton House. He waved as I pulled up.

"Morning, Brianna. How are you?"

"Fine, thank you. Last night was great. You were incredible!"

He laughed, embarrassed, and squinted at me. "Thanks."

Realising how it had sounded, and worse, how he had tried to ignore how it had sounded, threw me into a bit of a fluster.

"I mean, you and the band were fantastic. At singing." Why do I even bother? I just dig a bigger hole.

"It's okay, I know what you meant. And thank you. Again. Shall we?" He gestured towards the house.

"Good idea. Before I embarrass myself even further."

I made coffee and he got straight to work. It didn't take him long to get all the shots I needed, and he was soon off again. I stayed to greet the wedding party, hovered in the background during the ceremony and then handed over to the reception staff before leaving. It's the best part of my job; watching the whole day that has been in the planning for more than a year, take off without a hitch. Usually.

I checked my phone before driving off. A message from Julia.

*'Sorry if I've put my foot in it. I mentioned to Geoff about last night and seeing Niall at the pub. He didn't seem too impressed. Text me when you're home xxx'*

That's typical Julia, always making something more out of nothing. Why would Geoff be upset by that? I can imagine what she said though, probably emphasizing Niall's good looks and the attention he paid us. She knows how Geoff reacts to new people in my life, so why say anything at all. The fact that I hadn't, just made it worse now, as if I had something to hide.

I fretted about it all the way home, running through different scenarios in my head. Geoff doesn't have many faults, but jealousy and possessiveness are definitely his two strongest. However, I've learnt how to soothe and negotiate around them, so I don't know why I was so worried this time.

As it turned out, it was exactly as I'd initially predicted; Julia making a big thing about nothing. Geoff didn't mention anything about it to me. He'd made up a picnic and we drove down to Studland beach. It was busy but nothing compared to the masses that invade during tourist season - only two weeks away now. We found a quiet spot and had a lazy late lunch, watching Pip dart back and forth at the gently lapping waves.

"Did Julia get off alright this morning?" I asked, desperate to steer the conversation and clear the air about Niall. He nodded; eyes closed against the sun.

"Yes. A bit of a headache but she was fine. I made her beans on toast; that's all she wanted." He didn't ask about our evening out as I'd hoped, so I left it. Best forgotten now.

It wasn't until we were getting ready for bed, cleaning our teeth together in the bathroom, that he broached the subject.

"Did you see the photographer today?"

"Niall? Yes, he took photos before the wedding. I can't wait to start putting the website together."

"And last night?" He stared at me through the mirror. "Why didn't you tell me you were with him last night?"

My heart sank. I couldn't tell if he was angry or hurt. Betrayed. I should've said something sooner.

"I wasn't with him, Geoff. He was playing at the pub. I had no idea he's in a band. I think you'd like them," I smiled back at his reflection. He rinsed his brush and dropped it smartly into the holder, making me wait for his response.

"Would I? Pub bands aren't really our thing though, are they? They're just glorified buskers. When he plays The Pavilion, then maybe we can go." I tried not to wince at his cutting tone. "So, what's changed to make you all pally with him? I thought you couldn't stand him a few days ago."

"I know; you're right. I misjudged him. He was tired. Serious lack of sleep makes anybody grouchy, unreasonable. Remember how you struggled when they were teething?"

Geoff shook his head. "No. I don't think I struggled."

"That's because you stayed away as much as possible!" I teased. "But you did struggle with the broken nights; I remember it well." I took his hand. Should I say anything more? Yes, I needed to.

"Does it bother you? That I'm making a new friend, I mean. Because it shouldn't. He's *just* a friend. Besides, he's ten years younger than me, happily married with a baby. Why would he be interested in me?"

"But what about you? He's very good looking." There's that insecurity creeping through that he always tries to disguise.

36

"According to Julia, yes! According to me – not as good looking as you, by a long shot."

We hugged and kissed and then Niall was forgotten about. For now.

# Chapter Three

"Tell me about your music; how come you're a photographer and not a musician? That's not to say your photography isn't any good; it's just, how did you choose?"

We were taking a break in the gardens, drinking coffee and idly watching visitors stroll through.

"It chose me. Sounds daft, I know. I always dreamt of being in a band, touring the world, that kind of thing. The usual teenage fantasies. And I pursued it but not wholeheartedly, not enough to get me anywhere. My dad was on at me to get a proper job, to stop messing around. I did the busking, the pubs, the county show. Then I got disheartened and bummed about for a bit, doing nothing except odd jobs. I had a massive row with my dad – it'd been brewing for years – and so I left. Came over to England."

"When was this?"

"Seven years ago." He stared off into the distance, troubled. I'd obviously touched a nerve. I was aching to ask if he had reconciled with his dad, but I guessed that would probably trouble him further.

"And the photography?"

"Ah, well, after my dramatic exit from home, I went to stay with my aunt, to cool down a bit and beg some money for my journey. She went above and beyond to help. She gave me more than enough money, she bought me a plane ticket from Dublin to London and gave me a parting gift. It was a Nikon camera. '*Record your travels*,' she said, '*and send me photos*.' Which is what I did. And I discovered I was actually very good at it, without much effort. So, I practiced and practiced, then did a few weddings and christenings and slowly built up a name for myself. Then I branched out into wildlife photography and landscapes and discovered I'm not bad at that either."

"*Not bad.* You're brilliant!"

He smiled. "Thanks."

"But if you arrived in London, how did you end up in Dorchester? And why England in the first place?"

He gave a short laugh. "Well, I chose England because I knew it would annoy my dad. He hates the English! Then, on the plane, I got talking to this couple who were on their way to a music festival on the Isle of Wight, via London. So I tagged along. Met a girl there from Dorchester and the rest is history, as they say."

"Lizzie?"

"No, somebody else. It didn't last long. Story of my life."

"And did you make it up with your dad?"

He shook his head. I was aching to ask more questions, but I didn't want to be the nosy inquisitor, and I sensed his mind was drawn to darker memories. One day I would ask more about his dad – their relationship – but that would have to wait.

We both waved at the gardener as he passed by, his wheelbarrow laden with pots of bedding, fresh from the greenhouse.

"He's been here for years," I told Niall. "So long, he's like part of the family."

Niall stared up at the house, scanning the windows for signs of life. There was none.

"I can't imagine living here, raising a family. They must be so out of touch with the real world."

"Not at all! They're really down to earth and very much hands on. The kids go to the local school, they have local friends, all very normal," I said. "They're lovely."

"But it's been in the family for generations, right?"

"Yes. But it's nothing like *Downton Abbey*. You won't find footmen and lady's maids here."

He laughed. "Lizzie is obsessed with *Downton Abbey*."

"So am I! To be honest, I thought this place *would* be like Downton initially and that was half the appeal. I'd love it if we got to wear the costumes; can you imagine? That'd be awesome! Who would Lizzie be, if she was in Downton?"

"Mary. Without a doubt."

I nodded. "Good choice. Her clothes are beautiful. A bit bossy though?"

He laughed. "Yes. Like I said, definitely a Mary." There was no hint of malice. It was obvious that Lizzie likened herself to Mary and why not. A woman who stood no nonsense and no doubt would grow to be as formidable as her granny, The Dowager Countess.

"How about you, Niall?"

He raised his eyebrows. "You have to ask? I'd be Branson, the Irish rebel who hates all you aristocrats with a passion! Who would you be?"

"I'd be Sybil. She's my favourite. A bit quirky, a bit stubborn."

"Oh dear. You'll be stuck with moody Branson, then die in childbirth. You would've been better choosing Mary or Edith. Or Cora – she's American, so you've got a head start with the accent."

"You're right. And she's probably more my age. I just never think of myself as fifty."

"Are you?" The look he gave me was hard to decipher. Had he just not considered it and was surprised at how youthful I look or was he thinking I looked older than that. I'll never know.

"Well, nearly. Next month, actually. August eighteenth."

He was still studying my face. "Big party? Let me guess; a ball, somewhere really fancy?"

"No! A party at our house. Just a little gathering; family and friends. You should come. You and Lizzie." I watched him frown. "Please! I'd love it. You can help boost the peasant-side numbers. So far, there's just me, Julia and a few friends from here. The rest of the guests are Geoff's family and business friends, so I could do with the moral support." I joked but it wasn't far off the truth. I was getting nervous about it, to be honest.

"Okay. Thanks, that would be great. I think." He pulled a scared face and laughed. "How are Geoff's family with the working class?"

"Oh, don't worry, they won't even notice you. The hired help is usually invisible, don't you know." For some reason, we laughed for ages at the thought. It wasn't even that funny. But it felt good to have an ally. That sounds bad, doesn't it. I know I paint a negative picture of Geoff's family, but they really are a lot to take. So opinionated, so stuck in their ways, and so insufferably smug. Individually, they're okay but put them all together and it's enough to make me want to run to the hills. Thank goodness Geoff isn't like them. If it weren't for the striking family resemblance, I'd feel sure he was adopted.

All too soon, it was Niall's last day at the house. I felt really flat. I've had enough of people I care about leaving me. Niall seemed very low key too. We cheered ourselves up with cake and coffee at the garden café, sitting under a wide parasol. Despite its shade, the heat was still stifling. I fanned my face with the table menu.

"Brianna, I've had an idea. How about adding some location shots on the website; nearby attractions. Maybe Dorchester, Swanage pier, Corfe Castle; that kind of thing."

I stared at him, eyes wide. "I was thinking exactly that, only last night!"

"Me too. Last night. So … a good idea?"

"Yes! You should include Old Harry Rocks and maybe, Durlston Country Park, in Swanage." I pulled out my notebook to jot ideas down.

"I haven't been to Old Harry Rocks in years. I tend to forget about Studland, for some reason," he said.

"Oh, Studland is my favourite place. Pip's too. She and I walk for hours over there."

"Not Geoff?"

"Rarely. He did when the kids were little but nowadays it's just me and Pip. He's usually busy with work, you see."

"Come with me, then," he suggested. "Tomorrow? I could drive over to Corfe, take some shots of the village and castle ruins, then we could go on to Studland."

Our mood lifted, we sat for a while planning an itinerary. I wasn't convinced we'd need shots of all the locations we both came up with, but it was fun planning it and would be a great excuse for a couple of days out, away from the house but still under the guise of work. It was exciting.

Niall pulled up outside my house on the dot of half past nine. Pip darted out as soon as I opened the front door and greeted him like an old friend. She jumped up and down and ran rings round his ankles, barking joyfully, then threw herself at his feet.

"Don't mind her, she's a bit of an old floozy," I said, pulling the door shut behind me.

He bent to stroke her outstretched belly. "I'd be gutted if she didn't like me. I love dogs. We always had dogs when I was growing up."

"Me too. And a daft old cat who seemed to live forever."

We strolled down to the square, chatting about our childhood pets. Niall took photos of the pubs, the National Trust shop and café, and plenty of the castle ruins.

"Fancy a climb?" I asked. "The view of the castle from that hill is incredible." I pointed to West Hill, to the left of the ruins. We followed the path by the stream that runs alongside the foot of the castle mound, crossed the wooden bridge and began the ascent. It's a walk I do regularly and have done for many years. Pip raced on ahead, then turned, panting, watching us catch her up.

As I said, the view is spectacular. It looks down on the castle ruins and across to the adjacent sheep studded Challow Hill. In the distance, Poole Harbour – argued to be one of the largest natural harbours in the world – basks in that particular light you only find on the coast.

As if on cue, the ever-popular steam train puffed its way along the heritage tracks on the other side of the castle, shooting up a dense cloud of white smoke. Bright green carriages glinted in the early morning sun. Niall was in his element, snapping away, capturing a moment in time with

43

an ease I found fascinating. I pointed out other things of interest which he dutifully photographed, then we sat for a while in silence, soaking up the scenery.

"I could sit here all day," he said softly. I murmured agreement.

"I often do! But it's better with company. Pip's great but she doesn't share my enthusiasm when I spot a kestrel hunting over on that hill, or an Adonis Blue resting on the vetch."

"Can't say I've ever seen an Adonis Blue."

"Really? We should go to Durlston – there are loads of butterflies over there. Do you do much wildlife photography? I mean, butterflies and other insects. Flowers?"

"Yes. Getting into it more than before. I find it restful; more so than I thought I would. I didn't ever envisage myself being just a wedding photographer and I'm glad I pushed my boundaries. Did you see my feature in the *Dorset Magazine* last year?"

"No! Have you got a copy? I'd love to see it."

The church bell struck eleven, bringing us back to life. We headed back home, stopping at the bakery in the Square to get some warm pasties for lunch. I'd already packed a bag with water and biscuits for Pip and a flask of coffee for us. I shook my car keys.

"Shall we take my car?"

"What's wrong with mine?"

I shrugged, smiling. "Nothing. But would you rather travel in style in my open-topped beauty or bump along in your clapped-out old thing?"

"*Clapped-out*? Don't mince your words, will you." He shook his head in mock disgust.

"What would you call it?" I challenged.

"Pre-loved. Upcycled. Well-travelled. Oh, I know: *vintage*. Everybody loves vintage. It's all the rage." He spread his hands out. "Your choice: in-your-face privilege, or vintage."

"I am not privileged!" I opened the door for Pip. "Jump in, Princess Pip-squeak. Make room for the hired help – if he cares to join us."

"Fine, fine," he laughed. "But please tell me that is *not* her name!"

"Oh, but it is." I flashed him a smile as I put on my expensive, polished tortoise Ray-bans. He shook his head again, trying not to laugh.

"You really are something else."


Old Harry is one of the jewels of the Jurassic Coast, which stretches along the south coast from Exmouth in Devon, to Studland, on the Isle of Purbeck, in Dorset. There were huge parties locally when it became a World Heritage Site in 2001.

Old Harry Rocks are made up of three chalk formations, Old Harry itself being the solitary chalk stack standing furthest out to sea. Old Harry's Wife was the stack next to him but eroded and collapsed some years ago, and all that remains is a stump. I always feel she deserved a name of her own rather than just being 'the wife', but then again, maybe I'm just overthinking and personifying what is, essentially, a lump of chalk.

Studland has a special place in my heart, it really does. I came as a naïve tourist on a bit of a whim, fell in love – with both Studland and Geoff – and have since adopted it as my home. Initially, I wanted to settle in Studland but then fell for the romantic lure of Corfe Castle, five miles inland. I've made it my mission to explore every inch of the Purbecks and I instilled my infectious love for it in my children. I just didn't ever consider that one day they would grow up and leave, move further afield, and I would still be here to do the exploring, alone. Geoff grew up here amongst all this and doesn't have the same fascination or hankering to explore it as I do. Picnics and evening walks with Pip on the beach are about his limit, I'm afraid.

The walk up to the rocks from the car park in Studland is a tranquil heat trap, hemmed in by thick gorse bushes on one side and hedged farmland on the other. Birds flit, sheep bleat and cows rumble, instantly calming the senses. Pip knows this walk inside out but I always keep her on a lead; too many horror stories of dogs running full pelt off the cliff edge, have made me so cautious.

Niall ventured right to the edge by the rocks and wandered on to get as many different angles as he could. Pip and I watched from the safety of flat ground, near the edge of a wooded copse. He eventually re-joined us, looking pleased.

"I'd forgotten how stunning it is out here. And the way the light bounces off the chalk – a photographer's dream. Sorry, I don't mean to bore you." He watched me stifle a yawn.

"I'm not bored, honestly. Just a bit of a headache, that's all." I offered him a pastie and poured some coffee. "I'm glad you love it here. I knew you would."

He frowned at my face. "You look a bit peaky, actually. Shall I run back to the corner shop and get some painkillers? They're bound to have paracetamol or something, there."

Embarrassed by the fuss, I reassured him I was fine, and we slipped into a comfortable silence, watching the butterflies dance above our heads, and listening to the gulls screech as they soared across the washed sky. Pip stretched out on the warm grass and closed her eyes. I longed to do the same. My head was starting to throb and every inch of me wanted to lie down.

"Come on, Brianna, let's get you home," Niall said, watching my face with concern. He offered a hand to pull me up.

"I'm sorry. I think I'm coming down with a cold or something. I feel a bit fluey."

He took my backpack without asking and threw it across his shoulder, along with his camera bag. "Do you need an arm to hold?" he offered, taking Pip's lead. Two weeks ago, I would have blushed profusely at such a suggestion from him but now I linked my arm through his, as if we'd been linking arms forever.

The look on his face when I suggested he drive, was priceless. Like a little boy in a sweetshop, being offered the most expensive sweets but trying not to show his absolute delight at it. Ten minutes later, he pulled up outside my house and patted the steering wheel.

"Not a bad drive," he smiled. He jumped out and opened my car door, then followed me to the front door.

"Coffee?" I asked. He shook his head.

"No but thank you. I'll leave you to rest. And make sure you do!" He made a fuss of Pip, deposited my bag on the hall floor and turned to leave. "I'll phone you in the morning. Take care of yourself now."

47

I felt a little empty once he'd left. I had so wanted the day to last longer but my head was seriously banging. Pip followed me upstairs to bed and curled up by my knees. We were both fast asleep within seconds.

I didn't feel brilliant the next day. Nothing really specific, just achy all over and a dull head, as I explained to Annabelle when I phoned in sick. I've never phoned in sick before; I felt such a fraud. Especially as five minutes later, I was on the phone to Niall, inviting him round so that we could work from home. It would be the same as if we were working in the office, only with fewer distractions. I was dying to see the end result of all his efforts and equally excited to finally be getting to grips with building the website.

Coffee and paracetamol helped lift my head, so by the time he arrived, I was back to my usual cheery self. We got straight to work, scrutinising the photographs, which far exceeded my expectations. He has a way of capturing light and colour that make other professionals work pale by comparison.

Niall stretched and looked round the kitchen when I got up to put the kettle on.

"You have a great place here, Brianna. I love this kitchen." He pointed at the Aga, standing up to get a better look at it. "That is so cool! Does it work?"

"It does. It's the first thing I bought for the house. And it was my first mistake. But I'm glad you like it; I love it so much."

"Mistake, how?" He ran his hand across the barge art on the doors; bright posies of flowers in red, orange and blue, on a granite backdrop. I'd found this gem in a store in

Dorchester and fallen in love with its unusual, customised paint work. It reminded me of an Edina Ronay knitting pattern I once had for a cardigan, inspired by traditional Hungarian embroidery.

"Mistake because it's gaudy rather than classy. And it's not *the* brand of Aga that the others have. I had no idea, you see. I just thought, an Aga is an Aga."

"And isn't it?"

I laughed and shook my head. "No, it is not."

He watched me for a while. "I get the impression you haven't had an easy time of it with Geoff's family. Sorry if I'm overstepping the mark."

"You're not, it's fine. When they heard where I'm from, everybody expected this brash American. I think they were relieved when they met me; they thought I'd be easy to mould into what they wanted me to be. Sometimes, I wish I was that brash American rather than the meek and mild one I am. But I think I've stood my ground, in my own way, on so many things. It hasn't always been easy though."

"But Geoff supports you?"

"Yes, he does. He's not like them, really. He said his cousins always bossed him about, especially the girls. Matthew has three sisters, and their husbands are just as pompous. Sorry, that sounds so mean of me! I must sound really ungrateful." I busied myself making coffee, regretting I'd sounded so spiteful about the family.

"Not at all," he said quietly, then reading my mind, changed the subject. "Where did you grow up?"

"Brooklyn. A different world to Dorset. How about you?"

"Cork."

49

"I thought so, with that accent. My dad's grandparents were from Cork."

"Were they?" He took the mugs back to the table while I grabbed the biscuit barrel from the side. "And did they settle in Brooklyn?"

"They did, yes. And their son, my Pops, married my Granny, from Kilkenny. My mum's parents – Nana and Granda – were from Dublin. They both came to America when they were one and grew up together."

"Did the families emigrate together or was it just by chance?"

"Together. My great grandfather's cousin was killed in the Easter Rising and the family feared for their safety, especially the young men – they were all so close, you see – so he and his best friend fled with their wives and children to America. They arrived in Brooklyn with nothing more than the clothes on their backs but there was already a big Irish community there, so they were taken in and looked after, helped to get on their feet. His brother came out soon after with his parents. None of them ever left Brooklyn. Until me."

"And what made you leave?"

"I was on my way to Dublin, to see where they came from. Then I was going to go on to Cork."

"Have you been?"

I shook my head.

"Have you been to Ireland at all?"

"No. I met Geoff, had a family and then never had the time."

"You should go. You have time now. Besides, you're a hundred percent Irish so you have a duty to." He laughed but I could tell he was serious. I could also tell he was quite impressed with my heritage.

"Nana and Granda always dreamt of going back to see where they were born but never did. So yes, I suppose if nothing else, I should do it for them." Excusing myself, I disappeared into the front room, bringing a book back with me.

"This was my Nana's book. Granda gave it to her on her eighty-third birthday. He died five years later. She died six months after him." I handed him the book. A well-thumbed gold and black hardback, decorated with a Celtic knot design, entitled *Anam Cara – A Book of Celtic Wisdom.*

"It means *soulmate*. Look – he wrote a dedication to her. I love it." I showed him the handwriting I knew of old.

*For my one true love, my soulmate. Mo Anam Cara.*

"*Anam Cara.* Yes, it does. That's a beautiful book. And a beautiful story. I can't imagine knowing somebody my *whole* life. They must have known each other inside out."

"They did. They certainly taught us all about family values. They doted on us when we were kids. And they loved their great grandchildren. I go back to Brooklyn once a year to visit my family – always have done – so they got to meet their great grandchildren from England, too. Only a few times but I'm glad they did."

# Chapter Four

"I'm sorry. If I could spend the whole day shopping, then I would. There's nothing I'd love more."

"Right!" I laughed, hitting Geoff's arm. "You hate shopping and don't deny it."

We were off to Dorchester to buy him a new shirt for my party. Initially, we were going to make a day of it – have lunch out and take our time in the shops – but Geoff had been called in to work at the last minute, so could only spare an hour. Matthew had arranged to pick him up from Dorchester, leaving me to shop for a party dress alone.

"They do know you're the CEO, don't they? And Sunday is a day off?"

"You've just hit the nail on the head, Bree. I *am* the CEO and I need to be there when things go wrong. This contract is too important to ignore. Sorry."

"Not as sorry as you'll be when you see how much I spend in your absence," I teased. Yes, I was a little annoyed at the change in plans, but secretly, very proud of him. The contract he was fretting over, was a huge one for the company and it was down to his efforts alone that had secured it.

Geoff flicked on the CD player in my car and frowned.

"What's this? What happened to Ed Sheeran?"

"Oh, I fancied a change. It's Imagine Dragons."

"Who?"

"A band Patrick likes," I smiled.

"Oh, right." He stared at the passing hedgerow. "Has he said yet if he's coming home for your birthday?"

"He can't. I said we'd go down and celebrate with him there."

"I don't think I can. I'm busy."

I shot him a look. "I haven't said when it is yet." The silence that followed was weighted to say the least. "What is it with you and Patrick, anyway?"

"How do you mean?" He didn't look at me.

"You both seem so distant with each other."

"Do we?"

I sighed. "Yes. You know you do, just by the way you said, *do we?*"

"You're seeing too much into it, Bree. He's growing up. He doesn't need me."

"He doesn't need me either, but I still want to see him. I miss him."

He turned and gave me a sympathetic smile, suddenly remembering all the tears.

"Well, you go down and spend a weekend with him. I'll find you somewhere nice to stay that allows dogs. Okay?"

"Okay."

What is it with sons and fathers? You'd think after the way Geoff's relationship with his father had gone, he would do everything to avoid that happening with his own son. I couldn't understand it. They used to be fine, until Patrick left for university. Did Geoff resent him? University had passed him by. He had gone straight from sixth form to work for his father and learn the trade. And when he had suggested Patrick do the same, he had been deeply disappointed that he declined. Patrick wanted the uni experience; he wanted the education. As it is, he'll leave with a Masters in Geology and have a whole library of knowledge and new skills to bring to the family firm – if that's what he eventually chooses to do. I don't put pressure on them. I believe in them finding their own paths, making up their own minds. Another thing for the family to frown upon and tut at.

The week flew by quickly and Friday dawned bright and sunny, just for me.

"Happy Birthday, darling!" Geoff woke me with a breakfast tray of coffee, croissants, a bowl of strawberries and a bouquet of roses. I say *woke me*, but in fact I'd been awake for ages, feigning sleep so as not to ruin his surprise. I always get excited for birthdays, like a giddy girl, and this one was no exception.

Kitty and Sean were due later in the day and Patrick sent a text first thing. The tick list of party preparations for Saturday was complete – just flowers to arrive on the day and the catering, of course. I had initially suggested doing the food myself, but Geoff wouldn't hear of it, for which I was quietly grateful.

I was regretting not taking the day off; it was promising to be a scorcher and I quite fancied a day by myself in the garden and maybe a walk on the beach with Pip. But I'm glad I went in. Annabelle had stayed late the night before to decorate. She'd hung up birthday banners around the office and scattered glitter confetti on my desk. A bunch of pink and silver *50th Birthday* balloons hovered by my chair and a huge bouquet of mixed summer flowers sat in a beautiful crystal vase on my desk. The card attached told me they were from my boss, Martyn, his wife and children. A small pile of wrapped gifts and cards had been laid out on the couch, along with a packet of my favourite chocolate covered digestives. Annabelle had put a little sticky note on it; *No expense spared! xx.* She always jokes about my basic taste in biscuits. It's the same with chocolate. I'm not a fan of fancy chocolates; those overly decorated morsels with bits of gold leaf or dried fruit. Galaxy is my favourite, plain and simple. Or Cadburys. I'm not even keen on things like fruit and nut; I feel like I've somehow been cheated out of chocolate.

By the time the others arrived at work, I'd inspected each of the gifts, trying to guess what was under the wrapping paper, and made an indent on the biscuits. The tray bakes I bought to share were calling me from the kitchen, but I resisted. I had an inkling Linda had baked a cake for me. It's her hobby – one she's very good at.

She didn't disappoint. I was serenaded by the team and presented with a Malteser cake, adorned with a diamanté *50* and edged with sugar paste pink roses. The cake was heaven, the gifts were beautiful, and the Bucks Fizz was a pleasant surprise. We had such a relaxed, cheerful morning and despite all the reminders of my milestone age, I certainly didn't feel it.

"You never do," Linda said. "I dreaded fifty and then I dreaded sixty but nothing's changed. I'm sixty-two but in my head, I'm still twenty-five."

By the time I got home and took Pip for her walk, both Sean and Kitty had texted to say they were on the train. Both had finished uni for the summer weeks ago but neither had wanted to come home. Kitty loves London life too much, and besides, she had bagged herself a summer job at a little boutique just off Covent Garden. Retail isn't her thing per se, but fashion is.

55

Sean was off to Berlin with some friends, and before that, he'd opted to do very little. He makes me laugh. He's become such a cliché student; partying all night, sleeping all day and living on a diet of pot noodles and take-aways. I told him to embrace it. I haven't mentioned it to Geoff though. I know they will all adopt his work ethic when the time comes, but for now, they need to enjoy their last bit of freedom before adult life takes over. And before they know it, they'll be clapping their hands and watching the cake topper sparklers shine like cascading diamonds, on their fiftieth birthday cake.

Geoff had booked a table at the Old Granary, our favourite pub in Wareham. Right on the quay, overlooking the river, it's always been our place to go for birthdays, ever since the children were small. I tried to ignore the fact that Patrick wasn't with us.

"Happy birthday, my beautiful wife," Geoff said dramatically, handing me a small oblong package. I opened it and lifted the lid to find a key nestled in gold tissue paper. I frowned. He passed me an envelope. He'd written across a photo of a beach hut; *your new retreat.* I gasped loudly.

"You've bought me a beach hut? On Studland?" I recognised it. One of a row I always pass further up along on South Beach. Away from where the crowds tend to congregate by the National Trust café on Knoll Beach and the equally busy café on South Beach. More popular with locals than tourists, it's definitely my favourite spot.

"I have. I thought, you go there so often with Pip, wouldn't it be nice to have somewhere to make yourself a coffee or a bite to eat. Sit and read in peace. Somewhere just for you."

He looked a bit emotional, and pleased by my response – which was to openly cry.

"Dad, that's amazing!" Kitty grinned, hugging him. "That's definitely the best present ever." She passed me a paper napkin to dry my eyes. I genuinely couldn't speak. I just kept nodding and sniffing and laughing through a stream of tears.

"Let's go and see it after this!" Sean suggested.

And that's what we did; by-passing home to fetch Pip. It's exactly where I thought it would be, nestled under some windswept, spindly trees, halfway along the stretch of South Beach, with a spectacular view of Old Harry. All built from identical dark timber, I could tell which hut was mine in an instant, thanks to the *Happy Birthday* banner fastened to the door.

I opened the door and as I did so, we were greeted with a waft of trapped damp sand and seaweed. We all huddled inside, looking at the bare, freshly painted white walls, visualising what we could do to brighten it up. Kitty got busy reeling off a list of *must haves*, while Pip got busy sniffing every inch of the wooden floor.

"Geoff, how did you manage this? These huts are like gold dust," I said.

"I know. I just got lucky."

"Did somebody die?" Kitty asked. Geoff grimaced, shooting me a look, and nodded.

"Oh no," Sean laughed. "So, you literally jumped in their grave."

"Well, if I hadn't, somebody else would," Geoff defended. I kissed him on the cheek.

"I think it's perfect. And the fact that it's pre-loved, makes it all the more special. Whoever owned it before, will be smiling down on me when I'm sat in here on a windy day with Pip, watching the waves from the safety of our little retreat. I love it!"

Saturday dawned even warmer than the day before, with not a cloud in sight. Kitty was up early to join me for Pip's walk on the common. We left Geoff and Sean still snoring peacefully. By the time we got back, Geoff had left for work, leaving a note with a scrawled promise to be home by three.

"Mum, can you give me a lift to Wareham, please?" Kitty asked, stuffing things into a bag. "I'm meeting up with Kelly and Mia. Kelly's mum will bring us back in time for your party. Unless you need any help?"

"No, it's all sorted, thanks. You go and have fun."

I had hoped for a morning of planning my beach hut interior with her, but I know how much she values her friendships, and she does miss them when she's in London. Designing can wait for now.

By ten o'clock, Sean still hadn't stirred. The house was vacuumed, furniture rearranged slightly in the front room and surfaces cleaned ready for the food to arrive mid-afternoon. The flowers – three beautiful floral displays – had arrived and were in place in the front room and kitchen. I sat out in the sun, with Pip by my feet, taking a well-earned break.

My phone rang. It was Niall.

"Happy birthday! I'm in Corfe at the moment; been here all morning, in fact. I just wondered if you fancied a walk to meet me?"

"Yes, that'd be lovely. Where are you?"

"Up the hill. I came back to get some early morning shots of the castle and before you know it, it's ten o'clock!"

I quickly made a flask of coffee, told Sean I was off with Pip – he barely stirred – and headed up the hill. Niall was sitting in the same spot we had, just over a week before. I sat down next to him and offered him the flask.

"I've got some biscuits, too," I said. He nodded, pouring himself a cup and cradling it in his hands.

"It's very deceptive weather. The sun is shining but my hands are freezing up here."

We sat in silence for a bit, admiring the view. I could tell something was on his mind but also sensed he wasn't keen to talk about whatever it was.

"I have a present for you. Can I give it to you now, rather than tonight?"

"Of course! Thank you. You shouldn't have, though."

I opened it. Inside the small white box – tied up with a brown velvet bow – was a beautiful silver Celtic trinity knot necklace, set with tiny stones. It was breath-taking. I hoped it wasn't as expensive as it looked. I was a little lost for words.

"It's beautiful," I murmured. "Absolutely beautiful."

"It's from a jeweller in Dublin. I thought you might appreciate that, with your Dublin heritage." He smiled, then stared out across the landscape. "I'm in trouble, Brianna, and I don't know what to do."

"What kind of trouble? With the police?"

"What? No! No, that would be easier to deal with. No, it's more complicated than that."

"How? Tell me."

He squinted into the distance, watching low flying jackdaws coming in to land on the castle tower.

"I think my marriage is over."

"Oh, no. Why?" Instinctively, I touched his hand. He didn't react. He just looked troubled.

"I've met somebody."

"*You've* met somebody? You're having an affair?" It seemed so unlikely, but then again, maybe I didn't know him as well as I thought. He shook his head.

"No, no. I wouldn't do that. That's not … that's just not something I would do. But it's made me realise that what I have, is not what I thought I had. Sorry, this is all very confusing."

"No, it's fine, I understand. Go on."

"If I really did love my wife and we had the perfect marriage, then I wouldn't be falling in love with somebody else. Would I?" He turned to look at me, searching my face for an answer.

"You're in love with this other person?" I could see the torment etched in his face. He nodded.

"And does Lizzie know?"

"No, but we had a row last night. I don't even know what started it, to be honest. We do that, all the time. Row. For no reason. She hates me – she said as much last night."

I stared at him, feeling sad for him. What an awful thing to hear from your wife.

"But you have a child together. That must mean something."

"I know. That was a mistake. *She* said that, not me. But she's right. I'm not father material. I'm too selfish, too immature. She said she fell in love with my accent. The rest of me is a huge disappointment." He tried to laugh it off.

"I have to agree, it's a great accent."

"What, and the rest of me is a disappointment?"

"No, no, I meant…" We both laughed, a little forced, then fell into silence again, watching the tiny people in the castle grounds setting up tents for an event taking place over the weekend.

"It's you, Brianna."

"What's me?"

"The trouble I'm in."

My head spun round. What was he saying? "But it can't be me!"

"And yet, it is." He gave me a wry smile, watching my reaction.

"But I'm married."

"I know."

"*Happily* married."

"I know."

"Why are you telling me, then?"

"Because you're the only friend I have to talk to. You're the only one I can trust."

"But you're talking to me about *me!*"

We sat in awkward silence, neither knowing where to look or what to say next. In the end, I voiced what I was thinking.

"What am I supposed to say, Niall?"

"Nothing."

I stood up, ready to leave. He held a hand out to stop me.

"No, please don't walk off. I'm sorry. I know it's unfair of me but it's doing my head in. I can't think about anything else. God knows, I've tried."

"Try a bit harder!" My words came out tight and clipped.

"Thanks." He looked away.

"Niall, I can't…"

"Listen, just hear me out. I don't expect anything from you, but I have to tell you how I feel. Please."

I sat back down, staring at the ground.

"Thank you," he acknowledged. "I thought my marriage was okay. I thought all marriages were like that. Bickering, struggling, swiping at each other, then loving each other, cuddling up. It's a rollercoaster. It's unsettling. And we never really talk. Not like *we* do." He waved a finger between us. "*We* connect, you can't deny that." He willed me to look at him. "We do, Brianna. You're my soulmate, my anam cara. I know you are. And as soon as I realised that, I lost all interest in making a go of it with Lizzie. I'm living a lie, a sham. And I know you're happily married, and I don't expect anything from you, but I had to tell you."

We sat in silence for a long time. I ran my fingers through the flattened grass, deep in thought. I was finding it hard to breathe, not liking where my mind was going. I know he's right; there's a definite connection between us and I don't always feel I have that with Geoff. That intuitive way of knowing what each other's thinking or feeling. Of being so comfortable with each other that you don't have to speak to fill the silence. It's been bothering me ever since we'd met, that my first thought in the morning is of him. My last thought at night is of him. And I know it's wrong. And I know it's unfair to Geoff to even allow myself to think like that.

I touched Niall's hand lightly. "I can't let this happen. I'm sorry."

"I know, I know. And I love you all the more for that." He shook his head. "Jesus, listen to me! You've made me into a soppy, snivelling mess!"

I tried to laugh but it came out as a strangled hiccup. "Can we still be friends?"

He grabbed my hand and held it with both of his, studying my face for what seemed like an eternity. "I don't know. I want to, of course I want to, but it's slowly killing me. I think it would be better if I stayed away."

"Then why have you told me all this? What did you expect?"

He shook his head and shrugged. He stared at my hand in his, gently rubbing my knuckles with his thumb. I snatched my hand away. He drew in a deep breath.

"I should go." He stood up, hesitating, waiting for me to say something. I just nodded. He quickly packed up his bag. As he walked away, I found my voice.

"Will you still come to my party, tonight?"

He turned back to me. "I don't know."

"Please?"

He nodded, reluctantly. "Okay." And with that, he carried on his descent. I sat at the top, watching him. Pip raised her head and watched him too. I closed my eyes and let the burning tears trickle down my face. What a mess. What an absolute mess.

What should have been a feeling of excitement and joy as I got dressed into my new party frock, was now a feeling of dread and awkwardness. My dress, a joyous find in Monsoon, was bought to show off my figure, embrace my curves and say *to hell with being fifty!* But as I studied my

63

reflection, I just kept thinking about Niall's face before he left me. That sadness, that dejection, that knowledge that he couldn't have what he wanted. And here I was, about to flaunt it in his face.

I rummaged around for a scarf to drape across my chest, in the style of Grace Kelly, but that just looked ridiculous. I'm not Grace Kelly, for a start. I bet she had plenty of men clamouring for her attention. I bet she knew how to handle it too, without feeling like an absolute heel about it.

I took the box out of my drawer, looked at the necklace yet again, then put it back, under a pile of tops. Scouring my jewellery box, I opted for one Geoff had bought me for a birthday some years ago. A diamond studded heart. Patting it into place, I gave a determined nod and headed downstairs.

By eight o'clock, the party was already in full swing. Julia had been the first to arrive, with Curtis.

"Welcome to the Fab Fifty club, Bree! You look stunning! That dress looks so much better on, than in the photos. Gorgeous!"

I unwrapped their present and squealed. It was a digital radio and CD player, in a vintage floral design, that we had seen and swooned over, months ago, in Dorchester.

"For your beach hut," she grinned.

"How did you know about it before I did?"

"I badgered Geoff into submission. It took a few days, but I finally cracked him," she laughed. "I can't wait to see it."

Niall was one of the last to arrive. Alone. I went over to greet him, forcing a smile. His eyes dropped when he noticed my choice of necklace. Julia was hot on my heels

64

and introduced him to Curtis, then led him through to the kitchen, where all the food and drink was.

Unintentionally, the house had become divided; my friends and the twins' friends congregated in the kitchen and overflowed into the garden, whereas Geoff's family and work colleagues huddled in the front room. The chat was distinctly more low-key in there.

The hall had also become a gathering place, for those who couldn't decide which camp to join. Julia had been heading for the front room, under instruction from Kitty, to root out my *Mamma Mia* CD, but stopped dead in her tracks when she spotted the gathering. Geoff's mother gave her a subtle wave, whereas Matthew's mother turned her back. It's always been awkward when the family gathers and Julia's there. She may not be part of their pack anymore, but she is definitely part of my family. She is the children's favourite aunt and always has been. She played such an active part throughout their childhood and has been my most loyal friend, and I feel fiercely protective of her when the family dismiss her like a bad smell.

Strangely though, the men usually acknowledge Curtis, with a brief nod. Curtis, a successful barrister with a reputation for standing no nonsense, is in fact the sweetest man you could ever wish to meet. Hopelessly devoted to Julia – and she to him – he makes a point of waiting for that nod of acknowledgement before putting a protective arm around his wife.

Momentarily trapped in the hall, I told Julia about earlier with Niall. She didn't seem altogether surprised.

"He's been watching you like a love-sick puppy, all evening," she said.

"Oh God, has he?" I darted a look at Geoff. The last thing I wanted was for him to get jealous. He was oblivious however, deep in conversation with somebody I was introduced to earlier but didn't recognise.

"How do you feel about it?" Julia asked, pushing her way back through to the kitchen, pulling me along with her. We stood by the open doors, watching Kitty and her friends dance on the lawn.

"Sad. I thought we were friends, nothing more. We get on so well together, we seem to be on the same wavelength and that's been wonderful. It's been nice having a friend of the opposite sex who I feel comfortable with, but now I feel bad. I've been a bit flirty with him but only because I didn't think it would mean anything."

"And to you, it doesn't, but to him, it obviously does."

"Yes, thanks for pointing that out," I laughed abruptly.

"Sorry. I'm not much help, am I?"

"You won't tell anybody, will you?"

"Of course not." We were both watching Niall chat to Curtis on the other side of the kitchen. "He's very good looking though; lucky you, Bree."

"Yes, he is," I responded, without thinking.

"Aha! I knew it!" Julia said, eyes sparkling. "I said, right from the start, didn't I? You fancy him!"

"Well, it doesn't take a genius to see how good looking he is. But I'm married, Julia, and I love Geoff. And I feel bad even admitting I fancied him just a little bit – even though there's nothing more to it."

"But supposing you weren't married to Geoff, what then?"

"That's ridiculous!"

"Oh, come on, Bree; humour me. If Geoff wasn't around and Niall was, would you?"

"Would I what?"

She raised her eyebrows. I shook my head. "That's a dangerous game to play and I'm not going to. Not even for my best friend." I poked her side, annoying her. She took my empty glass and went to refill it, stopping on the way to say something to Curtis. Niall looked over at me and smiled. It was a sad, uncomfortable smile. I felt terrible but smiled back – equally uncomfortable. He looked away.

"I'm sorry, Bree," Julia said, putting a fresh glass in my hand. "I didn't mean anything by it, honestly. I know you love Geoff and if you ever did cheat on him – God forbid – I would disown you."

"I know. I would disown me too."

The party carried on until after midnight, by which time I was dead on my feet. Niall left shortly after ten, making his apologies. I saw him shake hands with Geoff, exchange a few words and then head for the front door. I couldn't believe he was leaving without saying goodbye. I followed him out to his car.

"Are you off?"

He turned in surprise, then took a few steps towards me. "Yes. Thank you for a lovely party." It sounded so trite; we both knew it.

"Niall, I …"

"No, don't say anything, Brianna. I'm sorry about earlier. You were right; I shouldn't have said anything."

I gave him a weak smile. "I'm sorry, too. If I ever led you on, I didn't mean to."

He stared at me, wide-eyed. "No, no, you didn't. Don't think like that." He sighed and unlocked his car. "Goodbye, Brianna. I hope the website works out for you."

"Oh, but aren't you going to help me with that? I thought we discussed it." I put a hand on his arm. Why do I keep doing that? His expression told me he was thinking the same thing.

"I can't. I'm sorry." And with that, he got in his car and drove off, without a backward glance.

I stood for ages staring after him. I couldn't decide if I was sad or angry. Either way, he had ruined our friendship and I was losing somebody special.

Geoff sat on the edge of the bed, whiskey glass in hand, watching me take my earrings out. The television was blaring through the floor from downstairs, accompanied by the sound of infectious laughter. Sean and Kitty had friends staying over and once the party guests had left, they set up camp in the front room.

"Everything alright?" I smiled. "It went well tonight, don't you think?"

He nodded. "Although, I'm not entirely happy about your friend."

"Which one? Surely not Julia?"

"No, the Irish chap."

I sighed heavily. "Niall. His name is Niall."

He muttered under his breath and took another mouthful of his drink.

"What about him, Geoff?"

"Why does he call you *Brianna*?"

"Because that's my name."

"No, your name is Bree. It always has been."

I shook my head wearily, niggled by his pettiness. "Geoff, *you* instigated the abbreviation. You said Brianna was too much of a mouthful. Maybe Niall doesn't find it a problem."

His eyebrows clenched together in an angry frown. "I don't trust him. I saw the way he looks at you. I saw the pair of you out by his car."

"I was just saying goodbye, as I did with all my guests!"

"No, he seems far too familiar with you. It's not right."

"He's just a friend. A work friend," I insisted. "Besides, I won't see him so much now anyway; he finished the job." My hands were shaking as I tried to undo my necklace. Geoff noticed and frowned.

"Good. I don't want you to see him at all. Don't look at me like that, Bree! You're very naïve and I don't want you to be taken advantage of."

"What does that mean? *Taken advantage of!* You're being ridiculous." I banged the jewellery box lid down.

"Am I?" He challenged my indignant stare. "And that dress…"

"What about it?"

"It's lovely, but … you're fifty now. It's time to dress more age appropriately."

"What does that mean?"

He stood up and headed for the door with his empty glass. "Less cleavage, more class. That way, you won't have Irish men drooling all over you." He left the room before I could retort, knowing I wouldn't follow him downstairs, with guests in the house.

# Chapter Five

"What's that?" Geoff asked, kissing my cheek as he passed by the table where I was sitting, an appointment letter in my hand.

It'd been two weeks since the party and although his words had stung, he had apologised unreservedly the following morning. He blamed the drink, he blamed his inexcusable jealousy, he blamed me for being too beautiful. The last statement was said in jest, but he kept reiterating how beautiful I am, and insisted I must ignore his comments about my style of clothes. *'More cleavage, the better!'* he had said. Which was ironic, considering the letter I'd just received.

"It's a belated birthday card from the Dorset Healthcare Trust." I said lightly, holding the letter up. He looked confused. "It's an invitation to breast screening. It's their way of hammering home the fact that you're fifty, just in case you'd forgotten!"

"Ah, I see. Nothing to worry about though?"

"No! Well, I say that, but Julia had hers last year and she described it to me. They squish your boob between two Perspex plates, like a flower press, and just when you think you can't stand the pain any longer..."

"Yeah, okay, enough!" Geoff held his hand up, wincing. "I don't need to know, thank you."

"Are you sure?" I teased.

"I'm sure. You'll be fine, won't you? When is it? Do I need to come with you?" It was an offer out of duty rather than willingness. I declined.

"I'll be fine. It's in twelve days. Buy me dinner that night though, somewhere nice."

"Deal!" he agreed.

Julia's description of the breast screening unit at Poole hospital had been so accurate, I felt like I'd been there before. She'd talked me through the whole process, offering more than once to be there with me. I'm not keen on hospitals but on the occasions that I've been for appointments, I prefer to go alone. Geoff came with me for my first antenatal appointment when I was pregnant with Patrick, but after that, it was easier by myself, and more meaningful, almost spiritual. Just me and the little being growing inside me.

Geoff is a worrier, a fretter, even when there's nothing to worry about. Just a whiff of hospital steriliser and he starts to panic. His mother says it stems from a traumatic tonsillectomy when he was small. The operation was fine but there were complications afterwards and he was kept in for over two weeks. That's a long time for a seven-year-old to be away from his mother. And in those days, hospitals weren't friendly places, unlike the children's wards nowadays, with their cheerful colours and painted murals on the walls.

The Perspex flower press was an interesting experience. At first, I thought Julia had been exaggerating; the pain wasn't too bad, it just pinched a bit under my arm. But then it carried on, and on, until it felt like I was hanging from the vice-like press by my left boob and the skin under my armpit was slowly being ripped apart. It hurt to breathe. *'Try to*

71

*relax'* has got to be the most laughable quote of the century and yet, the most used.

Despite the medieval torture, the whole process went quickly and very efficiently. The staff on the reception desk were lovely. They greeted me with a tentative yet cheerful smile, knowing exactly what was in store, then said *goodbye* with a huge smile of relief to mirror my own.

I drove on down to Poole Quay and treated myself to an ice-cream while texting Julia, before heading home for a long soak in a hot bath.

"They sent me a recall." I was on the phone to Julia the minute I received the letter from the breast screening unit. "'*Dear Mrs Hillingdon, following your recent mammogram we would like you to attend for the second stage of screening.'* Tomorrow. They want me there again, tomorrow."

Julia was quick to reassure me. "I told you they would. It's nothing to worry about. With me, it was a fatty cyst that showed up on the screening, but ordinarily, you wouldn't know it was there. But they always warn you that they may do a recall. Didn't they warn you?"

"Yes, they did," I was distracted, re-reading the letter.

"Bree, try not to worry. Do you want company this time?"

"No, it's fine. Like you say, it's nothing. But I wasn't expecting it to be so quick. I was only there four days ago."

"Yes, that's about right. Maybe a bit sooner than expected but they may have had a cancellation or some spare slots. Who knows? Don't worry."

I blasted Ed Sheeran on my way to work, singing along at the top of my voice, in a bid to calm my panic. I wasn't worried that they'd found anything – not at all – I was dreading another flower press episode. It really does scar you for life. Mentally, obviously, not physically.

I was sitting on my favourite bench along Swanage Pier, just near the start where the drop to the sand isn't too far for Pip to jump. We were playing her favourite game, where I throw the ball over the railing onto the beach, and she darts under the railing and takes a flying leap onto the sand to fetch it. She could play for hours without getting tired of the monotony.

I saw Geoff's car pull up and waved as he walked towards us. Pip sat down by my feet, sensing the game would be put on pause.

"Hey, I got your message," he smiled, looking out towards the sea. "Beautiful evening." He sat down next to me and put his arm round me, giving me a kiss. "I'm guessing you're angling for fish and chips?"

"Maybe. I just wanted some sea air, that's all."

He nodded, then looked closely at me. "Busy day? You look done in."

"I wasn't at work today."

"Oh?"

"I went to the hospital, for a re-call."

"I know, but that was yesterday," he frowned.

"They phoned yesterday evening and asked me to go back again this morning. I've been there the whole day, it feels like."

"So, they've seen you three times now? Is everything alright?" My heart ached when I heard the crack in his voice. "Why didn't you tell me they phoned?"

73

"I didn't want to worry you. Until I knew."

"And?"

"It's fine," I nodded. He breathed a deep sigh of relief.

"See? I told you it would be." He rubbed my shoulder, then scooped up Pip's ball and bowled it far across the beach, watching her leap into action to fetch.

"Except … it's not fine, Geoff." I focused on Pip, swallowing repeatedly as my throat dried up.

"What do you mean?" He twisted round, leaning in to my face. "Bree?"

"I mean … I've got breast cancer. It's … it's pretty bad, in fact."

"How bad?"

"Terminal kind of bad."

Looking back, his reaction was quite spectacular. He leapt up from the bench as if he'd been scalded, then looked like he wanted to run away. As far away as possible. He paced back and forth, questioning it again and again. "Are you sure? Can they be certain? Are you sure?"

I just kept nodding and reiterating. What else could I do?

He sat back down, wrapped both arms around me and squeezed me. Then apologised. Then squeezed me again. He rested his chin on my head and stared at the crashing waves, sniffing repeatedly. I knew he was crying. I was determined not to. I hadn't allowed myself that luxury yet.

"I need to tell the children. No, *I* need to do it, Geoff," I insisted, when he went to interrupt. I didn't want him to take over, to break the news as if I'd already died. This was my news to break, and I had to find a way of doing it, causing as little damage as I could. I wished they lived closer to home.

We slipped into silence again. I could sense a thousand questions stacking up in his head but not wanting to ask any of them. Not voicing them made it not real, I suppose.

"Will you look after Pip?"

"Jesus!" he hissed under his breath.

"Geoff, I need to know. I need to plan everything."

He stared at me; a mix of soul-crushing hurt and anger. Not at me, I knew that.

"Will you? I know you've never really liked her."

"I like her!"

Without thinking, I snorted and looked away.

"Bree, why are you cross with *me*?"

"I'm not cross with you. I'm sorry. I'm angry at life. At this *thing* inside me. I'm angry at the injustice. At the totally indiscriminate way it chose me. Why me?" My voice rose to a squeak. "Why me?"

"I don't know. I don't know." We clung together and let the tears flow. An angry, slow stream at first, followed by a snotty tsunami of desperation.

Finally spent, we watched the sun get lower on the horizon and a thousand twinkling lights appear across the bay and up onto the hills beyond. Street lights, harbour lights, house lights. The same lights appear each evening as the day winds down and the chill sets in. The gulls cease their screeching, and the distant nightjars and tawny owls take over for the night shift. Life goes on.

Geoff went and fetched the promised fish and chips. I didn't think I could eat but just one waft of the vinegar chips made my stomach growl with hunger. We ate in silence, both sharing our feast with Pip.

"So, what happens now?" he asked, screwing up our wrappers into a tight ball.

"I start treatment next week, to try and shrink the growth. Buy me a little more time."

"How much time are we talking?"

I shrugged. "It's pretty advanced already. Weeks, months; I don't know."

He shook his head. "I can't … I don't understand. You don't look ill! Do you feel it?"

"No. A bit flu-like, that's all. Tired but nothing new there."

"How can you be so calm? I'm shaking. I can't think straight." He put his arm back around me.

"I have to be calm. I can't not be. I have to be focused, for the children. For you."

"Don't worry about me!"

"Of course I worry about you." I patted his thigh. "I've looked after you for most of your adult life." I smiled at him, trying to make a joke. "What will you do without me?"

He looked away, blinking back tears. Badly timed joke.

"I'm sorry, Geoff," I whispered. I wasn't apologising for making light of it; I was apologising for destroying his world. I know it's not my fault, but I felt so responsible.

We slipped back into silence. I rested my head on his shoulder. Pip rested her head on my thigh. If it weren't for the devastating news we'd just received, this would have been one of those perfect moments. Full tummies, warm and content, listening to the sounds of nature.

"Bree, I need to tell you something."

"Is this about the weekend away you've booked? I was wondering when you were going to tell me."

He shifted slightly. "You know about it?"

"Yes. I was using your laptop the other day when mine crashed, and an email popped up about it. I'm sorry; it sounds amazing, but we can't do it, not now. Why did you book it though? It's already been my birthday." I turned to look at him when he didn't answer straightaway.

"It wasn't for you."

"What?"

"The weekend away. It wasn't meant for you. It was for somebody else."

"Who?"

"Her name is Francesca."

"Who is Francesca? And why are you booking the honeymoon suite for her? Is she from work? Is she getting married?" I fired the questions in quick succession. A prickly feeling crept over me at the change in his expression. "Geoff, what the hell is going on?"

"Bree..." He went to tighten his hold of me, but I pulled away, twisting so I could see his face clearly. He looked so shifty; a look I've never seen before.

"Tell me," I insisted.

"Francesca is someone I met, and we..." He looked away.

"Oh, my God, are you having an affair?" He nodded. "What? You *bastard*!" I lashed out, hitting his arm with such a force. He stared indignantly, shocked by what I'd just done.

"Hey! I'm only telling you so that you know you don't have to worry about me."

I stared at him in absolute disbelief. I stopped breathing, my mouth open. Stunned.

"Are you kidding me? I *want* you to be distraught. I want you to be completely and utterly heartbroken when I die. I

77

want you to think that nobody could ever replace me!" I stood up, tipping Pip to the ground. "But no, no. You're going to swan off to Paris and screw Francesca just as soon as they've buried me! I guess we'll both be in a hole then, won't we." I was spitting my words; I was beyond angry.

"Bree, that's so vulgar!"

"Vulgar? I'll give you vulgar! I'll be as vulgar as I please. How dare you!"

He stood up, not liking how I was glaring down at him. "I wouldn't have told you if you weren't..."

"Dying? Oh, that makes me feel so much better. Thank you for your consideration. Tosser!"

He looked round to see if anybody was in the vicinity. My choice language was clearly embarrassing him. It just fuelled me more.

"So how long have you been screwing Francesca, then?"

"I'm not going to discuss this with you when you're being so vile."

"Vile? Vulgar? Any other V words you've got there, Geoffrey? I've got one – how about very, very, very, *very* pissed off! How long, Geoffrey? A year? I'm guessing by the fancy hotel it must be a celebration of sorts. Celebrating your sordid little shagathon." I tried not to smirk at his displeasure. "Go on then – spill the beans!"

"Ten."

"Ten what? Months?" I gasped at his expression. "Ten *years?*" I sat back down with a bump, winded. How could he? "You tosser! Tosser. TOSSER!" I screamed.

"Bree, stop it! What's got into you?"

"Oh, I don't know – *cancer?*"

He grabbed my shoulders. "This isn't like you! I thought we could talk about it, sensibly, like normal people."

"This isn't exactly a normal situation though, is it? I'm telling you I've got cancer and you're telling me you're having an affair! Look at everything Matthew put Julia through. How did you *think* I'd respond?"

"It's not the same."

"By which you mean, you're not going to fall apart the way he did. The affair; that's the same."

"Matthew's okay," he said quietly.

"Really? What about all those nights of looking after him because… Oh my God, I'm so stupid! You weren't with Matthew! You were with her, weren't you?" I watched him nod. That nod shattered everything for me. That nod told me he had cheated not just on me but the children too. Ten years of wanting their dad to spend more time with them but accepting that he had to work or look after Uncle Matthew. I felt sick.

"I don't want you to come home tonight."

"But we need to talk!"

"No, we don't!" I snapped. "I need to be alone right now. You need to do the decent thing and give me space."

"It's my home too," he warned.

"One night, Geoff. It won't kill you! I'll be gone by tomorrow, don't worry."

"Gone? Gone where?"

I shrugged. "As far away from you as possible." I grabbed my bag and headed for my car, with Pip by my side. I didn't look back, but I knew he was staring after me, wondering if he should try and stop me. I'm glad he didn't. I think I would've punched him.

I didn't know what to do with myself once I got home. I didn't want to sleep upstairs in our bed, that's for sure. I didn't want to touch anything in our room; anything that *he* had touched or used. I couldn't bear it. I took the duvet and pillows from Kitty's bed, making a bed up on the large sofa by the fire, which I lit. I felt cold right through to my bones – a shaky kind of cold. Plus, the flickering flames would give me something to focus on while I tried to make sense of everything.

Growling with frustration, I got back up and went into the kitchen. I stared out at the dark garden for an age, then stared into the fridge. I made coffee. I didn't drink it. Instead, I opened a packet of biscuits and systematically ate five before realising what I was doing.

I sat at the kitchen table staring at my phone, debating. I should really have phoned Julia first, but it was Niall I wanted to talk to, Niall I wanted to turn to. I just wasn't sure how he'd react. I typed quickly.

*'Hello, I'm sorry if this message wakes you. Can you phone me, please? Brianna'*

The phone rang almost instantly. I bit my knuckle to stop myself from crying at the sound of his voice.

"Brianna, are you okay?" he asked.

"I'm sorry to disturb you…"

"You're not."

"Niall, can you come round? I'm on my own and I really need a friend. Please." I was anticipating the questions, or the excuses as to why he couldn't. I was ready to plead.

"Yes, of course," he said. He didn't even say goodbye before hanging up.

I sat by the window waiting for him to arrive. "Thank you," I said, inviting him in. He looked nervous, unsure.

"What's happened? Where's Geoff?" He saw my puffy eyes. "Have you two had a row?"

I nodded. "Yes. He cheated on me."

"Oh." He waited for me to say more. I didn't know what else to say, I couldn't find the words. He sighed. "So, you called me because you'd had a row?"

"I'm sorry, I ..."

"You can't do this to me, Brianna. You can't click your fingers when Geoff's been a naughty boy and expect me to come running."

"*Naughty boy*?"

He held his hands up. "Alright, sorry. I know he's been an absolute ... idiot; you don't deserve that. But the thing is, I haven't seen you for nearly a month, and I've missed you every day. I haven't seen my wife for nearly a month, and I haven't missed her at all. I've been hoping you would phone or text me, but nothing. Until now."

"I'm sorry. I didn't think."

"What I'm saying is, I *will* come running. I'm here, aren't I. But it's not fair for you to do that. Not after what happened between us."

I nodded, trying to fight back the imminent tears. "I just need a hug, Niall. I just need a hug from you."

He opened his arms and wrapped me up in such a solid embrace. I leant into his chest and caved. Tears, sobs, wails; it all came out for a second time. He let me weep for a while and then started to stroke my hair, making soothing noises. I started to tremble again.

81

"Let's move from the hall, shall we?" he suggested, guiding me through to the front room. He sat me down in the armchair nearest the fire, grabbed the box of tissues on the coffee table and crouched in front of me, offering them. I grabbed a handful, dabbing at my face and blowing my nose. I knew I looked hideous, but to be honest, I was beyond caring at that point. Sensing what I was thinking, he gently brushed back the locks of hair that had stuck to my face.

"You look fine," he smiled. "Although I wouldn't enter yourself into a beauty pageant or anything, just yet."

I laughed, a watery, sobby kind of laugh. "Thanks, Niall. For being here, I mean. I need someone I can trust."

He nodded. "What about Julia?"

"She's my best friend, yes, but when it comes to cheating husbands, she has her own issues, and I can't deal with them right now."

"Fair enough. I'm sorry for what I said; of course I'll be there for you. It's just been a tough month."

I looked at him properly, noticing the dark circles under his eyes and the haggard look about his cheekbones.

"I've missed you too, Niall," I whispered.

"Don't say that unless you mean it."

"I do mean it. I just haven't let myself admit it."

He took my hand in his, studying it. "Brianna, you've had a shock about your husband. I don't think you should say anything else that you might regret later. Or that I might believe, and you didn't actually mean after all. You're very upset right now and I know you're a devoted wife to Geoff."

I stood up at the mention of Geoff's name, anger creeping back again.

"I'm not crying about Geoff."

Niall stood up with me, frowning. "What then?"

I closed my eyes. I wasn't sure I could say it all again. *Cancer.* It's such a hateful word. Niall put his hands on my arms.

"Brianna?" I opened my eyes and he looked deep into them, seeing the pain and fear. "Oh Jesus; you're not well, are you? What is it?"

I swallowed hard. "Breast cancer."

He immediately wrapped his arms around me and cradled me, holding on to me as if absorbing my pain. We stayed like that for some time. I sank into his chest for a second time. He smelt of apples and woodsmoke, and the faint remnant of aftershave from the morning. It was comforting. Familiar.

"Does Geoff know?" he spoke into my hair.

"Yes. That's when he told me about *her.*"

"What a bastard!"

I pulled away to look at him. "Thank you! That's the kind of support I need. None of this *naughty boy* nonsense. I don't want you to feel sorry for him or dismiss what he's done. Yes, his wife is dying of cancer, but he's been sleeping with somebody else for *ten years*!"

"Ten years? Jesus, Brianna, I'm so sorry." I watched the delayed reaction to what else I'd said hit him. "What do you mean, *dying*?"

I sat back down. He took up his crouched position again at my feet.

"I've got stage 4 cancer."

"What does that mean?"

"There's no stage 5. It means there's no way out for me."

"At all?" I shook my head, watching the desperation in his eyes. "But surely, there's a way to fight it? You've got to fight it."

"I don't think I can. I don't have the strength. When they told me today what's in store, my world fell around my ears. My first thought was of my children; how do I tell them? What's going to happen to them? How will they cope? All these thoughts crowding my terrified brain. And then, just at the point when it felt like my head was under water, not able to breathe, Geoff pushed it down a bit further. Killing me. I don't have strength left to fight. I can't do it."

"But your children need you!"

"I know."

"I need you." He took my hand and kissed it. "I'll fight it with you. I won't let you give up."

I stroked his face. "I'm sorry, but I can't give you what you want just now," I said quietly. His eyes widened.

"What, you think me kissing your hand is a declaration of intent?" he joked. "Brianna, you know how I feel. That won't change but I don't expect anything from you. I'm here for you, regardless. I told you before; we're soulmates. Actually, I *do* expect something from you," he corrected, "I expect you to not give in to it. Fight it with all your might. There's no such word as *can't*. Okay?"

"Okay."

"Right," he straightened up, "What you need now is an Irish coffee."

"Do you know how to make them?"

"Is the pope catholic?" he laughed. "Do I know? Seriously?" He went over to the bottles of drink on the cabinet and drew in a sharp intake of breath, shaking his head in mock despair. "This whiskey is *not* Irish. You should've known not to trust him, Brianna. All the signs are right here!"

"And then he said that you were drooling over me!" I laughed.

"*Drooling*? I don't like that man at all."

We were sitting on the sofa by the fire, the duvet covering our legs, pillows stuffed behind our heads, and mugs of coffee with thick cream, warming our hands. I let out a deep sigh.

"I have loved him for so long that it feels bad – wrong – having any negative thoughts about him."

"That's only natural. It's in your nature to see the best in people; it's one of the first things I noticed about you."

"Really?"

"Yes. The thing is, ordinarily I'd say, take your time to get over this, give yourself time to grieve, but you don't have that luxury right now. You need to forget about Geoff – however harsh that sounds – and focus purely on yourself. On fighting the cancer. On not allowing yourself to give in."

"You're such a good man, Niall."

"Why, thank you."

"And I ruined your marriage. I'm sorry for that."

"No, you didn't. It was over before it began, really. I'm sorry I made out that you were the cause. That's not true."

"What happened then?"

"I didn't know what love is." He looked at me and smiled. "I thought I'd found it, but I was wrong. I was so desperate to find somebody to settle down with, you know, the whole *forty is looming,* kind of thing."

"I know it," I said with feeling.

"And now here I am, in love with a married woman who's..."

"Not going to make fifty-one."

"Yeah," he breathed.

"Life really is crap, isn't it?"

"Amen to that!" We clinked mugs together and watched the fire, wondering what the next day would bring.

# Chapter Six

I was on the phone, first thing, to book a holiday cottage in Studland. Niall and I had talked it all through and he was adamant he would stay with me.

"Besides," he said, "I'm slowly outstaying my welcome at Dan's place. He would disagree, as would his wife, but I hate feeling in the way."

"Well, you wouldn't be in the way with me," I assured him.

Dan-the-man, as he's known, is Niall's friend and drummer in the band. Niall had been staying with them since my birthday – since he left Lizzie.

It didn't take long to pack a bag of clothes and essentials. I wasn't sure what would be happening, so I took enough for the week. By then, I would've had time to plan my next step.

Once Pip and I were settled into the cottage, Niall shot off to Dorchester to collect his things, and a Sainsbury's shop. It felt so strange writing a shopping list with him and yet we both seemed to want the same things.

While he was gone, I took the time to phone Julia. I couldn't tell her the worst of my news, but I did tell her about Geoff. She was beyond livid with him. The air was blue as I sat back and listened to her rant for a good five minutes about the morals of the Hillingdon men.

"Where are you staying? I'll come over. Do you want me to stay tonight? We can get drunk and have a good bitch about them," she suggested. I hesitated. "Bree?"

"About that – yes, I do want you *and* Curtis to come over. I need to talk things over with you both."

"Ah, yes, of course. Curtis will put you onto a good divorce lawyer." I didn't want to tell her she had misunderstood, so I just agreed.

"Niall is here with me," I said quickly. She couldn't mask her surprise.

"But … already?"

"No, it's not like that. He's just here as moral support. A friend."

"I'm a friend. Surely you want me there, instead of him. He's a man, for a start."

I could see the way the conversation was going, so I feigned an incoming call from Kitty and said I'd see her and Curtis later. I hate lying.

Next on my list to phone, was the children. We have a group chat on Facebook and often do video calls. Geoff doesn't bother with social media, even though Kitty had begged him to join Facebook so she could keep in touch with him, too. I dreaded telling her about Geoff. Out of the three of them, I knew she would take it really badly.

I couldn't face it. How can I tell them about the cancer? Just the thought of their sadness and the inevitable tears, and not being able to hug them, set me off again. Equally, I knew I would have to phone my parents and siblings at some point. How can I do this? How can I break their hearts like this? I worried about my dad. He's already had one heart attack and I would hate to be responsible for another one.

Niall returned with a couple of suitcases, his camera equipment, guitar and bags of shopping. He'd only been back five minutes when Julia and Curtis pulled up. Julia swooped in with a canvas bag. I spied wine bottles and a huge bar of Galaxy.

"Essential stuff," she said, hugging me. Curtis was next to hug me, patting my back, murmuring words of encouragement. He shook Niall's hand.

I could see Julia was about to have a look round the cottage and make small talk, eyeing Niall with suspicion, so I went straight to the point.

"I have some bad news and I wanted you both here to hear it. You are my closest friends – the three of you – and I'm going to need all of your strength and support."

"Of course!" Julia interrupted. "We'll sort this mess, Bree. Make him pay."

I shook my head. "No, it's not about Geoff, although God knows, I wish that's all it was."

Julia's face crumpled when I said the C-word; Curtis looked immeasurably sad. They listened as I reiterated the diagnosis yet again. Julia wept and paced the floor.

"What can we do? Come and stay with us; we're only minutes from the hospital."

"I can't," I said. "I need my space. I need to find somewhere more permanent, too. I can't go back home to Geoff."

"But I can't leave you here!" she practically wailed.

"Stay here, with us," Niall said. "If that's alright with you, Curtis?"

Curtis nodded. "Of course it is. Although by rights, Bree, you should be back in your own home, resting in comfort, and Geoff should be the one living out of a suitcase."

"I can't think about that right now," I said. I didn't want to face the thought of never going home again but I knew Geoff wouldn't leave readily. And I was too spent to fight him.

We sat and talked a little while longer and before Curtis left, he called me aside.

"Bree, I know you don't want to cause a fuss and it's commendable, but I strongly advise you to reconsider. You need familiarity and security right now. It's all very well staying here with Niall and Julia but then what?" He watched me take onboard everything he'd said. "We have to put *you* first."

After he'd left, Julia opened the wine.

"I hope you've got spare pyjamas for me. And where am I sleeping? Not with you two!" She eyed us both, not quite teasing, not quite scolding. Niall shook his head, laughing lightly. For once, I didn't blush. She knew nothing was going on but couldn't resist stirring.

"There are two rooms. Julia, you can have the other room and I'll kip on the sofa," Niall suggested. "I'm used to it."

They were just the tonic I needed, Julia and Niall. We ate pizza for lunch, washed down with wine, chatting and regaling Niall with stories of our friendship. We avoided talk of Geoff and cancer. We sat in the sun, dozing on and off, then cooked the evening meal together. It was like being students again. Niall unzipped his guitar and strummed, and before long, we were shouting out requests to him. He's amazing; he knew every song we suggested. Fuzzy-headed from wine, Julia and I sang along to our favourite songs, not caring how terrible we sounded. And as is our tradition, we

90

ended the night with a couple of episodes of *Friends*, pre-empting our favourite quotes, as always.

By the next morning, I had drawn up a plan of action. Niall brought me an early cup of coffee (I wasn't sure he'd slept at all) and I ran it past him.

"I need to tell the children, face to face, about everything. I can't bear the thought of saying it over the phone. So, my suggestion is that we do a round trip tomorrow; drive down to Exeter to see Patrick, then up to Sean in Bath and on to Kitty in London. If we all go, we can share the drive. It would've been better going today – less traffic in the city on a Sunday – but I don't think any of us are in a fit enough state to drive all that way, are we?"

"No, we're not. She can put it away, can't she?"

"Yes, she certainly can," I agreed. "Thanks, Niall, for looking after her last night."

"Oh, you saw?"

I'd heard Julia crying outside in the small garden and got up to check on her, but Niall beat me to it. I watched from the bedroom window; saw how he held her, saw her lean on his shoulder and sob. He then disappeared and came back with a drink for her. I crept back into bed. I could hear their muted voices talking for some time before finally, I heard Julia come upstairs to her room. I lay absolutely still, straining to hear if she was crying again but I think she must've drifted off to sleep. I could hear Niall moving around downstairs for a while; it seems sleep was eluding him too. I debated going back down to join him, but my head was spinning and I felt a bit sick. Note to self: wine and stress do not mix.

Despite having walked the beach a thousand times, starting the day there before the rest of the world had even finished breakfast, and then going back to the holiday cottage, made it all seem very new. I left Niall promising to cook up a full English and I didn't even bother to try and stir Julia before nipping down to the beach with a very happy Pip.

There's something about the sea that is so restorative; the sounds, the smell, the way the water encourages your eyes to rest and mind to drift. I walked to the furthest point of the beach and sat on one of the fallen trees by the water's edge. The trees blew down years ago and had been left to embed their branches into the sand and act as a net for seaweed, a perch for robins and an exciting mini climbing frame for adventurous children.

I listened to the inquisitive robin having a chat to a fellow robin up on the cliff edge. Songbirds really have perfected the art of conversation, haven't they. One speaks, the other listens intently then responds. There's a slight pause as their train of thought takes a new turn and the dialogue starts up again. Back and forth, back and forth. And always so pleasant, so considerate of the other, making sure each gets a turn to be heard.

My mind went over the last conversation I'd had with Geoff. Screaming match, more like. I know I'd shocked him. He'd never heard me swear before, or even raise my voice. Yes, we've had arguments, but never more than frustrated squabbles, followed by silence. I hated the idea of the children hearing their parents bicker, so any disputes we had were usually hissed in the corner of the kitchen, shooting anxious glances at the door for fear of one of the children walking in.

I learnt early on that the secret to a quiet, level relationship with Geoff, was to allow him to think he's right even when he wasn't. I kind of adopted the way his mother treated him; like a petulant child that needed constant reassurance. I'm thinking now that if he'd been pulled up on things sooner or not pandered to so much, he may have thought twice about his actions.

*His actions* – why am I still so polite even when I'm talking to myself? He's been sleeping with somebody else for ten years! Living a double life. *Cheating* on me. How did I not spot that? How did he think that was okay? How was he able to carry on without showing any signs of guilt or remorse? Did he even feel remorse now? Or had he already written me off? I've had no texts, no phone calls, to see if I'm okay. Surely if he cared, he would've checked up on me. Or sought out Julia to see if she knows how I am. *Where* I am. It's as if I'm already dead and forgotten.

Curiously, I don't feel sad. Or angry. Well, maybe a bit angry. More than anything, I feel a sense of calm about it. Maybe Geoff was right after all; now that I know about his affair, I don't have to worry about him. I don't have to crucify myself at the thought of breaking his heart, destroying his life, by dying. Or maybe, subconsciously, I've taken Niall's advice – forget about Geoff and focus on me.

I don't *feel* like I'm going to die. I can't quite comprehend that. How can I be so near death and not feel it? I don't have any aches, I don't feel sick or weak or drained of life. I'd expect that, surely; to feel like I'm on my last legs. This is why cancer has such a bad press; it's unpredictable and it takes you completely by surprise. And by the time you have an inkling that something is amiss, it's too late. Cancer has already engulfed you; claimed its prize – your life.

"Good walk?" Niall asked.

"Beautiful," I smiled. He put a plate in front of me, laden with food. Steaming sausages, egg, beans and fried mushrooms. I gave a contented sigh. "This is the life!"

Niall watched me, his eyes narrowing. I already knew what he was thinking; *why is she so calm?*

"Maybe rest after breakfast," he suggested. I shook my head.

"No. I need to be doing things. I need to sort; I need to plan. I feel strangely positive. It's like, when you're a kid and somebody tells you, you can't do something – either because it's not allowed, or they don't think you're capable – you then focus all your efforts on doing that thing. Don't you?"

"What are you saying?"

"I'm not sure. I just feel like I'm not ready to accept somebody telling me I'm going to die."

"Is that what they told you? *'I'm sorry, you're going to die'.*"

"No, not exactly. They said, it's so advanced that there's not much they can do now. I'm going to have chemo to try and shrink the tumour to slow the progression but I'm not sure how that works. I'll know more when I go for my next appointment, I suppose"

"Can I come with you?" he asked quietly.

"Yes, please. But in the meantime, don't treat me like I'm ill. Okay? I'm not."

He laughed. "Well, I think some people would beg to differ. You *are* ill, with cancer. But I also think you're stubborn.

"I think I am, too. I never realised that about me."

"Maybe it's been hiding? Maybe that is going to be your superpower."

"God knows, I'll need it."

Niall put a mug of coffee next to my plate. "Make sure you use that power, Brianna. I know you can fight this. Be as stubborn as you possibly can." He squeezed my shoulder. I put my hand on his.

"Thank you, Niall."

"And stop thanking me! Otherwise, we are seriously going to fall out!" he laughed.


The calm didn't last. My phone beeped. I read the text from Kitty and let out a scream of frustration. "Nooooo!"

"What's happened? Julia and Niall leapt up from their seats.

"He's told them that I've got cancer – *by text*! I can't believe he'd do that! He *knew* I wanted to tell them myself."

Before I'd even had a chance to read Kitty's text to them, she phoned. And as I listened to her torrent of tears, I had two notifications of incoming calls, from the boys.

The next two hours were spent talking, explaining, reassuring as best I could, and trying not to weep down the phone to them, individually. Kitty cried uncontrollably, Sean with a little more control, and Patrick was just silent. He asked questions, spaced out with long pauses. I knew he was hurting but he's never been one to react dramatically. He internalises everything. That doesn't mean he's not feeling – far from it. He feels deeply. About so many things.

"And how did they react about Geoff?" Julia asked, once I'd briefly relayed my conversations with them.

"I didn't tell them."

"Why on earth not? They need to know."

"I couldn't. They've got enough to deal with, just hearing about me."

"And did you tell them exactly how bad it is?" Niall asked. I shook my head. He stood up and hugged me; no words, just a solid, reassuring hug.

"I hate lying but I couldn't. I just kept saying, '*I'm sure I'll be fine*'."

"They need to know about Geoff," Julia reiterated. "He won't tell them, that's for sure. And they'll be feeling sorry for him, having to cope with you being ill and having to look after you." She made a growling noise of disgust. "I can't abide it! He's going to get away with it, isn't he?"

"I *will* tell them," I said quietly. "Just not yet."

When I had a moment alone with Niall, I told him what Kitty had said to me.

"She was so angry with me. Upset, yes, but also, angry. She said she couldn't believe that I hadn't told her myself; that I thought it was okay for Geoff to send a text, as if they don't matter. As if they're acquaintances, not our children. I didn't know what to say. I couldn't even defend myself because that would let on that I'm not at home with Geoff." I stared out of the window. "I don't know why he's doing this. I'm not the guilty party here; he is. But he seems to want to turn the children against me. I don't get it. And I can't talk to Julia about it. You've seen how she reacts just at the mention of his name."

"Yes, I've noticed. Although she has a point."

"Does she? I don't want the children to hate him."

"Brianna, they're not children anymore. They can make their own minds up. They can decide whether they hate him or forgive him. Either way, you're not even giving them the chance to choose."

He was making sense. Calm, rational sense.

"Okay. I'll just give them a day or two to let the cancer news sink in first."

But as we all know, *the best laid plans* and all that, or better still, *don't put off til tomorrow what can be done today.* These old sayings came about for a reason.

Kitty did a group video chat an hour later. I was the last to join in, dreading it. It's one thing to lie over the phone but another to keep up the pretence, face to face.

We all waved, very subdued except Kitty, who seemed quite buoyant.

"Okay, I've had a long chat with my friend, Sally. Her mum had breast cancer a couple of years ago, so she's just talked me through it. You're going to feel really rough for about a year, Mum. The chemo isn't great, it makes you sick and your nails bleed but by the sounds of it, the worst that's going to happen is, you'll lose your hair. But I was thinking, we could go shopping for wigs together in London. Make a day of it!"

My heart sank. I should've said something sooner. Should've explained the prognosis. Instead, I was watching a flicker of hope grow in Sean's face, a look of relief in Patrick's.

97

Kitty smiled and took a deep breath, the way she always does when she's about to ask an awkward question or beg a favour she knows is a bit impertinent.

"The other thing is, Mum, I phoned home to talk to you. Dad said you've gone away for a few days. He said you needed time alone to get your head round everything – which I understand – but he needs you too. He said he understood and was fine about it, but he didn't sound it. I think you should go home. You need to support each other." She raised her eyebrows like a scolding teacher.

"Kitty, I'm sorry but …"

"No, Mum, I understand what you're going through, but you need to think about Dad, too. This affects him, too."

"I've left him."

"*What?*" Kitty and Sean exclaimed simultaneously. "What do you mean? When?"

"On Friday, when he told me he's having an affair."

"No! No, that's not right, he wouldn't do that!" Kitty shouted.

"He would. He is," I said, my confidence growing. Truth is good. "He's been lying for a long time, to all of us."

"I don't believe it," Kitty said defiantly. Sean and Patrick were quiet. Stunned, shocked. Not able to compete with Kitty's overt reaction. "Something must've happened. He wouldn't go off with somebody else for no reason. Was it a fling? Did you have a row?"

"A row? That made him so mad he went and had an affair that lasted *ten years*? No, I don't think so. Do you?" I know I sounded cross but her refusal to believe it, was annoying me.

"Wait, did you say it's been going on for ten years?" Patrick asked.

"I can't believe it, Patrick, can you?" Kitty interjected.

"Kitty, your dad has lied and cheated. He sent you all a text when he knew full well, I wanted to tell you all myself. I was coming to visit you all, tomorrow, so we could see each other. So I could be there to hug you. But Dad took that away from me. Just like he took our happy marriage away." I watched her process it all, a glimmer of doubt at Geoff's innocence.

"I believe it," Patrick said quietly.

"Do you?" Kitty asked. "Why? I can't believe it, I just can't."

"I saw them."

We all stared at Patrick, momentarily dumbstruck.

"I hoped it would go away. I hoped he would stop."

"When?" I croaked.

"Before I first left for uni. I was in Weymouth with friends, and I saw them together. Having a cosy lunch. Dad was shocked when I appeared at their table, but he played it off, saying she was a colleague from work." He smiled awkwardly. "I don't know why but I didn't buy it, so I followed them and saw them kissing. Sorry, Mum," he whispered. "And then I confronted him about it. It was the scariest and bravest thing I'd ever done, I think. He denied it, then when I showed him the photos I'd taken, he smashed my phone. He said if I ever breathed a word of it to you, he would make sure you believed I was lying. He said none of you would ever want to see me again."

"Oh, Patrick!" I choked on his name. "Is that why you never come home?"

He nodded.

"So, I miss out on seeing you because he's sleeping with somebody else?" I could feel a rage starting to burn. "How fair is that, Kitty? *Now* do you believe what he's done? Not just to me but to Patrick. To all of you. All those fun Fridays we had when you were kids, and he was never there. He lied about Uncle Matthew too. That was a cover for seeing her. Every weekend. Do you see now? Do you understand? And he told me this, *the minute* I told him I've got cancer." I swallowed hard, my throat painfully dry. Julia appeared by my side with a glass of water.

"Who's there with you?" Kitty asked.

"Julia," I said. "And Niall."

"Niall? The guy from your party? Why is he there?"

"They're both looking after me. Because your dad isn't." That statement was greeted with silence.

"I'm glad," Patrick said. "I haven't met Niall but I'm glad he's there with Auntie Julia."

More silence.

"Look, I'm sorry you had to find out about Dad like this. I am. I'm angry and hurt but above all, I'm scared about my treatment, and that's what I have to focus on now. And Julia and Niall are making sure that's what I do. I love you all."

"Love you, Mum," they all replied. We waved and I hung up. I phoned Patrick back immediately.

"I am so, so sorry for what Dad did to you, Patrick. I'm sorry he put you through that."

"I'm sorry too, Mum. Sorry I didn't say anything. I stupidly thought he would stop once I'd confronted him. But he really scared me. You won't go back to him, will you?"

"No! No, I won't. Besides, Julia wouldn't let me, would she! Will you come home soon to see me? I mean, my new home – wherever that may be."

"Yes, of course. As soon as possible, I promise. Love you, Mum."

"Love you more, Patrick."


"Done?" Julia asked. I nodded. She pulled a sad face at my puffy eyes and crossed the room to hug me. After Patrick, I phoned my parents, then Martyn, my boss. I'd toyed with the idea of going in to work to tell him but as Sunday progressed and Monday loomed, I opted to phone him at home and be done with it. Phoning my parents was hard; harder than anticipated. I even told my mum about Geoff too, not just the cancer. She promised to break the news to the rest of the family to save me from doing it.

I feel angry that somehow Geoff has managed to steal the limelight – not that I particularly crave it – and in a way, undermined my illness. There's not just the focus on what I'm going through with cancer but also with my marriage. And strangely, it's my marriage – or the destruction of it – and Geoff, that has dominated conversations. I'm sure I'm wrong but the children seemed more distressed by that than by the cancer. Especially Kitty. And I can't deny it – that hurts.


Julia left after lunch to fetch some things from home and check that Curtis was sorted for the week.

"He can cook – actually, he's quite good – but he tends to forget to, unless I remind him. So, I'll write out a meal plan

101

for the week. There's plenty of stuff in the freezer if he runs out of fresh."

The three of us had tentatively planned a course of action. Julia would take the week off work and once we knew the chemo schedule, she would probably take more time off or just flit between me and her job. The huge advantage she has regarding her job, is that she is Curtis's personal assistant. That's how they met, many years ago. He helped her through those dark days that followed her marriage break up. Nine years her senior and a confirmed bachelor – he thought – he fell in love and proposed once her divorce was finalised. They are so suited yet completely different. He's besotted with her and after all the trauma she's had in her life, she totally deserves it.

# Chapter Seven

"This is it!" Niall and I stood admiring my beach hut. "I'm not sure how to feel about it. I mean, I love it, but it was bought out of guilt, I'm sure." I unlocked the door, and we went in. "It needs chairs. It needs lots of things."

Niall nodded approval. "It's great. The thing is, Brianna, this is yours. You have the deeds, right?"

"Yes. Still wrapped up with a pretty bow."

"So keep it. This will be a great place to come and recuperate. You could spend the whole day here, listening to the sound of the sea. Resting. Sleeping. It's perfect. We should get it sorted, now."

I looked round at the white walls, visualising.

"I have a chair at home that would be great in here. It's in my bedroom. It's my end-of-the-day, sit-and-read, chair. Really comfy."

"Then let's go and pick it up. And get stuff you need for here. A table, kettle, mugs; all that. Then, by the time you start your treatment, this will be ready for you."

We sat on the doorstep, watching the waves. Pip lay by my feet, tired from her earlier sprint across the beach. I wanted to enjoy the moment, feel excited about my beach hut, but I just kept thinking about all the things Geoff had bought for me over the years, that I had been delighted with, thinking they were spontaneous gifts of love. Now I'm sure they were all guilt gifts. The car, definitely. Just after Patrick left. What a coincidence.

"If he'd done it just the once, had a fling in a moment of madness, then I think I could've forgiven him."

"That's a phrase – *moment of madness*," Niall said, shaking his head lightly.

"How do you mean?"

"Well, yes, there are people with genuine mental health issues but is it fair for 'normal' people to use madness as an excuse? To my mind, if you do something to hurt somebody – something you wouldn't normally do, something that is out of character or that isn't acceptable – of course it's a moment of madness; you're not thinking straight.  But is that a reasonable excuse when you have, in fact, destroyed someone?"

I stared at him, trying to fathom what he was saying. He kicked at the sand with his toes.

"I mean, in all seriousness, Brianna, would it matter if he'd slept with her only once or a hundred times? Could you ever trust him again?"

"Is this me we're talking about – or you?"

"Both," he sighed.

"Oh, Niall."

"It's okay; we were already broken."

"What happened?"

"We had a row – I told you, on your birthday – then she went out, met someone and slept with him. She said it was because she was so angry with me – as if it was all my fault. She didn't even say sorry."

"Is that why you've been staying with Dan?"

"Yes. I couldn't face her. And I knew we'd just argue even more and that's not good for Layla. But Lizzie couldn't understand why I couldn't forgive her. She said it didn't mean anything; it was just sex. But does that make it alright?

She said it was just the once and I would've done the same. That's when I realised, she doesn't know me at all."

I leant my head on his shoulder by way of comforting him. "What a pair we are!"

"What a pair, indeed."

The three of us headed for Dorchester, bright and early. Our first port of call was Goulds department store; Dorchester's answer to Debenhams, albeit on a much smaller scale. They had everything I wanted for the beach hut, from a sky-blue kettle, cute mugs with owls on, and some cheerful daisy print plates, to soft, fluffy throws, a door mat to trap the sand, and a dustpan and brush. We also picked up four beach chairs that could fold away neatly in the corner, from the camping shop, and two floral canvas prints to brighten up the bare walls.

"I'm not sure about going to pick up my chair," I said on the way back.

"Why not? You love that chair," Julia insisted. It's true but I hadn't allowed myself to think about home. It's all too raw. I said as much. Niall smiled at me through the rear-view mirror, taking his eyes off the road for just a moment. Julia wasn't as understanding – or maybe she was but wasn't prepared to let me give up what was mine.

"Best to go today; it's Monday, so he won't be there. I'll come in with you."

I spotted Geoff's car on the drive as we neared home. It wasn't unusual for him to leave his car and get a lift from Matthew; they tended to car-share, taking it in turns to drive. Who knows; maybe Matthew had been staying with Geoff.

I opened the door. I'd asked Julia to give me a moment by myself. I felt incredibly emotional; overwhelmed. I had left in such a hurry, and it already felt like a lifetime ago, not just the three days that it had been. I glanced back at the car. Three pairs of eyes watched me intently. Niall gave an encouraging smile; Pip strained her neck, pawing at the window. Julia waved me in with an impatient hand.

The house smelt different somehow; it's the first thing I noticed. Not a smell I recognised. Flowers? Air freshener? Perfume? It was perfume. I walked through to the kitchen. Geoff jumped up from his chair, tightening his dressing gown belt.

"Bree!"

I caught my breath. I stared at the woman getting up slowly from the chair next to Geoff's. She too tightened the belt of her silky robe. I tried to ignore her blond mane and tight figure. Geoff glanced nervously at her and stepped towards me; his arms outstretched as if he were about to hug me.

"Where have you been? I've been so worried," he blurted. Unbelievable! I snapped out of my momentary trance and stepped back.

"I've … just come for some things," I mumbled, heading for the door.

"Bree, I'm Francesca." I froze in my tracks. I didn't turn to look at her, but she carried on anyway. "Geoff told me about … you … and I wanted to say how sorry I am."

*Sorry that I'm dying or sorry that you slept with my husband?* I didn't say it – I wasn't that brave. I wish I had been. Instead, I pretended I hadn't heard and hurried upstairs, trying not to trip over my own feet. I frantically texted Julia. *'Help!'*

The bedroom was my undoing. That's when I found my voice; that's when my repressed rage and resentment was suddenly unleashed. Her clothes were carelessly draped over my chair. Her underwear was on the floor by the bed – *my* bed – and the duvet was thrown back, and sheets crumpled. It may as well have had *'night of passion'* stamped across it. Letting out a strangled roar, I threw her clothes across the room. Geoff was in the doorway.

"She's here already, sleeping in *my* bed! How long did you wait? Five minutes? You bastard, Geoff! I hate you!" I choked on my words, determined not to cry but doing so anyway. Francesca appeared behind Geoff.

"It's not like I've never slept in it before," she said. Geoff shot her a warning look and hissed, "*Shhh.*"

"When?" I demanded, staring at Geoff and refusing to look at her. "*When?*"

"Whenever you weren't here," she replied. She was goading me. "Weekdays, usually lunch time."

Geoff turned to her. "For Christ's sake, Fran, not now!"

"Why? She can't talk to you like that, Geoffy. Not in your own home." She turned to me. "He's been worried sick about you, and you didn't even phone him to say you were okay."

I blinked at her, stunned. I was still trying to register the way she had called him *Geoffy.* If anybody else had called him that, he would've sneered at them.

"What the hell is going on?" Julia appeared in the doorway behind Francesca. She glared at Geoff. "You really are something else! What the hell is *she* doing here?"

"*She* has a name, thank you," Francesca replied smartly, rounding on Julia.

Julia smiled. "Of course; where are my manners? What the hell is your cheap little tart doing here, Geoff?"

Francesca's eyes widened; quite scarily wide, actually. She looked Julia up and down.

"My sister was right about you. Common as muck, she said."

"Your sister?" Julia frowned.

"Tamzin. Surely you remember her? Your husband left you – remember – for Tamzin." She smirked at Julia, watching the colour drain from her face. I honestly don't know how either one of us managed to not slap her. We should've done, because she didn't stop there.

"It was Geoffy who introduced Matthew to her. We all got on so well. It's a shame it didn't last."

Geoff finally found his voice, pulling her into the room. "Enough, now." She wriggled her arm free and scowled at him.

"Did you?" Julia asked him. You could hear the raw emotion. I just wanted to leave. I felt sick. It's like he was a completely different person. How can that be?

Julia stood her ground. "How could you do that, Geoff? Never mind me – although, I will never forgive you – but how can you treat Bree like this? What would Jessica say?"

The mention of his mother hit a nerve. "She won't believe you, Julia. You mean nothing to the family. She'll think you're just being bitter, as always."

"But if I see it for myself, then what, Geoffrey?" His mother appeared, large as life, behind Julia. I felt my legs buckle and sat down on the chair. This was turning into a badly scripted farce. Who else was going to appear? I just hoped Niall would see sense and stay in the car.

"Mother! What are you doing here?" Geoff had turned a deep shade of pink and suddenly looked about twelve years old. She stood in front of him, eyeing him with disapproval.

"We had a visit yesterday evening, from Curtis. Your father is very disappointed in you."

"What's new?" he muttered, regretting it as soon as he'd said it.

"I am not in the mood for your impertinence. How dare you treat Bree like this? How dare you treat the mother of your children – my grandchildren – so appallingly. I am ashamed of you!" She waited for a response, but he knew better than to argue. I actually felt a twinge of compassion for him. Fleetingly.

"You didn't even tell me that Bree is ill." She glanced over at me, sadness in her eyes.

"I was trying to find the right time," he said quietly.

"Which is when? It's cancer, Geoffrey; there is no right time."

Nobody spoke for a minute, which felt like five. Jessica shifted her weight, turning to Julia.

"Could you go and put the kettle on, please, and make a pot of tea or something. Thank you. And make sure it brews for five minutes, would you?" She nodded, dismissing Julia then looked at Geoff. "And while I'm drinking my tea, you pack your bags with whatever you need now, and leave."

He stared at her, dumbfounded. I stared at her, too.

"What? Where am I supposed to go?" he stuttered.

"Home, with me."

"I am not going back home!"

109

"You are not staying here. This is Bree's home, too, and she has priority. I don't think for one minute she wants you here, so you have no choice, Geoffrey."

"I am *not* going home with you," he reiterated.

"Stay with me," Francesca interjected quietly. It's surprising how quickly her confident facade had slipped once Geoff's mother had appeared.

"And you," Jessica said to her, "Regardless of what you mean to my son, you will never mean anything to me or his father. Is that clear? Now, get out."

"I'm going to help him pack."

"No, he can manage. He's a big boy. You leave now before you do any more damage. And I don't ever want to see you here again. Do I make myself clear?"

Francesca tutted. "You can't tell me what to do. This is Geoffy's house and I'm staying with him."

I could see Jessica balk at the use of the pet name. She was about to reply, when Geoff stepped in, telling Francesca to go and wait in his car. Francesca tutted again, snatched up her overnight bag, ignoring the clothes on the floor, and flounced off downstairs. The door slammed behind her, and I heard Julia shout a choice parting greeting. I strained my neck to look out of the window. Yes, as I thought; she had indeed left the house in nothing but that silky gown.

Jessica crossed the room and offered me her arm. She's never done that before. I took it and we went down to join Julia, leaving Geoff alone upstairs. Before we sat down, she gave me a hug, holding on for a long time.

"I'm so sorry, Bree; for your news, for my son, for the way he has treated you."

We sat down and drank tea in silence. Jessica reached across and squeezed Julia's hand. I think she was trying to apologise to her, too; for Geoff's behaviour and for the bombshell Francesca had dropped. Jessica sipped her tea; very deliberately and slowly. Giving her son time to pack.

"Bree, who pays the bills here?" she asked. I wasn't expecting that kind of a question.

"Geoff does. He always has."

"So, do you have a joint account?"

"No. I have my own account. My wages go in it and Geoff transfers money for shopping, as he always has done. He says, because I earn a fraction of his wage, it makes more sense for him to be in charge of it all. It's always worked well. Why do you ask?"

She shrugged lightly. "Just planning ahead for you, that's all. It's not right that you are staying in a holiday rental. This is your home, and you need to be here for your own peace of mind and for your health. You can't possibly go through treatment living out of a suitcase." She was echoing Curtis's sentiment from a couple of days previously. I was getting a good indication of how their conversation had gone.

"And what kind of bills do you have for this place? Would you have any idea how much you'll need for utility bills, etcetera?"

"Umm, well, obviously the biggest chunk of Geoff's wage is the mortgage. Then there's council tax, gas, electricity, insurances. I'm going to have to ask him." My heart sank. I had never in my wildest dreams, ever envisaged having this conversation.

"Mortgage? Is he … still paying the mortgage?"

I nodded.

"How long is left?"

"I really don't know, sorry."

She could see how difficult I was finding this, so she just patted my hand and thanked Julia again for the *'lovely cup of tea.'*

"Oh, I forgot to mention; I told your friend to go home with Pip and come back later. I thought it was best that Geoff didn't see him."

"You sent Niall away?" My heart sank even further.

"No! Not *sent*. I just didn't want any scene, that's all."

"But he's not … he's just a friend, Mother."

"I know, dear. And he's a very polite chap. But Geoff won't see it like that, will he? That's all I'm saying."

And that is all she did say. We finished our tea and she stood up, telling us to stay seated. Julia and I glanced at each other, not daring to speak. We heard her call for Geoff. We heard the front door open and close, and we heard his car leave. Jessica reappeared, hovering in the doorway.

"Don't get up; I'll see myself out. Julia, make sure Bree settles back in, please. And Bree, I'll pop over in a couple of days and we can have a better talk then."

Ignoring her order to stay seated, I got up and hugged her, still not entirely sure what had just taken place.

"Thank you. And I'm sorry you felt you had to come over and do this. I was going to leave. It would've broken my heart but then again, it's already a bit broken." I gave her a weak smile. '*A bit*' is an understatement but she knew what I meant.

"This is your home," she said quietly. "You chose it, you decorated it, you filled it with love. You raised your children here. We all thought you were a little bit mad at first, but actually, I fell in love with your home too. Including that hideous Aga," she chuckled. "You have been a fantastic mother and a fantastic wife. Don't ever think you haven't." And with that, she quickly kissed my cheek, waved at Julia, and left. I could tell she was on the verge of tears.

We sighed simultaneously and sat back down.

"Well, I think I should die more often; you certainly see people in their true colours when they know there's a death in the offing."

Julia put her head in her hands. "Oh, God," she breathed.

"What?"

"With all this business with Geoff, for a moment I'd forgotten that you're ill. Sorry."

"Don't be sorry. And don't give me that sad face again! I don't want to spend every day being sad. I'm going to fight this cancer. I'm going to fight for my home. I'm going to divorce Geoff before I die."

"Really?"

"Yes. I need to write a will, and I need to leave everything that's mine, to you and the children."

"Bree..."

"I know; you don't want to hear it, but I need to sort it out. Having heard how Geoff behaved with Patrick fills me with dread. What'll happen after I'm gone? I don't think *she* will step into my shoes and be their surrogate mum, will she?" It didn't bear thinking about.

I sent Niall a message telling him the coast was clear. He hadn't gone back to the cottage; instead, he'd parked up in the Square and walked with Pip down by the stream at the foot of West Hill.

I told him what had taken place. He's a good listener; what I like is the way he takes it all in but doesn't react dramatically. However, as I relayed events, he swore under his breath on a few occasions. When I told him the bit about Geoff being the one to introduce Matthew to Tamzin, he couldn't hold back any longer.

"Is this really the same guy that you've been married to for all these years? Is he some sort of Jekyll and Hyde? How can he behave like this and think he can get away with it?"

"Well, he's not, is he? His mother will see to that," I replied.

"Except he has," he said, shooting a look at Julia's closed face. "He's destroyed your marriage; he destroyed Julia's. He engineered it so that Patrick doesn't come home. He told your children the news, without even considering how they would react. Is there no end to what he'll do?"

A brooding silence loomed over us. I slammed my hands down on the table and stood up. "Come on, let's get out of here. I can still smell her nasty perfume. I need some air!"

We sat on the beach chairs outside the beach hut, christening my new mugs. I passed the matching biscuit barrel round, helping myself to four chocolate digestives. I balanced them precariously on the arm of the chair. Niall watched me, amused.

"If I get too ill to shop, would one of you make sure this is always topped up with biscuits, please," I said, dunking one in my coffee.

"Of course. Consider it done," Niall nodded.

"Make sure you do, Niall; otherwise, she'll have a full-blown melt down," Julia chipped in. She'd been very subdued since earlier, but she seemed to be perking up a bit. I wanted to broach the subject but wasn't sure if she'd want to talk about it. It would be digging at old wounds. A time best forgotten.

"How do you want to work this evening; pack up and eat before we leave or eat when we get back to yours?" she asked. I pulled a face, staring out at Old Harry.

"I'm not sure I want to go back now."

"Why not?"

"Two reasons: it's been really fun staying in the cottage. Like a holiday. As soon as I went back home today, it hit me. I've got cancer. My marriage is over. I know it sounds daft but it's all suddenly very real now." I sighed deeply in unison with Julia. "And the second reason is – where do I sleep? I can't bear the thought of sleeping in my bed. Not after what I saw today. I need to throw it out; get a new one."

"Beds take weeks to be delivered," Julia said.

"Not if you go to IKEA," Niall suggested. "I can go there tomorrow. Pick up a frame and a mattress. Just tell me what you want, and I'll fetch it."

"Thank you," I murmured, reaching for his hand. My biscuit tower was knocked over in the process. I let out a dramatic wail.

"Get some biscuits while you're there," Julia laughed.

Coffee break over, Niall went into the hut to hang the canvases. I took my chance to talk to Julia, undisturbed.

"I'm sorry for what Geoff did to you and Matthew."

"He did me a favour, Bree. I'm so much better off without him. Look what I have with Curtis now; Matthew seems like such a child in comparison."

I murmured agreement.

115

"I can't believe how fake Geoff is, though," she continued. "The number of times I cried on his shoulder, and he said things like, '*he's an idiot, Julia*', and, '*you're reams better than her*'."

"I know."

We slipped into silence again, smiling with closed eyes at the sun. I reached for the biscuit barrel.

"Do you think I eat too many biscuits?"

"I know what you're thinking, Bree."

"Do you?"

"Yes. I spotted her skinny little arse, too. She makes me sick."

I laughed. This is why Julia's my friend; she always knows the right thing to say at exactly the right time.

"Over the years, when I've had moments of self-doubt – usually every summer, when it's time to bare all – Geoff has always said, '*I love your curves. You have such a great figure. Who wants a stick, anyway?*'" I took a bite of my biscuit. "Clearly, he does."

# Chapter Eight

My phone woke me with a start. I had well and truly drifted off, lulled to sleep by the warm sun and sounds of the sea.

"Mum! Where are you?"

"Hi, Kitty. I'm at Studland beach. Why?"

"We're at home. We wanted to surprise you but you're not here."

"Oh! Okay, I'll be right there." I waved a frantic hand at Julia who was eyeing me sleepily from her chair. Niall had his eyes shut tight, headphones in.

"Don't rush; we let ourselves in. I'll put the kettle on, shall I? Can't wait to see you!" Kitty chirped, then hung up.

I tapped Niall on the shoulder. He opened his eyes, startled.

"Everything alright?"

"I think you're about to meet Bree's children," Julia said, before I had the chance to.

We packed away the chairs and locked up the hut.

"The thing is – like I said earlier – I'm just not ready to go back there yet. But they can't stay at the holiday let. I mean, it's fine with you two because it sleeps four anyway."

"Tell them to meet you at the holiday cottage, and Julia and I will go elsewhere. I can go back to Dan's," Niall said, putting a plan into action.

"No! I don't want you to go anywhere. Neither of you." We walked back to the car slowly, trying to work a way round things. In the back of my mind, all I could see were Francesca's clothes strewn across my bedroom floor. I had refused to pick them up before we left. I was regretting that now. As if I didn't have enough explaining to do.

"Right," Julia stopped in her tracks to emphasise the point she was about to make. "We all go home with you now. Have dinner, or whatever. We can be there for moral support when you tell them about Geoff in more detail…"

"Must I?"

"Yes! Then, when everybody's going to bed, Niall and I will go back to the holiday let and sleep there. Then back to yours for breakfast. How about that?"

I felt a pang of jealousy at the thought of them spending the evening together without me. Not in *that* way obviously but just knowing I'd be missing out on the laughs we'd been having together, was not a great feeling. I desperately wanted to see the children, but equally, desperately didn't want to talk about Geoff or cancer; I wanted to bury my head in the sand for a little bit longer. Until Friday.

Kitty was at the door, waiting. She threw her arms around me and squeezed me hard. Sean hovered behind her, waiting his turn.

"Patrick's on his way," Kitty said. "He's driving – stuck in traffic."

I thought I was going to cry at the mention of Patrick but checked myself and put on a bright smile.

"So, did you two meet at Wareham station, or what?"

"No, I went down to Bath yesterday and we got the train together." Kitty made it sound so casual but for her to leave her beloved London and head for Sean at the drop of a hat, spoke volumes. I could see the pain lurking. I knew there would be tears later and I suspected there had already been plenty.

Julia hugged them in turn, then introduced Niall. There was a little chat about my party and how Sean had briefly said *Hi* to him, and how Niall had noticed how Kitty spent the entire evening barefoot in the garden. It was all very amicable. For some reason, that made me nervous. Ridiculous, because I had nothing to hide or reproach myself for.

I carried a tray of teas and coffees through to the front room and right on cue, Patrick pulled up. We held each other for the longest time, silent tears rolling down both our faces. Then he shook hands with Niall and hugged Julia, Kitty and Sean, who had been patiently waiting their turn to greet him.

"So, what happens now? When do you start chemo – I'm assuming you will have chemo?" he asked.

"Friday," I nodded.

"This Friday? That's quick! Is it always that quick?" Kitty asked, looking from me to Julia. I'm sure she caught the look that passed between us.

"The thing is, your mum is …"

"Very scared," Niall interrupted. "So it's great that you're all here. We've been trying to cheer her up, but I think she needed to see you all."

"Oh, Mum," Kitty put her mug down and smothered me, holding me tight. And as soon as she sniffed, it started me off, closely followed by Sean. Patrick struggled to hold it all in, watching me quietly. Julia got up and stared out of the window. Niall busied himself with clearing mugs away and returning with a box of tissues.

I thought I'd cried it all out but apparently not. Hardly surprising, I suppose. I settled back, with Kitty on one side

119

and Sean on the other. Patrick sat on the footstool by my feet, holding my hand. All we needed was a couple of teddies and a book, and it would be like old times, reading a story to them before bed.

Niall hovered in the doorway. "I'm going to order food for us; what does everybody fancy?"

Half an hour later, we were sat around the kitchen table, eating fish and chips, washed down with cider and tea.

"I've missed this," Kitty sighed, licking her fingers.

"Don't they do fish and chips in London?" Niall joked.

"Probably, but they wouldn't taste like this. Nothing beats proper fish and chips from the coast."

"I know what you mean," Sean agreed, "We have a chippy near our house in Bath and it tastes nothing like *proper* fish and chips. It's almost fake, somehow."

I closed my eyes, content to listen to the children chat about food and compare notes on the taste of water. I felt Niall's hand on my shoulder.

"Any more tea wanted?" he asked quietly in my ear. "Coffee?"

I shook my head and smiled, briefly opening my eyes to acknowledge him. Kitty was staring intently at me.

"You look tired, Mum." She watched Niall clear the table, then got up to help him. "More cider, anybody?" She turned to me. "Mum, why don't you go upstairs and lie down. We can clear away in here."

"I'm fine, honestly. And besides, I'm sleeping down here. I can't bear to be upstairs at the moment."

"Why not?"

"Because," Julia interjected, "*she* has been staying here, with your dad." She looked triumphant. I wish she wouldn't do that; pour all of her own rage into every syllable uttered about Geoff. Yes, I agree with it all, but he is still their dad, and they are still only just about coming to terms with it.

"So, your mum is going to move into your room, Kitty. You'll have to do a swap."

Kitty stared at the two of us, open mouthed, realisation dawning.

"Were those *her* clothes on the floor? I did wonder at the mess."

I nodded, apologising.

"You've got nothing to apologise about, Bree," Julia snapped. She looked at my children. "I know this is a lot for you to take in, but things are going to change around here, and as you're home, it would be great if we can all pitch in to get it sorted for your mum, before her treatment starts."

My heart ached, watching their crestfallen faces. I was ready to backtrack and leave things as they were. Try and cope with sleeping in my room. The bed would have to go, though.

Patrick was the first to snap out of the trance they seemed to have slipped into.

"I think that's a great idea. But how about you swap rooms with me, Mum? I quite fancy a view of the front and you can have the garden view – I know you'd like that. Besides, my old room could do with decorating, so now's the perfect time."

Niall told Patrick about his planned IKEA trip and Patrick asked to go along with him. Julia busied herself loading the dishwasher while Sean came over and hugged me. Kitty stood quietly and watched. There was a look in her eye I couldn't fathom.

Pip was beyond ecstatic when we took her for her evening walk, en masse. We did a complete circuit of the village; the mood lifting again after Julia's little talk. It was the tonic I needed, listening to their banter back and forth. We stopped at the play park for Kitty to have a go on the swings, laughing and screaming intermittently, as Sean pushed her as high as he could. Patrick persuaded Niall to have a go on the adult exercise equipment adjacent to the swings, and soon enough, they too were laughing as their legs strode comically on the health walker and slalom skier.

It's a neat little play park on the edge of the field that runs between East and West Street. Part of the field is sectioned off as a dog exercise area, away from the cows, and has provided Pip and the children alike, hours of fun over the years.

Back home again, we played a round of *Harry Potter Scene It* – thrashed by Patrick, who has remained the unconquered hero of the game for the past ten years – before Niall and Julia headed back to the holiday cottage for the night.

"I'll sleep down here with you, on the other sofa," Kitty said, helping me make up my bed.

"Me too!" Sean chipped in. He and Patrick dragged their mattresses downstairs and set up camp in the middle of the room. The TV went on quietly and I fell asleep to the sound of them chortling at old episodes of *SpongeBob SquarePants.*

Everybody keeps telling me to rest but my brain obviously didn't get the message. Wide awake again at five and my mind racing, I crept out to the kitchen to make coffee and toast. Pip followed me, yawning and stretching each leg in turn as she walked, like a ballerina doing a warm-up.

I'd been to the common and back with Pip, had a shower and was on my second cup of coffee by the time Kitty stirred. She found me in the garden.

"Mum, can I ask you something?"

"Sure. What is it?"

She put her teacup on the round, cast iron table and sat down opposite me.

"Is Niall ... the reason Dad left?"

"What? No!" I sat up, stunned. "The reason Dad left is because he's having an affair. I've already told you."

"And Niall?"

"Is my friend. He's just a friend."

She sighed and shook her head. "That's not what I see. The way he looks at you - there's more to it."

"If he looks at me in any particular way, then I can't help that. But it's one-sided."

"That's just it though, Mum; you look at him that way too."

I stared at her, incensed by what she was saying. "I don't believe this! Your dad destroyed my world, Kitty. He's been sleeping with that tart for ten years. He moved her in here the minute I was gone! The only reason they left is because Granny told him to go. She's appalled at his behaviour. Everybody is. And yet, you're taking his side."

"I'm not!"

"I know you love him. I understand this is hard to get your head round. But to accuse me – and not him – is so far off the mark."

"I'm not accusing."

"Niall is here – with Julia – to look after me. That's all. Next, you'll be accusing me of having a threesome!"

"*Mum!*"

I could see I'd gone too far. She had the same shocked expression as Geoff, when I didn't curb my tongue with him last Friday. I tried to rationalise with her.

"Kitty, I've done nothing wrong. I feel sick to the bone when I think about how much love I have poured into my marriage, and all the time, he was with someone else. I feel so stupid."

"You're not stupid." She reached for my hand across the table. I really struggled not to pull away. Her words had hurt. So much.

Julia appeared at the kitchen door.

"Morning! Patrick let us in. Shall I put the kettle on? Have you had breakfast?"

Kitty excused herself and disappeared upstairs. Julia frowned at me.

"Everything alright?"

"Not really." I quickly relayed the conversation, begging her not to react loudly. For once, she listened. Kitty came back downstairs.

"Mum, you're wanted upstairs in Patrick's room. And Niall is asking for a tape measure."

I grabbed it from the kitchen drawer and headed upstairs.

"Morning, Brianna," Niall smiled, hugging me. "We're just measuring up and seeing what's needed for in here. The rooms are all about the same size, aren't they?"

I nodded, opening the windows wide. "It's so stuffy in here!" I looked around the room, at the pale grey walls,

124

dotted with Blu Tack marks where posters had once hung. Patrick was right; it really was time for a revamp.

"The wardrobes are fine, and we can just move my chest of drawers … actually, no. Can we swap them round, Patrick? I'll have yours and you have mine. Or should I get new stuff? I really can't think."

"Mum, we'll get a new chest of drawers and a bed. What about your chair?"

"That's going to the beach hut," Niall said.

"Great! So maybe we can find you a comfy chair, like a Sherlock Holmes kind of thing?"

"Shall I come with you?" I was suddenly thinking of all the little things I would need, too. I hadn't really thought it through, but it would need more than just a new bed. I wasn't really au fait with IKEA. I had readily agreed to a new bed but anything more was now making me feel panicked. It had taken years of careful window shopping to create my bedroom, and now I was entrusting Niall and Patrick to redesign it, with no planning whatsoever.

Julia's raised voice broke my train of thought. It wasn't an angry tone, more of a scolding one.

"I don't understand why you're not backing her up one hundred percent, Kitty. She has been through so much in just a few days and she needs our support. That includes you."

"I know, but I still want to see Dad. I need to hear it from him."

"Are you saying we're lying?"

"No, no, but…"

"What then?"

"I think there is something going on between Mum and Niall."

"There isn't. Trust me, I know. He is the loveliest man and he's a great friend. Exactly what your mum needs right now. Don't begrudge her that."

"I also think Mum's lying."

"About what?"

"About how ill she is. I can see it. She's *really* ill, isn't she?"

There was a pause. *Please don't say anything, Julia.* Too late.

"Yes, she is. I'm so sorry, Kitty."

I closed my eyes, breathing slowly to calm the trembling that engulfed me.

"Mum?" Patrick was right behind me, eyes wide with childlike fear.

"I'm sorry, Patrick. Julia shouldn't have said anything."

"How bad is it?"

I hesitated. How can I do this? "I have a fight on my hands. It's not good, I'm afraid."

"Why didn't you say?"

"I … I'm trying not to think about it myself. Not until I've started the treatment. I'm hanging on to what little bit of sanity and normality I have for now. If you can call this normality." I waved a hand around his room.

Kitty appeared in the doorway. She let out a strangled sob and ran into my arms.

"I'm sorry, Mum."

"I'm sorry too, Kitty. I shouldn't be angry with you; it's not fair. He's your dad and of course you should see him. Of course you should let him explain."

The next half hour was the one I had been dreading the most; explaining my diagnosis and watching their terrified faces absorb the news. I think the silence was the worst part. Too stunned to cry, too shocked to speak, too scared to even look at me – or each other.

Julia was the one to break the silence.

"So you see, kids, Mum really does have a battle ahead of her. I know the outcome is … well, no outcome … but we're not prepared to give up just yet. Your mum isn't ready to die and I'm not ready to lose my best friend. So, like I said before, we have to rally together and be as strong as we possibly can – for each other."

"And Dad knows?" Kitty asked quietly.

"Dad knows," I nodded.

Sean stood up abruptly and stormed out of Patrick's room, loudly slamming his own bedroom door shut.

"I'll go," Patrick offered. He knocked lightly on Sean's door and closed it gently behind him.

Niall shot me a look, then smiled at Kitty.

"Kitty, I heard what you said earlier, to Julia."

Kitty looked mortified. "Oh."

"I'm going to be honest with you; I love your mum. Very much. However, there is nothing but friendship between us and there never has been. I understand this is all very confusing and alarming, but I want you to know, I am going to be here to look after her and I hope the two of us can get along. Like you do with Julia. Okay, she's been around for a long time, and I haven't, so it's not quite the same but I'd like to…"

"Yes," Kitty nodded, interrupting just in the nick of time before Niall started to gabble. "And I'm sorry if I was rude."

"You're not rude, Kitty. You're in shock; we all are. And our instinct is to lash out; find someone to blame because we don't understand what's happening."

There was an awkward silence, and I was suddenly aware of all three of them looking at me; waiting for me to say something. What could I say that hadn't already been said? So, I just smiled. A weak, watery kind of smile.

Kitty took that as her cue to leave. "I'm just going to check on Sean."

Once she'd closed Sean's door behind her, Julia let out a dramatic sigh.

"Well, say it how it is, Niall, why don't you!"

"What? You said last night we needed more honesty. So that's what I did. At least now, everybody knows what's going on."

"Wait, did you two *plan* this?" I asked. There was that intense, unwanted, stab of jealousy again at the thought of them together, having meaningful conversations.

"Not plan exactly," Julia conceded, "We just said if the opportunity arose to make things clearer for the kids, then that's what we should do. I hadn't expected Niall to make a declaration of undying love, though."

"I did not!" He held his hands up defensively then turned to me. "That's not what I did. I just want them to understand why I'm here, instead of their dad. That's all."

"It's okay, Niall," I nodded. "I'm sure she understood what you meant. And thank you. It was very sweet."

"Sweet," he repeated under his breath, clearly unimpressed with my choice of words. Julia raised her eyebrows at him; he responded with a sardonic smile. Again,

I seemed to be invisible to them. They have their own secret language going on, neither one thinking I can see them.

I stood up. "I'll be in the garden if anybody needs me."

"Oh, I thought we were deciding what you want from IKEA. No?" Niall asked.

"I don't know. I … it's all a bit too much now." I sighed, summoning up the courage to look at them both. "I hadn't wanted to tell the children any of this. Not yet. I understand how it happened but now you're saying you both planned it. Without consulting me!"

"No, that's not what we meant," Julia said. "We were just talking, that's all."

"About?"

"About everything."

What kind of an answer is that? I suddenly felt completely drained; a combination of talking – yet again – about the cancer, and feeling totally overwhelmed. I just want to be in control but as each day passes, I feel less and less like I have a handle on things, and more and more like I'm drowning.

Niall followed me downstairs and into the garden.

"I'm sorry if I overstepped the mark, Brianna. I didn't mean to upset you."

"You haven't upset me. You make me feel panicked."

"Panicked?"

Conscious of the acoustics, I moved to the far end of the garden so we wouldn't be overheard.

"When you say things like, you love me very much. I can't love you back. Not yet."

"Again?" He looked exasperated. "We've been through this; I don't expect anything from you but…" he raised his hand to stop me interrupting. "But I'm not going to lie about

129

how I feel. Kitty thinks there's something going on between us *because* we lie about how we feel."

"We?"

"Brianna, I know how you feel about me." He lifted my chin to look at me, making it impossible for me not to look at him. "I *know*. And I know this is the wrong time completely for us. And I know you're hurting about Geoff, and I know you're terrified about what's happening to you. And I know you're trying to be the super-mum of the century, wanting to protect your children – even though they're adults, not children, and can protect themselves and think for themselves. And I know that deep down, you're actually quite glad that it's all out in the open now, however painful or awkward it is."

"You know a lot, don't you," I said quietly. He smiled.

"I do. I also know that you feel trapped here. And even though you wanted to see your children…"

"They're making it worse," I finished. He nodded.

"Can I tell you something you probably don't know?" I asked.

"Go on then."

I paused for a minute, trying not to laugh at the face he was pulling, feigning impatience, challenging me.

"I'm jealous of you and Julia, spending time together, without me."

He laughed lightly. "Oh, I knew that, too."

"How?"

"Because I know you. How you tick. I told you before."

"Soulmates," I smiled.

"Yep." He kissed my hand then clasped it in his. "Now, we need to get you sorted with somewhere to sleep. So, tell me what you need for Patrick's room. Start with the basics and then when you can think with a clearer head, I can go shopping again. It's not hard, you know."

"I'm sorry, I do seem to make it more difficult than it is."

"That's understandable. And stop apologising." He pulled me in for a hug. My whole body seemed to melt. It's becoming a bit of a habit; me, sinking into his chest, but he makes me feel so safe there. Cocooned. Protected. Exactly what I need right now. I'm so busy protecting everybody else when in fact, I just want Niall to protect me. To take over and make everything alright.

Julia called us over to the patio table. "Coffee! And biscuits. Come and get them before they melt!" She smiled, watching us walk towards her, Niall's arm around me.

"I was thinking of going back home tonight, if that's alright with you two. I'll be back in the morning, don't worry. I just need to see Curtis."

"Why don't you ask Curtis over here for dinner tonight, so he can spend some time with the children," I said, "Then you two can go back home together, later. And Niall – you can sleep on the sofa, maybe? Rather than the cottage, by yourself."

We made a short list of things needed from IKEA.

"Just a bed, mattress and chest of drawers for now," I reiterated.

"What about bedding?" Niall asked. I looked to Julia.

"Shall we go to Goulds?"

"I can get it all from IKEA," Niall interjected. "Save you going out."

"Thank you, but I'm a bit fussy about sheets. I'd rather choose them myself."

"Fair enough," he nodded.

"Don't spend too much; I'm not sure it's what I'll want long term."

Julia gave a knowing smile. "What she means is, if it's cheap, it can't be any good."

"Says you!" I laughed.

We all turned to the house when the front door slammed. Patrick appeared in the kitchen, pulling a face.

"Everything okay?" I asked. He came out to the patio.

"Kitty's gone for a walk."

"And Sean?"

"Still in his room." He grabbed a biscuit from the plate, grimacing when he realised, too late, that the chocolate had melted.

I stood up, offering him my seat. "I'll go and talk to him."

As I left, I heard Niall ask if he was still up for the IKEA trip.

Sean was sitting on his bed, shoulders hunched, scrolling through his phone. I sat down next to him.

"I'm sorry, Sean; I know this is all too much to take in. Are you okay?"

He shrugged.

"Do you want to talk?" I leaned in closer, trying to get eye contact but his were fixed on his screen. "Sean, please; put the phone down."

He sighed, doing as I asked. I waited. He's always been a reluctant communicator, so I played the waiting game as I'd done so often during his teenage years. Eventually, the silence got the better of him.

"I'm so angry with Dad. I hate him for what he's done."

"Me too," I said gently.

"But Kitty is doing my head in! She's adamant we should go and see him. I said *no*, so she stormed off, saying I was taking sides. Well yes, of course I'm taking sides! I hate him! I don't care if I never see him, ever again." He blinked back angry tears, sniffing. "It's not just that he's been … doing that … but that he told you about it when he knew you were ill. That's just …"

I could tell he was aching to swear, to scream with rage or punch a wall. He was remarkably controlled, all things considered. He hasn't always been. Yes, he'd been a happy, gentle, sensitive soul in his early years but once puberty hit, all that changed. He became withdrawn, troubled and would bottle things up until he reached boiling point. Then he would vent on inanimate objects such as his bedroom wall, his door, and once, next door's greenhouse. He hadn't meant to smash it; he'd angrily hurled half a brick from the raised bed I was constructing, into the dense hedge, forgetting that on the other side of said hedge, was Ron's greenhouse. Ron was fine about it. Sean was mortified and for a short while, curbed his anger.

Sixth form changed him. He mellowed, became calmer and more level-headed. That's when I discovered his tormentors had left school. My poor boy had been the butt of their teasing and cruel goading for over three years, without ever telling us. Yes, of course I had asked regularly about school and friendships, but he had never let on that there were any issues. And I had never been any the wiser.

My heart ached for him now, watching him battle with new emotions, new conflicts.

"We all react differently, Sean. Kitty is an organiser; always has been. I don't think she can cope with this situation

133

because she can't be in control. She can't organise us and sort it all out."

"I bet she'll try though," he said gruffly.

"Maybe. And we just have to let her work it out for herself."

"But why does she want to see him? I don't. Do you?"

"No."

"And look what he did to Patrick. And Patrick never said anything! He kept that from us. From you. For three years. How can he do that?"

"Trying to protect me. Hoping it would go away. I know you think he was wrong, but I can see how he was in an impossible position. And he was scared."

We sat in silence for a while. I watched the tension slowly leave and his shoulders relax. I put my arm round him.

"I love you, Sean."

"Love you too, Mum." He rested his head on my shoulder; quite an uncomfortable manoeuvre for him, as he's so much taller than me now.

Patrick knocked on the door. "Are you coming with us, Sean?"

Sean shook his head. "No, I'm going to stay here."

Patrick nodded and looked at me. "We're off, then."

I wanted to follow him downstairs and wave them off, but instinct told me to stay put. I knew Niall would understand. I heard voices outside, then the car pull away. Sean and I sighed simultaneously.

"Breakfast?" I suggested. He shrugged, not wanting to move.

"Mum, are you going to die?"

I think my heart stopped for a second. There was a definite sharp pain in my chest, making me catch my breath, followed by a pounding in my ears.

"I'm going to do my best not to."

"Are you just saying that?"

"Probably. But I need to believe it and so do you. Deal?"

"Deal."

Kitty was back by the time we went downstairs. Julia had brewed tea and was making a round of toast. Kitty glanced at us both, smiling briefly before resting her eyes on Pip sitting at her feet, waiting for a piece of toast to 'drop' her way.

"Kitty's coming with us to Dorchester," Julia said pointedly, "but not to shop. She's meeting Geoff there."

"In Dorchester?" I stared at Julia. The last thing I wanted was to bump into Geoff. I wouldn't be able to focus on shopping now.

"I suggested he pick her up from there and they can go somewhere else to talk," she nodded slowly. Sean glared at the back of Kitty's head, muttered thanks to Julia and left the room with a piece of toast in his hand.

"Mind the crumbs," Julia called after him brightly.

"I have to see him, Mum." Kitty looked more vulnerable than defiant. I could see she was struggling to hold it all together.

"Of course you do," I said, kissing the top of her head. "But please – for me – don't stay in Dorchester with him. I don't want to see him."

"I won't. I might suggest we go and see Granny."

"She'd like that," I smiled. I didn't say it but if Kitty was expecting to find an ally for Geoff, the last place she should look is at her granny's.

# Chapter Nine

There wasn't the same buzz, shopping in Goulds, as there had been the day before. Something was missing. Or should that be, some*one.*

I don't know why I had automatically chosen Goulds for bedding. It's where I've always shopped and as I scoured the shelves for something I hadn't seen before, my heart sank. Everything was familiar; everything screamed of domestic bliss with Geoff.

I phoned Niall. "Can you add duvet covers to your list, please."

"Will do. I'll do a video call when we get to that department," he said.

I picked up some pillows and a duvet, deliberately choosing microfibre rather than Geoff's preferred choice of down, then we headed for the café. Coffee and cake were needed.

"Is it possible to love somebody else when you've loved your husband for more than twenty years?" I asked.

"Yes, it's called a rebound," Julia replied. I shook my head.

"No. It started before I found out about Geoff. I just tried to ignore it."

She looked at me, visibly enjoying my honesty. "And yet, we can all see it."

"Can you? How?"

"When he walks in the room, you light up like a Christmas tree. Not just your face; your whole body language comes alive. I never saw that with you and Geoff."

Damn my stupid, transparent face. And body, apparently. Julia smiled – a reassuring kind of smile. She wasn't shocked by my confession; quite the opposite. She really does hate Geoff.

"Look at me and Matthew. I thought he was the one. My everything. But compared to Curtis, he's nothing. Not just because he cheated. We really weren't *that* connected."

"That's how I feel! I was trying to recall the last time Geoff and I had a proper conversation, and I honestly can't. It's like we've just bobbed along for so many years. Used to each other. But not really connecting, mentally. Not like I do with Niall. And yet, I feel so bad admitting it."

Julia took a sip of coffee, watching me. "And are you going to admit to Niall how you feel? Put the poor boy out of his misery?"

I shook my head.

"Of course not!" she exclaimed. "Don't tell me – you don't want to upset the children."

"It's easy for you, Julia! Sorry, but …"

"Easy because I don't have children of my own, you mean? You're forgetting that I am as close to your children as I possibly could be, and I know for a fact that you are just hiding behind them right now."

"I'm not! But I can't just flick a switch and pretend my marriage was over months ago. It's wrong, surely, to fall in love with somebody else the minute your marriage is over."

"Except you said you already felt like that about Niall *before* your marriage was over."

"Yes, and that's wrong too! Don't you see?"

She sighed, licking remnants of sticky cake from her spoon. "What I see is a woman – a beautiful soul – denying herself happiness in what could potentially be her last months on this earth. And I won't let you do that." She choked on her words, quickly ducking her head down and grabbing a serviette from the table to dry her eyes. I swallowed repeatedly, struggling not to follow suit.

"You don't have the luxury of time, Bree."

"Don't say that. If you believe that, then I'll lose all hope." We held hands across the table, watching each other's unchecked tears.

My phone made us both jump. I quickly brushed a hand across my face, wiping it dry. It was Niall, on video chat. His expectant smile froze.

"Oh, are you alright?"

"I'm fine. Fine." I sniffed and put on a bright smile. He nodded, knowing I wasn't, but played along anyway. His camera panned the shelves of bedding, and above them, a long row of duvet covers hanging on display.

"Take your pick!" He showed me a close up of each design – of which there were many – describing the colours as if I couldn't see for myself.

"That one!" I shouted. "The blue and purple one."

"The paisley one?"

"Yes."

"Really?" Julia wondered. "Not quite Dorma, is it."

I turned to her. "No. Precisely. Besides, it reminds me of my dad's favourite shirt when I was a kid."

"How about this one, too?" Niall asked, hovering the camera over a floral cover. Tiny mulberry flowers scattered over a grey background, with green vines weaving through them.

"Yes, perfect," I nodded. "Thank you."

"No worries. I'll get sheets to match. We're nearly done here. How's it going with you?"

"Fine. We're done here now, so we're heading home soon. We'll see you in a couple of hours, then."

He waved and hung up, not before turning the camera on Patrick, leaning on the trolley, who also waved. They looked very happy and relaxed. Unlike us. I shot a look at Julia's blotchy face, not holding out much hope that I looked any better.

"Home?"

"Home," she nodded.


I was upstairs with Niall in Patrick's room when Kitty came home. She'd already texted to say she was on her way. I'd assumed Geoff would bring her back, but she'd caught the train from Dorchester and a taxi from the station in Wareham.

I felt stupidly nervous about what she'd have to say; to the extent that I didn't go down to greet her. I heard her come through the door, heard Julia call out *Hello* and offer her tea. Then, as luck would have it, they went into the garden to talk, where I had a prime spot to eavesdrop through the window.

"He didn't deny it."

"Did you expect him to? Come on, Kitty, how could he? The evidence is all there."

"I know but I was expecting some kind of denial. Apology. Regret. But he said none of that."

"What did he say, then?"

"Not a lot. He didn't talk about *her,* and he didn't want to take me to see Granny. But he did ask how Mum was."

"And what did you say?"

"I said she's doing okay, considering. And that we've all had a long talk and we're just spending time together."

"Did you mention me? Or Niall?"

"No, not really."

"What does that mean? Did you tell your dad that Niall is staying with us?"

"No."

"Good."

"Why is that good? I thought there was nothing going on."

"There isn't but your dad can be very jealous, so it's best he doesn't know."

There was silence for a while – I think they were drinking tea – then Julia asked Kitty if she felt better having seen him.

"I'm not sure. I hate what he's done but I can't alienate him."

"Why not? I think the boys have."

"But what if Mum dies – we'll be without parents altogether, if we do that."

"You've got me and Curtis."

"I know."

Silence again.

"Do you think Dad will ever change?"

"No. Do you?"

"Not now, no."

"Can I give you some advice, Kitty? Your mum needs you, more than ever. Your dad doesn't. Get your priorities right. And if anything does happen to her – God forbid – you know who you can turn to for support, don't you. We will always be here for you."

141

Niall was standing behind me, also listening. He tapped me on the shoulder and put his arms around me when I turned to him.

"Are you okay?"

I nodded. He nodded too, resting his cheek on mine.

"You were right earlier," I said tentatively.

"About what?"

"About how I feel."

He moved to look at my face. "Sorry, I'm not following."

Was he just saying that, or did he genuinely not know what I meant? Julia's words echoed in my head; *You don't have the luxury of time, Bree.*

"I love you, Niall." I saw how his eyes softened and how he tried to stop an elated smile from taking over his face. He rested his cheek back on mine and whispered in my ear.

"I'm not going anywhere; you know that, right? We'll fight this, together."

"I don't deserve you," I whispered back. He couldn't help but laugh.

"Are you kidding me? I don't deserve *you*, more like."

"Yes, you do!"

He looked at me again, grinning now. "Shall we just agree that we absolutely deserve each other? Otherwise, this could go on forever and get very tedious."

"Agreed," I laughed. He looked at me for a long time, studying every inch of my face. I thought he was going to kiss me – for an insane moment, I hoped he would – but he didn't. Instead, he moved away, just as the door opened and Patrick walked in.

"I found him," he said. "Up on the hill, where I thought he'd be."

Sean wasn't home when we'd got back. Neither was Pip. I'd assumed they'd gone for a walk but when they hadn't returned by the time Niall and Patrick got back from IKEA in Southampton, I began to worry. His phone went straight to answerphone. Patrick had been quick to go looking for him.

Niall patted him on the shoulder. "Good work. I don't know about you but I'm starving. Shall we do another take away and pretend we're being healthy?"

"Why bother pretending? You should see my diet at uni. I am a walking pot noodle!"

Patrick helped Niall finish emptying the room of furniture, ready for decorating. I went downstairs to find Sean. He and Pip were stretched out on the sofa.

"Sorry, Mum. I didn't mean to worry you."

"It's fine; I just wondered where you were, that's all."

Julia called us from the kitchen. "I've made a late lunch. Come and get it!"

We all gathered round the table, appreciating the simple, standard, Hillingdon lunch of sausage rolls, beans and salad.

"I've never had baked beans with salad before," Niall commented.

"Mum's idea," Patrick replied. "She always insisted we have salad with every meal – even things like this."

"I was trying to keep you all healthy," I said.

"It didn't work," Kitty laughed. "We used to try and sneak it under the table for Pip but even she wouldn't eat it."

"But you're eating it now," I pointed out.

"Brainwashed, that's why," she replied smartly, flashing me a winning smile. I could see she was trying to make amends. I shouldn't begrudge her seeing Geoff, but I do. I can't help it.

"I think it's a great lunch, thank you, Julia," Niall smiled. Everybody murmured agreement.

"Yes, thank you, Julia. Not just for this but for everything you've done. I can't remember the last time I saw you so productive in the kitchen." I raised my glass of water to her. She raised hers back.

"Yes, I think it was probably just after you had the twins."

"It was! You made tea on demand for all the visitors."

"And mopped up after Patrick because he decided that was a good time to try potty training."

"He did, yes!" I laughed at the memory.

"Do you remember how he'd be running across the room, stop suddenly, pull down his trainer pants and pee on the floor? Then stare at the puddle and exclaim, '*Whoopsie!*'"

"Hey!" Patrick laughed indignantly, "Thanks for telling everyone."

"My pleasure, sweetie," Julia winked.

"You're an idiot if you think she's never told that story before. Probably to the whole neighbourhood," Sean teased.

"You haven't, have you?" Patrick asked Julia. She just shrugged innocently.

"Of course not. Why would I do that?" She hurriedly cleared the table, chuckling to herself. She dropped a fork on the floor and bent to pick it up. "Whoopsie!"

Even Patrick joined in with the laughter at his expense, muttering jokey threats of *'just you wait til you're old and incontinent, Auntie Julia.'*

"Your kids are great," Niall said as we walked arm in arm along the pavement later that evening, watching them ahead of us. Sean led the way with Pip, closely followed by Patrick and Julia. Kitty had her arm tucked through Curtis's, chatting nineteen to the dozen with him.

We were finishing off the day with a repeat circuit of the village, after a late Chinese take away once Curtis had arrived, straight from work. He takes a huge amount of interest in the children and demanded to know all their news as we ate.

"Don't tell me about your studies – it's your social lives I'm interested in. What's the latest gossip?"

Kitty told him all about the second year Freshers week that had just ended, and Sean described the dynamics of the new student house he's sharing with five others for the next two years.

"So, all's well," Curtis nodded. "I'm pleased."

"It is, except … I don't want to go back," Sean announced. "Not now. Not with Mum being so ill."

"Neither do I," Kitty agreed.

My heart sank. I stared at them, not sure what to say. Curtis said it for me.

"Listen, both of you; I completely understand what you mean and how you're feeling but giving up now – just as you're starting your second year – is folly. This chance won't come around again. If you give up now, it'll be so much harder to start again later. And it's the last thing your mum wants." He turned to me for confirmation. I nodded. "Besides," he continued, "the three of us are here to look after her. The best thing you can do is carry on with your studies and come home at weekends. That way, you bring some sunshine into Mum's life after what I can only assume, is going to be a crappy time with each chemo session." He

145

raised questioning eyebrows, waiting for them to agree. He lowered his tone. "I understand, really, I do. Trust me though, it would be better all round for you to stay at uni while Mum's treatment is going on; then come home to visit as often as you can. We need to keep a routine and we need to keep it calm. Okay?"

Kitty and Sean nodded reluctantly but I could see they'd listened and taken onboard what Curtis had said. There had been a look between Niall and Patrick, and I suspected that would be another conversation to be had later, probably without other ears.

"Curtis is right, darlings. I have no idea how I'm going to react to the chemo and the last thing I want is to be worrying about you worrying about me, and seeing me being – possibly – very unwell from it."

"But what if ..." Kitty started. I knew what she was going to say.

"If things take a turn for the worse, then yes, come home. But let's not think like that now. Let's have a positive plan. Take it a week at a time."

Back from our walk, Julia beckoned me into the garden while Curtis loaded her bags into his car.

"I'm going to stay away for a few days – give you all some space," she said, hugging me.

"Do you think?" I really didn't want her to go.

"Mmm, yes. I think Kitty needs to get to know Niall and she won't do that while I'm here. She'll just use me as a distraction. I'll be back on Friday, though. Is that alright?"

"Yes, of course."

"And then I can stay whenever you want, for as long as you want. Let's just see how you are after the chemo starts."

We stood, arms round each other, watching Kitty and Sean in the kitchen, hunting the cupboards for snacks.

"I'd always thought Kitty was my ally but she's actually quite a daddy's girl, isn't she," I said.

"Yes, absolutely! And that's why she's finding this all so hard. Give her time, Bree. She needs to see Geoff for what he really is. And she needs to trust Niall."

I looked at her. "I told him."

"I thought you would," she smiled, squeezing me.

"Nothing's going to happen."

"I know."

I blinked, surprised. "How do you know?"

"Because we talked about it."

"What? Not again, Julia! How could you talk about something like that behind my back?"

"He was about to burst, Bree. He needed to get it off his chest, tell someone how he feels about you. He's tormented by grief. And he knows nothing can possibly happen now. But at least you both know where you stand."

I sighed and we hugged again. "How did it all get so messy, Julia?"

"*How*? Don't even get me started on that one!"

"Right, we're going to get a second coat on the walls now," Niall said as we waved Julia and Curtis off. "That can dry overnight, then we can assemble the bed in the morning."

"Can I help?" Sean offered.

"Absolutely," Niall and Patrick said in unison, then laughed – also in unison. It was bizarre to watch.

Kitty slipped her arm through mine.

"We can watch a film together, Mum. You choose."

"Are you sure, Kitty? It'll be either *Mamma Mia* or *Leap Year*, if you let me choose," I laughed.

In the end, I opted for *Mamma Mia*. I prefer *Leap Year,* but I couldn't very well sit and swoon over an American falling in love with an Irishman, when I had my own Irishman upstairs decorating my bedroom, and my philandering husband's little girl, analysing our every move.

As it is, I fell asleep halfway through the film, waking again at the end credits. Kitty appeared with an armful of bedding.

"They've finished upstairs. They're out in the garden getting some air and having a beer. I've told Niall he can have my room tonight and I'll sleep down here with you."

I'd wanted some time alone to talk with Niall, but I knew that would have to wait. So instead, I smiled and said what a good idea that was.


Wide awake at five again, I stole upstairs and knocked softly on Kitty's door before opening it. Niall woke up and smiled.

"Morning."

"Morning. I was wondering if you fancied a walk with me and Pip?"

"Absolutely," he said, stretching.

Five minutes later, we were heading up to the common; Pip ecstatically leading the way, enjoying these extra early walks of late.

Once we'd passed the houses and crossed the cattle grid that separated the lane from the common, Niall took my hand and squeezed it.

"How are you holding up?"

"Okay, I think. So much is happening, it's hard to keep up. But I'm glad they all came home. I'm not so glad that Kitty saw Geoff, but I know it had to be done."

He nodded agreement, keeping a firm hold of my hand. I liked it. It's been a long time since I held hands with someone other than my children. Geoff wasn't one for public displays of affection and that even stretched to holding hands.

"What's going on with Patrick?" I asked. Niall raised his eyebrows and sighed.

"I think he needs to be the one to tell you."

"Should I be worried?"

"No, no, it's nothing bad. Maybe not quite what you had planned but … just hear him out."

"Okay. I'll wait until he tells me, then."

I didn't have to wait long. Patrick was up by the time we got back – another early riser.

"I couldn't sleep," he said, offering us coffee. "Mum, can I talk to you?"

"Shall I leave you to it?" Niall asked him. Patrick shook his head, ushering us to the kitchen table.

"Mum, I'm deferring my Masters for a year."

"Oh no, Patrick, I don't want you to do that for me!"

"It's already done."

"When?"

"I spoke to my tutor, the minute you told us about the cancer." He studied my face, looking earnest. "Look, I agree about Sean and Kitty, but I've already got my degree. And they're more than happy to keep my place for a year, especially with the grade I got."

"He got a first," I said to Niall. He smiled and nodded; clearly, he already knew that.

"I've been asked to write some papers which no doubt will be published, and I can do some studying to keep me in the loop. But I really want to be here for you. Especially as Dad isn't."

He looked at the both of us, waiting for my response.

"What do you think about this?" I asked Niall. He looked surprised.

"Me? I think it's a sound idea. I'm going to be here too, obviously, but I do need to work, and with Patrick being here, I can go out on location and not worry about you being on your own. I think it's great."

I reached for Patrick's hand. "Thank you, darling. I'm really grateful." I hadn't intended to cry but cry I did. The thought of Patrick being here with me, lifted me in an unexpected way. The fact that he'd discussed it with Niall – involving him in the family – lifted me even more. I suddenly felt very blessed and a little less scared.

Sean didn't take the news too well. He couldn't understand why it was okay for Patrick to give up uni but not him. Kitty agreed with him initially but quickly changed her tune.

"Actually, I think it's a great idea for Patrick to be here for Mum." She smiled at me, nodding her approval.

"And Niall will still be here, of course," Patrick added. I caught the way his eyes challenged Kitty. She looked away.

"That's great," she said.

Patrick put his arm around Sean's shoulders. "I'll keep you both up to date, every day, I promise."

"And keep Dad away?" Sean asked.

"Yes. Not that I think he'll bother us, anyway."

I wish I shared his confidence. I just had an uneasy feeling it wasn't going to be a simple case of Geoff moving on with his new life. Something was going to happen to upset the balance.

# Chapter Ten

"Are you sure it's not too cold for body boarding?" I asked again, dutifully packing the boards into the boot of Niall's car. My question was greeted with groans of frustration and shouts of *No!*

We had decided to put decorating on hold for the day and make the most of the weather. The children opted for Worbarrow Bay, our favourite spot along the coast. Not the usual sandy beach but one of large shingle. I say *shingle* — the stones are more the size of saucers, in parts. However, it's a great spot, sheltered from the breeze and not too popular, affording us with space and privacy.

I made up a quick picnic and Niall nipped down to the village store with an order of crisps and fizzy drink. It doesn't matter how old they are; as soon as you mention *picnic*, they instantly want crisps and cola.

It's a short drive down winding roads, flanked with sheep-studded fields, then a fifteen-minute walk from the car park to the sea. It's a route we know well but Niall hadn't been before. He was captivated by the scenery, and I could tell he was making a mental note of ideal spots to return to with his camera.

"Last shout for the toilet, kids!" I called, as I shut the boot, checking we'd unloaded everything.

"Mum, we're not five!" Kitty retorted, walking ahead. She stopped and turned around. "Actually, I do need to pee. Sean, hold my stuff." She passed her body board and bag to him. He tutted loudly.

"I need to pee, too. Take your own stuff."

I flashed Niall a smile. "And so begins a standard family day out."

"I think it's great," he said scooping up Kitty's discarded bag and body board. "Do you need to pee, Brianna?"

"Yes." I pulled a face, apologising, as I piled my bags by his feet. He laughed when both Sean and Patrick dropped their bags by his feet too and disappeared into the old, brick toilets, hidden behind a swathe of bramble and undergrowth.

Re grouping and gathering up our belongings, Kitty eyed Niall.

"Don't you need the loo? It's a long walk."

"I'm fine. If I need to go, I'll just go in the sea."

"Ewww!" She recoiled dramatically, screwing her face up in disgust.

"Kidding!" he laughed, throwing his bag for her to catch, before heading to the toilet.

It took longer than the usual fifteen minutes down to the beach, due to a pack of deer silently moving through the wooded copse adjacent to the path. Five phones were trained on them, recording their every move.

"Are there always deer here?" Niall whispered.

"Yes," Kitty whispered back, "but we don't often catch them in a group or for very long. They usually run when they hear people."

The moment was shattered when Pip, not fussed by the deer, spied a squirrel abseiling through the tree nearest us, and barked loudly. The deer took flight, everybody sighed heavily, and our journey continued.

I felt ridiculously pleased at the low whistle of appreciation Niall emitted when we turned the corner. Bathed in sunlight and an intoxicating perfume of gorse and woodruff, Worbarrow Bay did not disappoint. A perfect, sweeping crescent of beach, with a rugged backdrop of chalk and sandstone cliffs, stretched before us. A couple of anchored boats bobbed on the glinting water a few meters out. Seagulls swooped effortlessly back and forth, and above the cliffs, the unmistakable silhouette of a lone buzzard soared in the still sky.

"This is astounding," he said. "Why have I not been here before?"

"Not many people have," I replied. "The locals tend to favour West Bay, and the tourists head for Swanage or Weymouth. This is ours," I spread my arms out wide. "And that is where we usually set up camp." I pointed to the far side of the bay, where the cliffs climbed to reach their peak. "It's a real suntrap."

I sat on a pile of towels, watching the four of them splashing about in the water, half-heartedly paddling out on their boards but more content to just float on the ebb. Their laughter and loud chatter rebounded off the cliffs, resonating across the bay. Such a joyous scene.

Kitty shouted for me to come and join them, more than once, but I waved happily, declining. I'd given my board to Niall, saying I'd rather just chill and read on the beach. To be truthful, I felt completely drained. The heat from the sun and stones combined, had such a soporific effect and I just longed to sleep. This spot always makes me feel tired and I've often been lulled off to sleep, only to wake up with a burnt face.

Sean came trotting across the hot stones, bending over me as I lay on the towels. Beads of water dripped on my face.

"Sorry, Mum," he laughed, "Just checking you're okay."

"I'm fine; just dozing," I smiled. He turned and stuck both thumbs up to Niall, who nodded and waved, then said something to Patrick, who also waved.

"Are you having fun?" I asked Sean, pleased at how buzzy he looked.

"It's great! Did you know Niall's a surfer? He's got a board I can borrow next time I'm home, and he's going to take me surfing." He beamed, squinting at me, then glanced back at Niall paddling further out. "Anything you need?"

I shook my head. "No thanks, darling. I'm fine. You go and have fun."

I watched him hurry back to the sea, splashing Kitty as she lay sunbathing on her board by the water's edge. She shrieked and splashed him back. Laughter rang out again and I dozed back off to sleep.

Giving in to Kitty's pleas and reasoning of '*it's my last night here for ages*', we stopped off for fish and chips on the way home, then spent the rest of the evening assembling the bed and chest of drawers in my new room. Kitty and I systematically moved all of my clothes and bits. I thought maybe this would be a good time to weed my wardrobe and sort through my drawers, but a bigger part of me just didn't have the energy or inclination. It could wait.

Kitty joined me in the front room again, giving my new mattress time to settle after being unpacked. For once, she was asleep before me. Fresh air and exercise does that every time.

"How come the only part of me that got burnt is my ankles?" I studied my otherwise pale legs.

"My ears got burnt," Kitty said, "But nowhere else. It's good stuff, that Nivea sun cream. I obviously just missed my ears."

We were all out in the garden, having a lazy breakfast. Pip had already had her walk and was now stretched out on her sunny spot by the patio doors. She suddenly scrabbled to her feet, looking alert, moments before the door knocked.

"Granny!" Kitty jumped up from her seat to hug Jessica. Patrick hovered behind her, having shown her in.

"Tea, Granny?"

"Yes, please, and then I want to hear all your news, young man. We haven't seen you for far too long."

Patrick smiled, looking embarrassed, not sure how to respond. Jessica mellowed, dropping the matriarchal act that she does so well.

"Don't worry, Patrick. I know about your father. You don't have to hide from me."

I don't think I've ever known her to spend as much time with the children as she did. They laughed and joked, interspersed with moments of serious conversation. I noticed that Patrick didn't mention his deferral, and neither did the twins.

When the twins went to pack, Jessica sat in the front room with Niall and myself, wanting to know all about Friday's appointment; what would be happening, where it would happen and what was the name of my consultant. She then wanted to talk about finances and bills, and eventually, about Geoff. She didn't have a single good word to say about him and for the most of it, I just listened. It wasn't so much a conversation; more a monologue, interspersed with the odd question, which only required a limited response.

156

I'm not sure how I felt, if I'm honest. Granted, I don't have a good word to say about him either, but when I think back on all the times I've been made to feel inferior, or '*just the wife*', or '*Bree, with her American attitude*', and just accepted it because Geoff is her golden child, to hear her pull him to pieces now, annoyed me. But then again, maybe it wasn't her making me feel inadequate in the past; maybe it was Geoff's father. And by her not contradicting him, she was only guilty by default.

"You know Jeremy had affairs, don't you?" she announced, snapping me back to reality. I shook my head.

"No, I didn't." It wasn't a surprise; far from it. I'd always suspected Geoff's father of it.

"Yes. But they never lasted. Not like Geoff and this woman. That's what makes it so wrong."

I wasn't sure what to say to that and I was going to just nod and agree, but the other part of my brain got the better of me.

"You mean, if he'd had several affairs but only brief ones, that would be okay?"

"Well, yes. Think about it, Bree; a short affair wouldn't have demands on him. He wouldn't have got so involved. But this Francesca woman has dug her claws in, well and truly. And that has destroyed your marriage."

"I think *any* affair would've destroyed our marriage."

She studied me for a moment. "Well, maybe. You're very sensitive, I suppose. Whereas, I have the stiff upper lip, and *carry on regardless* attitude, that you Americans seem to lack. Not that I'm criticising," she added quickly, "But my father made it very clear to me when I married Jeremy, that if I wanted any of my inheritance, I would have to remain married, whatever happened. He didn't like Jeremy, you see. He thought he was just after my money. Maybe he was but I saw him as my ticket to freedom. So, I put up with any of his nonsense."

I was certainly seeing Jessica in a new light, that's for sure. Niall had disappeared into the kitchen and was missing her revelation. I think it was intentional.

"I'm sorry, I can't do the same," I said meekly.

"Heavens, no! That's not what I'm saying at all, Bree. Don't you dare forgive him! He has overstepped the mark, well and truly. He's made his bed ... and she's keeping him in it."


Jessica stayed until after lunch, leaving in a flurry of hugs. She hugged me too; again, for much longer than was comfortable. Not unpleasant though. I could get used to it.

"Keep me posted," she said to Niall.

"Of course," he nodded, accepting her offered arms.

"Since when did Granny become so emotional and ... human?" Kitty laughed, once we had waved her off.

"Since her son became an A grade wanker," Sean replied quickly. Kitty was about to retort but thought better of it. She just looked immeasurably sad. I should've pulled him up on his language but instead I pretended I hadn't heard it. He needs to vent.

It was soon time for the twins to leave. I watched Niall load their cases into his boot.

"I need to get a different car. One with a bigger boot," I sighed.

"Oh Mum, don't get rid of your car! I love it so much," Kitty said. "Besides, you only need a bigger boot when we come home from uni. I know; buy *me* a car with a big boot instead," she smiled angelically, batting her eyelids. I laughed, hugging her.

"Thank you for coming home, Kitty."

"I'll be back soon. Next weekend, maybe?"

"Whenever you want," I said.

"And if you're feeling lousy, I can wait on you, and we can watch films together." She nuzzled into my shoulder, not wanting to let go.

"Sounds perfect."

Sean's train was first to arrive. He gave me the biggest hug, squeezing me tight, then apologising. He hugged Kitty and Patrick, then without any hesitation, Niall.

"I'll phone you Friday evening," Patrick said. Sean nodded, forcing a smile. He hugged me again and jumped on the train at the last minute. We waved until he was out of sight.

Soon enough, it was Kitty's turn. She clung to me, brushing away tears. Patrick handed her a tissue. She gave him a quizzical look.

"I always have tissues," he said. "Allergies." He glanced at me. Kitty nodded, putting her arms out to hug him. I watched, wondering if she would hug Niall too. I could see her thinking about it and yes, she did. Quite a long, appreciative kind of hug.

"Thanks for such a great day yesterday, and all the take-aways," she said.

"My pleasure," he replied. "See you next weekend."

The blackbirds were serenading us with their evening repertoire, and I could hear a subdued rustling from the far end of the garden by my compost stack. Hedgehogs. For some reason, our family of hogs are not very nocturnal; they don't wait until the dead of night to emerge. As soon as the merest hint of dusk starts to settle, they venture forth to systematically rid my borders of slugs. They're a joy to have in the garden.

"Blackbirds always remind me of home," Patrick said. "It was always the last thing I heard at night before I fell asleep."

I nodded, distracted. I was watching Niall in the kitchen, leaning against the counter while on the phone to Dan. The patio doors were shut, scuppering any chance of eavesdropping but judging by his face, it was a good conversation.

I became aware of Patrick watching me watching Niall. He smiled. My face was obviously doing its transparent show-and-tell thing that it does so well.

"Mum, I hope you're not waiting for approval from any of us. But just for the record, I think he's great. Perfect for you."

"It's not like that, Patrick."

"Well, it clearly should be."

"We've both just ended our marriages. We're not ready for anything more. Not with everything else that's going on."

"But surely…" he stopped abruptly, not wanting to voice what he was thinking. Time isn't on my side. I could see it in his face. He took a deep breath. "I've hated Dad for so long, so I'm just relieved that he's not here anymore. And if Niall makes you happy … why not? Don't wait, Mum."

I didn't ever envisage the day when my son would be giving me relationship advice. I couldn't decide if it was tragic, comical or just very endearing.

"The thing is, I spent so many years with your dad, just accepting his way of life. I didn't always agree with it but went along with it, because I loved him. But now I wonder – did I love *him* or just the idea of him? Which one has kept me here for all these years?"

"*'The idea of him'* – what do you mean?"

"You wouldn't understand, Patrick. You never read the *Famous Five* books."

"Because they're boring, Mum!"

I pulled a face of mock horror, making him laugh. "What I mean is, your dad's so English, which was appealing. But now, I just see it as annoying. And false."

"That's not the English – that's Dad. *He's* false."

"I suppose, yes. I just had this ideal in my head. And he made it come to life. Everything. This house, this village. Dorset. The coast. It's all I wanted, since I was a little girl."

"And now?"

"It's … boring, to quote you. I feel restless; panicked that I've wasted so much time." I looked at Patrick's earnest face, listening to me. "But I can't have regrets. That achieves nothing. Besides, I have three beautiful children as a result. And I wouldn't change that for anything."

# Chapter Eleven

I looked at my alarm clock for the third time in as many minutes. Twenty past four. I'd been trying in vain to fall back to sleep for the past half an hour. It wasn't happening. Ordinarily, if I couldn't sleep, I'd be up, making the most of the morning stillness. But today, getting out of bed was one step closer to starting my treatment, which terrified me. The day I had been dreading – the day when I finally had to face reality – had arrived.

I sat on the edge of the bed, staring at the little white box with the velvet bow in my hand, deep in thought. I kept telling myself, *it's just a necklace*, but it's so much more than that. I know it. Niall knows it. And if I wear it today, Patrick will see it and he'll know it too.

"What are you doing, Bree? Everybody knows it anyway," I told myself out loud.

It certainly sparkled; such a beautiful piece of jewellery. Silly, I know, but I felt an overwhelming sense of peace and determination putting it round my neck, as if my ancestors were radiating through the Irish silver. Willing me on. Bringing me luck. Lord knows, I needed it.

I could smell the coffee halfway down the stairs. Niall was in the garden, his back to the patio doors. Pip ran out ahead of me to greet him and when he turned, I saw a cigarette in his hand.

"Are you smoking?" I blurted in surprise. Startled, he dropped his cigarette to the ground, quickly stamped on it and picked it up, concealing it in his clenched hand. I watched him, waiting for an answer. Suddenly, I felt like a chastising mum.

"Sorry, Niall. That sounded like an attack. It really wasn't meant like that. I just didn't know you smoked."

"That's okay. I kicked the habit when Layla was born – well, just before – but today …"

"Today you really need it," I finished his sentence for him. He nodded, putting his other arm out to hug me.

"How are you this morning?"

I pulled a face. "Couldn't sleep. You?"

"Not much, no. Coffee? Or walk Pip first?"

We took a subdued walk. Even Pip was subdued, trotting ahead dutifully but lacking in her usual enthusiasm. Niall took my hand again, holding it firmly in his; although this time, he didn't wait until we were out of sight of the other houses. He'd noticed my necklace earlier but didn't say anything. He didn't need to; his pleased smile spoke volumes.

Back home, he busied himself making me poached eggs on toast.

"First and last coffee of the day. Sorry," he said, putting the mug in front of me on the kitchen table. "And have some Weetabix at nine."

He'd made a list of foods to eat and foods to avoid, before and during chemo. I'm so glad he took responsibility of that; I really couldn't do it myself. I think once I've started the treatment, I'll feel more able to cope with things, but the prep has been solely down to him. I thanked him yet again and yet again, he told me not to.

"Niall, I have something to ask you," I said, mopping up egg yolk with the toast. He watched me from the opposite side of the table.

"Okay."

163

"You've been here a week and I know you came without any hesitation or questions."

"Yes. And?"

"How long are you staying?" I looked up to gauge his response. His steady gaze met mine.

"Are you asking me to leave?"

"No! I'm asking you to move in. Bring all your stuff."

"I have my stuff here," he countered.

"Well, that's not all of it, is it? Sean said you have surfing gear. And I'm sure you have other things, too." For once, I couldn't determine the look he was giving me. It made me feel nervous. "I mean, if you want to, that is," I added quickly.

"Would it make you feel better if I had all my stuff here?"

I nodded.

"Okay, then."

"But?" I saw the pensive look on his face.

"It just means I have to see Lizzie."

"Do you think that will be a problem?" It hadn't occurred to me that it would be. Was that bad? Selfish of me?

"It means leaving my little bubble here and facing reality again. I'm not sure I'm ready for that," he said. We sat in silence for a while, mulling that one over. "I cancelled a gig for this weekend," he said quietly.

"No! Why?"

"Same reason. It's been comfortable being here and shutting the world out, even just for a few days. Hasn't it?"

"It has," I agreed. "Are we in danger of becoming hermits?"

"Maybe. I couldn't think of anybody better to do it with though."

By the time we left a few hours later, I felt sick with dread. The journey across the bay to Poole seemed to take forever. Niall drove in silence but Patrick – normally the subdued one – sat behind me, chatting endlessly about nothing. It was pressured, it was well meaning, but I wished he would stop. Silence would have been preferable. My brain was screaming with the overloaded burden it was forced to carry.

Patrick hugged me, wished me luck and headed for the sprawling park opposite the hospital, book in hand. He intended to find a bench by the boating lake, to wait.

"Phone me when you're done. I'll meet you back at the car park," he said.

As soon as we reached the waiting room for my consultant, I had the urge to cry. One look at Niall told me he felt the same way. We simultaneously squeezed each other's hand, willing each other on.

"He's very nice," I told him, nodding towards the consultant's door. "Very down to earth."

It wasn't long before we were shown in by the nurse. Mr Jakowitz stood up to greet us, smiling encouragement.

"Hello again, Brianna."

I shook his offered hand. "Hello, Mr Jakowitz."

"Please, call me Peter." He extended his hand to Niall.

"This is my friend, Niall," I explained. He smiled at him and glanced at me, astute eyes assessing the situation, indicating for us to sit down.

"No Mr Hillingdon today?"

"No," I replied firmly. "He left."

"Because of the cancer?"

"No, because he found somebody younger, thinner, with pretty nails." I hadn't meant to divulge so much. It just seemed to tumble out of my mouth, at speed. Peter drew in a breath, his nostrils flaring in the process. He nodded.

"I see. So, shall we change your next of kin details?"

"Yes, please," I nodded back. "Niall has moved in to look after me, and my eldest son is home from university now, for a year."

"Good." He tapped away on the keyboard, asking Niall for his details. I had the urge to cry again, but this time, with happiness. It felt right to have Niall as my next of kin.

Peter talked us through the procedure, most of which went over my head. I was aware of making appropriate noises but honestly, I couldn't tell you what he said. My brain refused to hear or retain it. Niall asked some questions, about the additional medication and about the side effects of both that and the chemo. Peter was very patient and answered everything thoroughly, impressed by Niall's involvement and knowledge. As was I.

"Brianna, before you have bloods taken, do you have any questions?" Peter asked. I stared at him, willing my brain to think of something.

"Is there any chance I can beat this?"

He was quick to answer. "Well, I never say never. In your case, you have at best, an eight percent chance. At best. If I were you, I would take that and relish it. Mindset is key. Focus on staying strong but don't obsess; by that I mean, enjoy your time now, as best you can. Live each day." He watched me, keenly. "Does that help?"

"Yes. Thank you."

"Of course, as we discussed last week, you may respond remarkably well to the treatment and if that happens, your chances may improve. Keep that foremost in your mind."

As soon as we'd shaken hands again, to end the meeting, the nurse led us through to the treatment ward. It looked like any other ward, really; I'm not sure what I was expecting exactly but I thought it would be more daunting, more isolated, sterile. I was asked to sit on the chair next to the bed and put my arm on the wide arm rest. Niall hovered nearby, watching intently as the canula went in. I tried not to look, tried to focus my mind on other things. There was no view to speak of from the window, not like the other wards. I'd been on a ward on the top floor before, where the view is spectacular, stretching out across the sunny bay. A real tonic. But the treatment ward is in the bowels of the hospital, affording nothing more than a view of brick walls and windows. Suddenly, I appreciated why the phlebotomy cubicles always have posters plastered across their thin walls – distraction tactics.

Once the drip was up and running, Niall sat next to me. He pulled a magazine from his jacket pocket.

"I did the most cliché thing, I'm afraid, and bought you a word search puzzle."

I pulled a face. "I'm rubbish at those."

"Whereas, I am king," he smiled, offering me a pen. "Let's do it together."

It was all over remarkably quickly, or so it seemed. After my lengthy day last week, I'd expected more of the same, but no. Once the transfusion had gone through, there was no ceremony, no long goodbyes; just, *'that's all fine, see you next week'.*

I stared out of the car window, absently watching the greenery fly by. Niall tapped along to OneRepublic on his steering wheel, joining in with the chorus – he has such a great voice – and Patrick was regaling us with the story of a persistent seagull, who wouldn't accept that he had no food to share.

I didn't feel any different, however hard I focused on my body. Nothing had changed. Business as usual. I'm not sure what I was expecting but I was expecting *something.* My arm didn't even ache from the canula. The only discomfort I felt, was from the plaster she'd stuck on my arm afterwards – one of those flimsy, round things – and it had rucked up, pinching my skin. That, and the vile taste in my mouth. Even the chewing gum Patrick offered me, couldn't get rid of it. Small price to pay, though.

"Well, if this is what it's going to be like for the next six weeks, I think I can cope with that," I said, stretching in my seat.

"So, it's the same time, once a week?" Patrick asked.

"Yes. You don't have to come with me every time, if you don't want to," I replied.

"I know, but I will. Besides, I don't usually get time to read, so this is a good excuse."

I'd instilled the love of books in them from the word go. It was by far my favourite time of day; story time before bed. They'd be scrubbed and in their pyjamas, with full tummies, snuggled up in front of the fire, eager to discover which story would be read that night. I loved buying books for them but equally loved taking them to our local library. It was a fortnightly outing; a fortnightly debate on how many books was *too* many. Kitty always insisted ten was not enough.

But they soon grew out of the library and out of reading so voraciously. The summer *Reading Challenge*, which had once been the highlight of the long school holiday, lost its appeal as primary years came to an end. Teenage life took over and childhood favourites were quickly forgotten.

As soon as I got out of the car, I felt it. I let out a shaky *oooh* sound.

"What is it?" Both Niall and Patrick were by my side in an instant.

"Not sure. My legs feel like jelly. I feel very shaky all of a sudden."

Niall tossed his keys to Patrick, instructing him to get the door, then without any warning, scooped me up in his arms and carried me into the house. I didn't object. Who would?

Satisfied that I was comfortable on the sofa, with cushions padding me out, he stood back and watched me, assessing my pallor. I fidgeted with the cushion by my shoulder. He shook his head, giving me a knowing laugh.

"If I take Pip out for a walk, you're not going to stay on the sofa, are you?"

I pulled a face. "Sorry. I just feel restless. Maybe I'll sit in the kitchen, instead."

"On one of the hard, uncomfortable chairs, you mean?"

"Are they uncomfortable, though? They've got cushions on."

"You know what I mean, Brianna. You need to let me make a fuss of you, okay? I need to know that you're comfortable."

I sighed. "Okay. But can you make me comfortable in the kitchen, please? I can sit and look out at the garden. I won't move until you're back, I promise."

Patrick had gone next door to collect a parcel that the postman had tried to deliver while we were out.

"Expect me back in two hours at least," he joked. "They'll quiz me on all my news from the past three years, I bet you."

Niall left with Pip; not before putting a tall glass of water in front of me and instructing me to drink. He means well but I can see his insistence in doing everything by the book – that big, cancer manual of do's and don'ts, called the internet – could get very tedious. I shall have to learn to accept it, grin and bear it, with a little more grace than I'm feeling right now. If I was incapacitated, it would be fine, but I'm not.

It'd only been five minutes, when I heard the key in the door.

"Everything alright?" I called out.

Geoff walked through the kitchen door, bold as brass, as if he still lived here.

"What are you doing here?" I asked, hating how my voice trembled.

"I just came to see how you are. How did it go today?" He stood by the kitchen table, debating whether to sit down or not. He looked at me, waiting for me to invite him to take a seat. I didn't.

"What do you care?"

"For Christ's sake, Bree; I care! I love you. I haven't stopped loving you, just because ..."

"I found out about her?"

"Yes." He lowered his head, studying the floor. "I've always loved you."

"More? Than her, I mean."

He paused. He actually paused to think about it.

"Yes," he said, "But she's different."

"You're unbelievable!"

"I'm just trying to be honest."

I could've made so many snide remarks to that, but I stopped myself. I didn't want to slide down that slippery slope of bitterness. I remembered all too vividly what it did to Julia.

Surprisingly, Geoff took my silence as a sign that I was relenting. He really doesn't know me. I eyed him as he sat down opposite me, keeping a respectful distance; I'll give him that much.

"Bree, I'm sorry. I wish I could turn back the clocks. I wish I hadn't told you about her, the way I did."

I was listening but was distracted by his immaculate hair. Had it always been so immaculate? There wasn't a hair out of place. There was a chunky, gold ring on his pinky finger. That was new. It didn't really suit him.

I snapped back to reality, realising he expected some kind of reply to his apology. If you can call it that.

"Do you wish I hadn't found out?"

"Yes. I just want to go back to how we were."

"How far back is that?"

He blinked, confused. "What do you mean?"

"Well, are we talking two years? Ten? Twenty?"

171

"You see! We've had a lifetime together. Let's not throw that away." His simpering smile was nauseating.

"*You* threw that away! Not me. *You* cheated. *You* destroyed my trust."

"And I can rebuild it. Tell me what you want."

I stretched my open hand across the table. He smiled, reaching his hand towards mine.

"I want the door key, Geoff."

"What?"

"Your key. I don't want you in and out whenever you please. I don't trust you. I don't particularly like you."

"That's not fair!" he said hotly, snatching his hand back. "I know I messed up, but you love me – I know you do."

"Past tense. Not anymore."

"You need me!"

I shook my head. "No, I don't. The children might need you, so perhaps you could start with them. Build some bridges."

"And then will you trust me again?"

"Geoff, listen to yourself! Of course I won't. Ever."

He sighed deeply, sitting back in his chair. There was an uncomfortably long silence. He was thinking of something cringeworthy to say, no doubt, and I was ready to shout him down. I wasn't expecting what he said next, though.

"I never wanted kids. I wanted it to be just us."

"What? You never said."

He gave me a half smile. "No, because it's what *you* wanted, and I just wanted to make you happy. I never wanted them, Bree. I didn't realise how much they would sap you."

"Sap me? They've never sapped me."

172

"No, alright, but what I mean is, they got all your attention. I didn't get a look in."

I stared at him; a thousand thoughts flashing through my head, each joining the dots together. All Geoff has ever wanted, is attention. Like a spoilt or insecure child. Or both. He was certainly that. And if he didn't get the attention he needed from me, he was bound to look elsewhere. And if he hadn't wanted children, no wonder he resented them; no wonder he avoided family life whenever he could. I was in danger of feeling sorry for him. Almost.

"I made a mistake; I know that. I love you, Bree. More than her. And things were perfect between us since the twins left. You can't deny that." He paused, waiting for me to respond. I just focused on the table, listening. "I was going to end it with her. That was what the weekend in Paris was about."

"You were taking her to Paris, to end it?"

"Yes. I chose you."

"Because the kids had left?"

"Partly. It meant time for us."

"So, why didn't you end it?"

He frowned. "Because … because you told me you had cancer and I told you about her, and … why are you asking me this? You *know* what happened."

"I want to hear you say it."

He took a breath. "If you hadn't got cancer, we would be fine. I would've ended it with her, and you would be none the wiser."

"But you cheated."

"You didn't know. And you never would have."

"And that makes it okay?"

173

"Yes. No. I … I don't know. All I know is, I cocked up and I'm sorry." He blinked repeatedly. I thought he was going to cry. "I want to be with you – now – look after you til…"

"Til I die?"

"Yes," he nodded slowly, looking pained.

"Well, there's a thing."

"Bree, I'm serious."

"What if I don't die?"

"What do you mean?"

"What if, by some chance, I survive. What then?"

"We live happily ever after." He made it sound so simple. Unlikely. Laughable. Does he honestly believe that?

"And Francesca?"

"Is history."

"You'd do that for me?"

"Yes. Of course I would." He shuffled his chair closer to mine. I met his hopeful eyes with steady ones, holding my nerve. Just about.

"And who would pay the mortgage?"

He leant back. "What?"

"The mortgage on her house. Which is in your name."

"How do you know that? What are you talking about?"

"It's worth more than twice our house, Geoff! Why does she need that?"

He didn't answer; he looked worried. Trapped in a corner.

"Because," I continued, "you were planning all along, to leave me and live with her, that's why!"

"No!"

"Yes. Stop lying.

"I don't know what you're talking about, Bree."

"I'm talking about the fact that your mother owns this house, not us. She bought it. She intended to leave it to us in her will. She intended for you to not have to worry about a mortgage; instead, you could save your money for the kids, for our retirement, for living an easy life. What she didn't realise was that you were spending it on a luxury home for your tart. That came as quite a shock to her when she found out."

"H… how?" he stammered.

"The good, old-fashioned way. She hired somebody to snoop, dig around. Access your bank accounts. You thought doing it all through the company accounts was a smart move. You thought nobody would check. That was dumb, Geoff." I watched the colour drain from his face. I have to admit, it felt good. I was the one with surprises, for a change. And he had no idea it was coming.

"I never knew it was your mother that had all the money. I know your father and his brother worked hard to run a successful company, but it was her money that set them up in the first place."

His eyes darted from side to side as he processed what I was saying, what I was privy to. I left the silence hanging. I had no wish to fill it. I wanted him to panic. To feel betrayed. To wonder what would happen next.

"I want a divorce, Geoff."

His head shot up, incensed.

"What's the point? You'll be dead soon."

I'm not sure who's eyes widened the most at that attack. He was quick to back down.

"Oh God, I'm sorry, I didn't mean that. I'm sorry." He hit the side of his head with the flat of his hand, in frustration.

"Bree, I can't live like this. I need you. This has been the worst week of my life."

"And the house?"

"What?"

"When were you going to tell me that my home, is not *my* home."

"Does that matter?"

"Yes, it matters to me."

"Why?"

"Because it's another lie, Geoff. How many more are there?"

"None. That's it. I'm done with lying. I'll leave her. She can pay her own mortgage. I don't care about her. It's you I care about. This is where I belong."

Just then, the front door opened. Niall called out.

"You were right; two wees and a poop. I can't believe how predictable she is!"

Pip came scurrying into the kitchen, closely followed by Niall. The grin on his face froze. Geoff jumped up from his seat.

"What the hell is *he* doing here? Does he have a key?" He pointed an accusing finger at Niall.

"Yes, he does," I said calmly. His face turned crimson with rage.

"So, I'm being kicked out of my own home to make way for that leprechaun?"

"Not your home though, is it?" I challenged. "It's your mother's, and yes, she's absolutely fine about Niall being here. She told him so herself, yesterday."

"You bitch!"

"Now, easy," Niall tempered, raising his hands. "You need to calm down."

"Don't tell me what to do, you pikey filth!"

"Dad! What are you doing?" Patrick appeared from nowhere, stepping in front of Niall, just as Geoff raised his fist. He punched Patrick full in the face. Niall caught him as he stumbled backwards. Niall stared in horror at Geoff.

"Jesus, are you insane?"

"Apparently so. Better than a scheming runt, sliding into a dying woman's bed the minute her husband's back is turned. That makes you a man, over in Ireland, does it?"

"You're pathetic. You don't even care that you've hurt your own son!"

"He'll get over it. Look, he's already run to mummy."

Niall shook his head in disgust. "Your mother was right about you; you're a despicable coward."

Mentioning his mother was a mistake; I knew that, the moment Niall uttered his insult. I'd already goaded Geoff enough. I heard the clunk of Geoff's fist on Niall's jaw; I saw his head rebound and then his legs fold away underneath him. Patrick lurched forward, too late to catch him. His head cracked against the stone floor.

I screamed, crouching down by Niall's head. Patrick followed suit. Geoff stood towering over us, sneering, still pumped with rage. He pointed at Patrick, taking a step towards him.

"I warned you."

"Get out!" I bellowed at the top of my voice. "Get. Out."

He left, slamming the front door behind him. I grabbed my phone and called an ambulance.

I don't know when I stopped shaking; certainly not for the first hour. Patrick had gone with Niall in the ambulance. I wanted to go with them but once the paramedics ascertained I'd had my first chemo session only that morning, they refused to allow it.

Niall had only blacked out for a few seconds and there was no obvious swelling on the back of his head, but they needed to take him in for a check-up, just to be certain. They also wanted to get Patrick's nose checked and told him to hold damp gauze to his split lip.

Julia arrived as the ambulance was leaving.

"I got here as fast as I could. Are you alright? What's happening with Niall?"

"They want to check for concussion. And they think Patrick's nose may be broken."

The next three hours were spent waiting for one of them to phone and update me. Julia tried really hard not to, I know she did, yet couldn't resist ranting about Geoff and his despicable behaviour. I just sat and listened; my head getting heavier and the rest of my body turning to jelly. I felt like one of those weighted dolls that Kitty used to have; the one with a lead head and lightweight body, enabling it to do forward rolls. Who thinks up these things? And how did it even pass health and safety? Anyway, that's how I was feeling – a lead-headed, lightweight.

Finally, a call came through from Niall. Mild concussion for him and a broken nose for Patrick. Julia set off immediately to pick them up and they were soon back home again.

"I'm sorry to tell you this, Brianna; I don't think Geoff and I are going to be friends," is how Niall greeted me. I cried when I saw Patrick. His nostrils had been packed out with gauze, and the gash across the bridge of his nose sealed together with Steri-Strips. I could see the pain in his puffy eyes. Not just physical pain but emotional too.

"I'm going to make him pay for this," I said hotly. "He can't get away with it. Let's see how being arrested goes down with his fancy woman."

"No, I don't want the police involved," Niall said firmly.

"Why not? Look at Patrick's face!"

"Brianna, I don't need to remind you that you had chemo today. And yet, somehow, he's managed to make this day all about him. I won't let him dominate this. I won't let him worm his way back in – because he will."

"By being arrested?"

"Yes. Even negative attention is still attention. And what better sob story than him defending his marriage; him being under duress – devastated by his wife's illness. Racked with guilt for his wrongdoing." He raised his shoulders. "Need I go on?"

"Niall's right, Mum," Patrick said. "Don't give him the satisfaction."

"I don't agree," I argued.

"I know," Niall smiled gently. I looked to Julia for support. She shrugged.

"Don't look at me; I just want to smash his stupid face into the wall."

"That's not going to help."

"Maybe not, but it would make me feel a whole lot better."

Niall held his hands up, addressing us all. "Look, we're not going to smash faces – that's not really the done thing, Julia

– and we're not going to phone the police. We are just going to …"

"Carry on as normal?" My voice was heavy with sarcasm.

"Yes." He looked at me steadily.

"You don't know him, Niall. He'll see that as a weakness. Not a strength."

"Then we'll just have to take that chance, won't we. Now, you need to rest."

"*You* need to rest!" I said. "I'm fine. No, really, I feel okay at the moment."

Julia stood up. "I'm making risotto. I hope that's alright with everyone?"

"Back on the kitchen duties," I smiled gratefully.

"Wouldn't miss it for the world," she smiled back. "But you really do need to rest, Bree."


Cursing, I stumbled out of bed for the second time that night, to pee.

"All that damned water he's making me drink," I muttered. My legs were still like jelly and my head felt like it was in a metal vice. Suddenly, my stomach lurched, and I vomited spectacularly across the bathroom floor. I continued retching, trying not to choke.

Niall banged on the door. "Brianna, are you alright?"

"I'm fine." My hoarse voice told him otherwise.

"How can you be fine? I heard you throwing up!"

And just to prove him right, I vomited again.

"Brianna, I'm coming in!"

"No!" I croaked, "I'm on the loo!"

"I'm coming in." He pushed the door open, hesitating only for an instant to assess how to navigate around the spreading pool of vomit on the floor. As my stomach lurched again, I added to said pool, splashing onto his bare feet. Any feelings of mortification were quickly surpassed by the overwhelming need to just lie down. I can't quite put into words how completely wretched I felt. At that point, I no longer cared that Niall was in the briefest pair of boxers, and I was on the toilet, with my nightie bunched up around my waist. To top it all, my hair - which is always wild when I wake up – was dripping with the contents of my stomach. I just needed to lie down. Anywhere. In my own vomit, if I had to – I didn't have the strength to care.

"Is there a bowl anywhere?" Niall asked, eyes scouring the bathroom.

"Is there any point?"

"Maybe not."

"Oh no …" As I retched again, he crouched in front of me, his legs wide apart, holding back my hair. I tried to aim between his legs but failed miserably, vomiting on his shins.

"I'm sorry," I muttered. He shook his head.

"Don't be."

Finally done, he gently let go of my hair and turned on the shower.

"I've got you," he said, guiding me across to it. He stepped in with me, still holding me, then proceeded to wash my hair.

"Do you need to sit down?"

I nodded. He crouched behind me, lathering and rinsing, and repeating, until all trace of vomit had gone. He helped me back to my feet.

"You need to take your nightie off."

I hesitated. The warm water was having its reviving effect, and I was aware of his close proximity.

"Turn your back to me. I won't look." He lifted it over my head and dropped it outside the cubicle. "I'm not convinced that will wash up clean and stain-free, I'm afraid."

"That's okay," I said. It had been my favourite nightie, but I certainly wasn't going to try and salvage it.

"Shall I leave you to wash, or do you need my help?"

"I can manage but can you stay here with me, please? My legs …"

"Yes, of course." He stood behind me, all the while making encouraging noises, holding my hair up and even washing my back when I couldn't reach.

Showered and wrapped in a warm towel, he scooped me up once again and carried me to my room, skilfully dodging the puddled floor. He disappeared back into the bathroom, only to re-emerge fifteen minutes later, also showered, with a towel wrapped around his waist.

"The floor's clean. How do you feel?"

"Like my head is too heavy for my neck, and it's throbbing."

"Have you been drinking enough water? You need to flush the chemo through."

"I know, I know, and I have been drinking it. I think it may be caffeine withdrawal, though."

"Maybe that too but I'm pretty sure this is the chemo."

"Not so great after all, then."

"No," he nodded. "Not so great."

"And now you've seen me on the loo, covered in vomit."

He laughed lightly. "I have a feeling I'm going to see a lot worse."

"Don't say that!"

"But I don't mind. I'm here to help. Anything. Cooking your breakfast, plumping your pillows, washing vomit from your hair. Which is insanely curly, by the way!"

"I know! My kids were convinced that Pixar modelled *Brave* on me."

He smiled, a heart-stopping kind of smile. "I think they were right. She certainly has your spirit." He sat on the bed next to me. "Turn around so I can dry your hair for you, and then you need to sleep."

"I can't sleep now."

"It's just gone three, Brianna. Please don't stay up and take Pip for a walk and start your chores. Give yourself a chance to recuperate. Stay in bed. That's an order!"

# Chapter Twelve

"You were naked in the shower with him?"

"Yes."

"And he didn't …" Julia's eyes sparkled, revelling in what I was confiding.

"No."

"Did he even … react … you know, down there?"

*"Julia!"*

"What? Men can't hide these things, can they?"

"I don't know. I didn't look."

She tutted and rolled her eyes.

"Well, would you?" I retorted.

"Yes!"

"Even if you were covered in vomit and feeling like death?"

"Point taken. Even so, you and Mr Gorgeous, naked in the shower together. That's going to go down well with Maxine."

"You are *not* telling Maxine about this. You're not telling anyone. Okay?"

"Okay." She reached for a biscuit from the tea tray perched on my bed. "But you saw his chest, I'm assuming?"

"I did."

"Muscly?"

"Very."

"Thought so. Nice." She let out a long sigh. "Very nice."

Niall tapped lightly on the door. "I'm just off with Pip for a walk. Can I do anything for you ladies, before I go?"

He looked bemused when we both guffawed, and Julia choked on her mouthful of biscuit. I shook my head, not trusting myself to speak.

"Alright, then. Patrick's coming with me, so we'll see you in a bit. I'll leave you to whatever you were talking about."

"The weather," I said quickly.

"Smallpox," Julia said, at the same time. He laughed and shook his head in confusion.

"Right, well, enjoy talking about the weather and smallpox, I guess."

"*Smallpox?*" I mouthed, as he turned to leave. Julia gave a helpless shrug. We waited until we heard the front door shut, before laughing til we cried.


By Sunday, my headache started to lift but I still felt wiped out. Julia had spent the previous day with me, sitting with me on my bed when I was awake, and pottering about downstairs when I was asleep.

Niall brought me breakfast in bed again. "One cup of coffee for the lady of the house. Make it last," he smiled. "Toast, buttered just how you like it, and a banana."

"Thank you, Niall," I said, patting the bed for him to sit next to me.

"Do you feel up for a walk in a bit? I've already been with Pip, but I know she'd love another one with you, too," he asked.

"I think so, yes. I definitely feel better today. I bet I'll be back to normal by Thursday, just in time for the next onslaught."

"Well, at least now we know what to expect. I bought two bowls from Sainsburys yesterday; one for the bathroom and one for wherever you happen to be. You don't want to get caught out like that again."

"No, I don't. And neither do you!"

We laughed – what else can you do, really? – and he squeezed my hand.

"You do look so much better today," he said quietly. Relieved.

We sat in silence for a while, listening to the birds in the garden trying to drown out the distant sound of an early morning lawnmower.

"Niall, you know the other day, in the shower?"

"Yes?"

"Did you…"

"Did I what?" he turned to look at me. I knew I was going to blush.

"Want to?"

He laughed awkwardly, looking away for a second.

"Want to? Under other circumstances, yes. But there are rules about things like that."

"Are there?"

"Mm-hmm."

"Like what?"

He thought about it for a moment. "You don't take advantage of a woman when she's drunk or unwell. You don't take advantage of a woman who is emotionally compromised. You don't take advantage of a woman whose husband is messing with her head. Actually," he corrected, "You don't take advantage, full stop. And you don't sleep with a woman when you're still married to somebody else." He looked me dead in the eye. "Sorry."

I thought I was going to cry. That was a rejection, wasn't it? I'd just put myself out there, hoping for a flirty comment back; not that.

"You're very principled," was all I could say.

"I am," he nodded. The silence – our lovely, comfortable silence – stretched into a painful one. He finally broke it.

"Brianna, if I thought you were going to die, things would be different. I'd want to spend every minute with you in my arms, naked, in a shower, in a field, in a bed. Wherever. And we'd never leave." He tipped my chin to face him. "But you're not going to die. So, I have to wait. And I will."

I looked at him, trying not to smile.

"In a field?"

He chuckled. "Yeah, why not?"

"What kind of field?"

"Does it matter?"

"Yes. There's the kind that's full of sheep and all their poop. There's the kind that's full of thistles and stones. There's the kind ..."

"Oh, my God, woman!" he exclaimed, "A romantic field, bursting with wildflowers, overlooking the sea. Will that do?"

"That'll do nicely." I leant my head on his shoulder, relieved that the rejection hadn't been a rejection after all. "Do you honestly think I'm going to survive this?"

He kissed my head. "Yes, I do. I honestly do."


As predicted, by the end of the week I was feeling back to normal; just a little more tired than usual, but otherwise fine. Kitty and Sean were due to arrive in the evening. They had planned to come home the week before, but we agreed to leave it for the first session, to see how I was. I'm glad we had. I don't think they could've coped seeing me so unwell or coped with the aftermath of the incident with Geoff – which we had kept from them. But the truth would have to come out, especially as Patrick was sporting two black eyes and a very swollen nose.

The second chemo session was very similar to the first, with less nerves and more smiles. This time though, I felt distinctly wobbly before we even got back home. I listened to my body and went straight to bed.

"Mum, we're home," Kitty whispered, kissing my cheek. I opened my eyes to see the twins' beautiful faces smiling down at me.

I couldn't eat much but sat with them in the kitchen, listening to their news. Patrick had already explained his injuries when he and Niall picked them up from the station, and nothing further was said about it. Sean told me later, that Niall had specifically asked them not to discuss it in front of me.

"He's really looking out for you, Mum, isn't he?"

"He is. He's been incredible."

"I wanted to go and watch him play tonight in Dorchester, but Patrick doesn't want to go with his face like it is, and I think I'd rather stay here with you, anyway. We can play a game or watch a film, can't we?"

As it is, the four of us sat out in the cool evening air after Niall had set off for his gig. We talked and reminisced, just enjoying each other's company. The pristine bowl was by my side. I did feel very nauseous but the fresh air was helping.

And then it started again. I was prepared this time and my aim was better. I even had a scrunchie in readiness for tying back my hair. Patrick fetched the second bowl, and they quickly devised a chain gang system to empty, clean and return each bowl in turn. Once the sickness subsided, we went inside, and they helped me upstairs to bed. Kitty settled in my Sherlock Holmes chair, with her MacBook and headphones, to watch a film. Patrick and Sean watched me from the doorway for a few minutes, then, satisfied I wasn't going to be sick again, headed back downstairs.

I closed my eyes and before you know it, Niall was leaning over the bed to kiss my forehead.

"Hey," he said softly, stroking my hair. "I hear it happened again. How do you feel?"

"I'm okay. Just tired. Where's Kitty?"

"She went downstairs to get a snack. She's going to sleep in here with you, tonight. I'll be right next door if you need me." He went to leave.

"I need you, Niall," I mumbled. He smiled.

"A hug?" Without hesitation, he lay next to me and cradled me. I instantly felt better.

"How did it go tonight?"

"Fine. Loud. Busy. The usual." Something in his voice told me it hadn't been *'fine'*, but I didn't push the issue. Instead, I asked him to sing to me. I rested my head on his chest, listening to the deep vibrations, as he sang *The Parting Glass*. Not the cheeriest song, I know, but his voice is so incredible when he sings it. I was asleep again before he'd finished.

The weekend went by too quickly, and we were once again waving Kitty and Sean off at the station on the Sunday evening. Julia and Curtis had come over, complete with a

189

hamper full of food that Julia had prepared earlier, and we spent the afternoon lounging in the garden. It wasn't until Sunday evening, once we were back from the station, that I had a chance to talk to Niall alone.

"Talk to me. What happened on Friday night? And don't say, '*nothing*', because I know better."

He sighed heavily. "Lizzie was there."

"At the gig?"

"Yes."

"And?"

"And she wants me back. She wants us to make another go of it."

My stomach plummeted. "Are you going to?"

He looked up sharply, frowning at me. "No! I can't."

"Why not?"

"Because I don't love her. You know that."

"What about Layla?"

"I love Layla, obviously, but it's not fair on her to carry on with a marriage that isn't working. Lizzie and I make each other so unhappy, so miserable, and that must have an effect on Layla." He shrugged, looking defeated. "I'm not even sure Lizzie loves me, even though she claims she does. I think she's scared of being on her own. A single mum."

"Does she have family nearby?"

"Oh yes, they were all there on Friday night, scowling at me. I tell you, it's a wonder I managed to sing at all!"

"I'm sorry, Niall." I hugged him, feeling the tension in his rigid back. "Will you make arrangements to see Layla?"

"I want to, but she wasn't keen. It was more of an '*all or nothing*' scenario. If I'm not interested in her, then she's not interested in me seeing Layla."

190

"That's not fair!"

"I know. But to be honest, I'm not in any mood to fight my corner just now. I have more important things to think about."

"Do you?"

He gave an incredulous laugh, shaking his head. "Yes. *You*."

"I can't be more important than your daughter, surely?"

"Well, you are. You're more important than anything. I told you before, I'm not father material. I'm really not. I mean, it's great that I get on with your kids but that's because they're adults. I can cope with that. I can't cope with Lizzie and Layla; they make me feel so trapped. And I know that's wrong. I know I'm a terrible person for even thinking it, but I can't spend any time with them, or even time thinking about them, because that takes me away from you. Time with you. That's all that matters to me. You. Not them. Not anyone or anything else."

"Niall…"

"I even resented doing the gig because I wasn't at home with you. All I kept thinking was, *is she okay? Has she choked on her own vomit? Is she drinking that bloody water yet?*"

I laughed, thinking he was laughing too but then realised he was crying. I put my arms around him again and we clung to each other. He spoke into my shoulder.

"I can't lose you, Brianna. When I'm away from you, even for an hour, I'm terrified I will. I can't think straight, I can't see straight. I've got work to do but I have no inclination to actually do it. And it's easy work, you know; just point a camera and shoot. It's not brain surgery."

"Niall, look at me." I waited until he did so. "You said that you honestly believe I can beat this. So, you're not going to lose me. I know it's been intense; we've had more to deal with than just cancer, and we're exhausted. Completely. I think you could be right about Lizzie – I don't know her but from what you say, she may be trying to make you feel guilty because she's scared. And you can't really blame her for that."

"Should I be guilted into staying with her, then?"

"No! No, that's not what I'm saying. What I mean is, she may be trying to manipulate you, especially by not letting you see Layla. She's using Layla as a pawn, and that's not fair on you. So, don't beat yourself up for feeling the way you do. And as for your work; you know there's more to it than just point and shoot. But it's creative and you have to be in the right mindset for that. Now, hear me out," I took a deep breath, knowing he would shout me down. "Take a break from work. You need to. I have money."

"No."

"Yes. I do. And it's *my* money, not Geoff's. Okay? You want to look after me. I need you to look after me. So, let's work together. Have a break. Don't fret about earning just now. We can manage. Honestly, we can. Together."

Niall closed his eyes, rubbing the back of his neck. "I'm sorry. I shouldn't be burdening you with all of this."

"Yes, you should. If we're going to be a team, then we have to share things. That's what a team does. I filed for divorce, by the way."

"You did? When?"

"Last week, after Geoff attacked you and Patrick. Curtis brought the paperwork round today, for me to sign."

"I should do the same."

"Don't rush. Work out what you want as far as Layla is concerned, first. And just remember, she won't be little forever, but she will always be your daughter. Don't turn your back on her. I think you'll regret it if you do."

"Thank you, Brianna," he said quietly.

"Thank you, Niall, for trusting me with this."

"I trust you with my life."

"Snap! And I really am trusting you with mine, and I'm sorry that it's affecting you as badly as it is." I took his hand and headed back towards the patio doors. "Now, let's go in and get a drink. Water?"

And so, the days merged together, ruled by a rollercoaster routine of rest, walks, sickness, meds and drinking endless water. Two days after my third session, my hair started to fall out. I'd noticed a few strands on my pillow and in the shower but when I woke on the Sunday morning and ran my hand through my hair, clumps of it came out between my fingers. For some reason, I rolled it up into an auburn ball and placed it on top of the chest of drawers, where I could stare at it, trying to fathom what to do. I didn't want to leave my room. I didn't want anybody to see me. I phoned Julia.

"What do I do? What do I do?"

"Well, for a start, calm down. How bad is it?"

"Bad enough, and I know it's going to get worse."

"You have plenty of hair, Bree! Does it actually show? Are there bald patches?"

I studied my reflection, scrutinising every strand. "Well, I can't see any glaring patches but it's shedding by the minute. Oh wait..." I twisted my head round. "Oh God, yes! Yes, I can see my scalp!"

"Okay, I'm coming over now. Sit tight."

Niall tapped on the door before opening it.

"Morning, here's your breakfast."

"Don't come in!" I squealed.

"Why ever not?"

"Because I'm hideous!"

He pushed the door open with his foot. "Don't be ridiculous. What's going on?" He put the tray down on my bed. "Ah," he said softly, noticing the back of my head. "We knew this would happen, so don't panic. And you're not hideous. It's only hair, Brianna."

"No, it's not. It's *my* hair. It's my, '*Bree has such amazing hair*', hair. It's my trademark, Niall, and now I'm losing it!" I was aware I was wailing like a child on the verge of a tantrum, but all rational thought had escaped my head. Along with my hair.

Julia stepped back to study her handiwork, scissors in hand. Niall and Patrick were sat on the opposite side of the kitchen, watching.

"What do you think, boys?" she asked.

"It's ... definitely shorter," Patrick ventured.

"Oh, God," I groaned. "It's hideous. Hideous." My beautiful auburn locks carpeted the floor. I stared at the alien reflection in the mirror I was holding. A nineteen-sixties Mia Farrow stared back at me, with that iconic, jagged, pixie cut. Except I'm not a twenty-year-old starlet and this isn't the sixties.

"Niall?"

"I'd shave it all off. It's going to fall out anyway. I mean, you've done a good job, Julia, but it's still patchy and it's going to get worse. Sorry, but there it is."

"I've never shaved anybody's head before," Julia said.

"I'll do it," Niall volunteered. "I've done it lots of times."

"Have you?" I turned to look at him.

"Yes. My brother's."

"You have a brother?"

"Two."

"Really? You never said. Do you keep in touch?"

"On and off, yeah."

"Do they live in Cork, or...?"

"One's in Dublin, the other's in Waterford."

"Are they married? Do they have children?"

Julia sighed, shifting her weight from one foot to the other.

"Much as I'm loving the family history session, can we focus on the job in hand, please? What am I doing here? Snipping some more or shaving it off?"

"I don't know," I whimpered.

"Shave it off," Niall said.

"I agree. Shave it off," Patrick reiterated.

"Fine, then," Julia stepped back. "She's all yours, Niall."

Niall crouched next to my chair. "Do you want me to do it, Brianna? Personally, I think it'll look great – definitely better than a patchy, cropped look – but it's up to you."

I looked at him for a long time, wanting to ask if he'd still find me attractive with a bald, shiny head. I didn't need to voice it; he heard me anyway.

"I'll still love you, hair or no hair."

I nodded. "Do it, then."

195

He disappeared upstairs and came back down with his shaving kit.

"My beard trimmer should do it," he stated, giving me a wink of reassurance.

It was depressingly quick and easy to turn me from a Hollywood star to a skinhead. I couldn't decide how I felt. Humiliated? Liberated? Or just plain devastated at the abrupt loss of my identity.

"A bit of make-up, some nice earrings, and you'll look amazing," Julia smiled. "It really suits you, Bree. I didn't think it would, but it does."

"Would you like me to do yours too, Julia?" Niall offered, grinning. She slapped his hand away.

"Not a chance!"


The phone rang just as we were about to leave for a walk on the beach. I hadn't wanted to go but Julia had insisted. Correction, Julia had shouted me down, reducing me to tears.

"If you don't go out straight away, you'll stay at home, staring at yourself in the mirror, talking yourself into a depression about your lack of hair. And then you'll never leave the house. Start as you mean to go on – it's the only way. I know you think I'm being a bully, but trust me, Bree, it's for your own good."

I'd found an old, pink denim baseball cap of Kitty's in her room, which fitted perfectly. It didn't look that bad, to be honest.

Patrick answered the phone, chatted brightly for a bit then handed it to me. It was my mum. She was due to come over in a week. I took the phone into the front room and sat down heavily on the sofa, listening to what she had to say.

Dad had another heart attack. A bad one, this time. He was in intensive care; Mum was camped out in the hospital corridor, waiting for more news. She sounded calm but there was no mistaking the fear in her voice. I felt completely useless. A million miles away. All I could do was listen, console, and reassure.

"Nana won't be coming over, then, will she?" Patrick asked when I relayed my conversation.

"No, she won't. She's devastated but she can't possibly leave him. We're not even sure when he'll be out of intensive care."

The three of them crowded round to give me hugs. Niall held on to me. "Shall we forget the beach?"

"No, I think it'll do us good to get out. I can't do anything else, can I?" I rested my head on Niall's shoulder. "Is it my fault?"

"What? His heart attack? Of course it's not. He already had a problem, didn't he?"

"Yes, but have I made it worse?"

"Brianna, you cannot take responsibility for this. He wouldn't want you to and neither would your mum. It's just bad timing, that's all."

Well, I certainly wasn't going to forget this day in a hurry.


Curtis joined us at the beach hut, and, as was becoming the norm on a Sunday, they came back to eat with us and spend the evening together. I loved how Curtis and Niall were forming such a good friendship. It wasn't a father/son kind of relationship as their age should dictate; no, it was a

197

real, close friendship. They talked about all sorts, from politics to music, and photography to craft beer.

Curtis had never really got on with Geoff. They held a polite conversation about nothing in particular, each breathing a sigh of relief when it was over. It used to bother me that Curtis was so distant with Geoff, but I could see it from a different perspective now. Geoff really isn't very likeable, after all.

Dad remained in intensive care for over a week. Mum sent me a text every day with an update. Nine days after his admission, he was transferred to the coronary care unit to recuperate. Mum was scared that it was too soon, but the hospital staff seemed confident that he was doing well.

It was Monday. My fourth session on Friday had gone according to plan – only another two to go. Kitty and Sean had been home for the weekend, this time fully prepared for what to expect. Kitty brought gifts in the shape of colourful turbans, floral beanies, and a baker boy cap with a bow on the side. Sean brought chocolates and dubbed me *Captain Picard*. Not the beautiful Sinead O'Connor or Gail Porter, no. He chose to liken me to Patrick Stewart. I mean, what can I say?

They'd been troopers, all three, sending their Nana messages daily to keep her spirits up, as Kitty and Sean did with me, too.

The phone rang.

Niall came into the kitchen to find me with my head face-down on the table, sobbing.

198

"Oh, Jesus! Brianna? Is it your dad?" He gently pulled me up to cradle me. I tried desperately to stop crying long enough to speak.

"That was Peter."

"Peter, who?"

"Peter Jakowitz."

He froze, eyes wide with dread. I swallowed several times, tapping my nose to stop the tears. I don't know why but it works. Niall pulled up a chair to sit next to me, still holding me in his arms.

"What did he say?" His voice was so low I could just about hear him. I lifted my head and took a deep breath.

"It's working, Niall. The chemo's actually working."

"What? Seriously?"

I nodded. "He wants to see us on Friday, before my session, to discuss things."

"Things?"

"He's considering surgery. He thinks I'm in with a chance!"

# Chapter Thirteen

Friday couldn't come around soon enough. I felt guilty at being so elated, when Dad was still critical, but I couldn't help myself. I was buzzing. Niall and Patrick were buzzing, too.

I'd phoned Kitty, Sean and Julia as soon as I'd composed myself after Peter's call, but I held off from telling Mum my amazing news. I wanted to wait until I had all the facts from our Friday meeting.

And facts are exactly what I got. It was the first time I'd actually absorbed everything I was being told. Niall made notes, regardless; this was a momentous meeting, and he didn't want us to miss any detail.

Peter had been both pleased and surprised at how well I had responded to the chemo; the rate was far greater than predicted. He outlined a plan for a full mastectomy, and scheduled surgery for five weeks after my final chemo session. That would give my body a chance to recuperate from the chemo, enough to then cope with such extensive surgery. He would also be removing the lymph glands. He discussed success rates of surgeries of this kind but also reminded me that aggressive cancers such as mine, are exactly that; aggressive. And as such, hard to eradicate. He also discussed rates of the cancer recurring.

I watched Niall write everything down, faltering only twice when he gleaned something he didn't want to hear. He asked questions – questions I hadn't thought of and questions I didn't want to consider just yet. I knew that as soon as we got home, he would be googling every detail about the surgery and the aftercare.

I went straight to bed when we got back, as usual, and Niall did a video call to Kitty and Sean, on our group chat.

"They send their love. They were elated with the news," Niall told me when he came to wake me up with the obligatory water, a few hours later. "Up to eating?"

"Maybe, yes. I'm not sure if it's psychosomatic but I don't feel anywhere near as bad as I usually do."

"Oh, Brianna," he sighed, shaking his head slowly. "You've just tempted fate."

He was right of course, but nevertheless, it didn't seem to bother me. I was on the up.

We were sitting propped up on my bed, the breakfast tray on the floor next to me. Pip was stretched out by Niall's knee.

"I don't even think she cares anymore that I don't walk her first thing or get her breakfast. She's completely smitten with you now," I laughed.

"She cares," Niall said. "She told me so only this morning, but she knows you need to rest."

"Nice try."

I straightened out the duvet across my thighs, smoothing the wrinkles in the soft cotton.

"This is what I need more of in my life."

"What, paisley? A seventies revival?"

"No, a complete change. Things that are more *me*."

"Like your Aga."

"Yes, exactly!" I stroked the duvet, admiring the pattern. "It's quite liberating, buying something that is so far removed from what's expected."

"Brianna, it's just a duvet cover."

201

"Ah, that's where you're wrong, Niall. This is no ordinary duvet cover."

"Well, it's not an M and S duvet cover. I know – I was there." We both laughed.

"No, it's … freedom. It's me, choosing something for me. My gut response – an impulse – rather than settling for what I think other people will expect me to have. And what they expect, is never really what I want."

He gave me a searching look. "Is that how you live your life?"

"Yes. Okay, I'm not always towing the line as far as raising the kids is concerned, but actually, even then, I was always dictated to about certain things. I started out being individual, when I first arrived here, but then I slowly conformed. I worried too much about what the family would think, and I fell into their mould." I flashed him a smile, trying to cover up how emotional I was feeling, baring my soul. "I think it's time to be *me*."

"I'm all for that. More paisley it is, then."

I wriggled down the bed a bit, to rest my head on his chest. It had become my favourite place. We stayed like that for a long while, listening to the dulcet tones of the garden, and fields beyond. The usual bird song, the sheep and cows, the rumble of distant traffic. It was all so familiar, so peaceful. And yet, I was starting to wonder if this was it for me now; would I ever hear something different, see a different view, walk a different street. Do I even want to? Yes, I think I do. I really think I do.

"What did you want to do when you left college? Apart from travel, that is," Niall asked. Reading my thoughts again.

"Interior designer. That's what I studied."

202

"And did you ever pursue it?"

"No. I wanted to. That was the plan, but I ended up here instead. How about you? Did you ever want to pursue music?"

"What, apart from playing in a band regularly, you mean?" he teased.

"No, I mean, didn't you ever want to record an album, be famous?"

"Of course I did. Doesn't everybody want to be famous when they're a kid? Do something amazing. Be noticed. Remembered."

I twisted my head round to look up at him. "So why don't you? It's not too late."

"I know but I've just … it's not easy."

"Why not?"

He shrugged. "I have this problem called lack of confidence."

"Really? But you're brilliant!"

"I think you might be biased," he smiled.

"No. I know it. I've heard you. And you write your own stuff."

"It's hard enough selling myself with my photography. To put myself out there, with the one thing I want to do the most, is really scary. It is. Maybe if I was younger, you know, with all the confidence of youth. All the resilience to bounce back."

"Not all youth have that," I said.

"No but I might have, if I'd been more disciplined. More inclined to apply myself and less inclined to drift. I don't know."

"I wish I'd known you when we were younger."

"I don't think you would've liked me much. I was very argumentative."

"Creative, you mean," I corrected.

"No, definitely argumentative," he laughed. "And very cynical. I've probably not changed that much, to be fair."

"I don't think you're argumentative."

He thought about it for a moment. "No, maybe not. You've done that."

"Me? How?"

"I'm not sure. I just know that I'm a better, calmer person, since I met you."

"I still wish I'd met you before all this."

"Why?"

"I look hideous! I'm bald, I'm blotchy, I'm about to lose my boobs."

"There's more to you than body image, Brianna. I'm not interested in your boobs."

"Said no man ever!"

He laughed. "Okay, I may be *slightly* interested in your boobs. But I'm all for that cliché; it's what's inside that counts."

"But is it? For me to be happy, I need to feel good. Losing my hair has not felt good. I can't even begin to imagine how I'll feel after losing my boobs, too. I know it's all about adapting. I'm just not sure I have the confidence."

Niall put his hand on my head to stroke it.

"See!" I exclaimed. "You went to stroke my hair, didn't you!"

He kept his hand there. "No. I was stroking your head. I actually like you with no hair. It shows off your face more – which is beautiful, by the way."

I closed my eyes, willing myself to believe him.

"Would you have reconstructive surgery?" he asked.

"I don't know. I haven't thought that far."

"Maybe now would be a good time to," he said gently.

"But …"

"But what?"

I didn't want to say it. Didn't want to ask if *he'd* rather I had it done. We're reaching that awkward stage where we both know how we feel about each other, but nothing is happening. Nothing. He hasn't even kissed me more than a peck on the cheek or forehead, which feels more paternal than anything else. Is he going to stay? Does he want to have a future with me? I'm guessing he does but I don't want to just assume. That's too presumptuous, isn't it? I'm not sure how to handle this; It's not a situation I had ever thought I'd be in. Dating as a twenty-year-old was agonising enough – this is a hundred times worse. And technically, we're not dating, anyway.

"I'm not sure how I feel about my boobs, to be honest. They've always been there, you know, larger than most. They're my trademark – like my hair – but deep down, I have this love-hate relationship with them. Every summer, I envy all those flat-chested models who escape the heat. You have no idea how hot these things get," I cupped them for emphasis. "They're heavy, they're restricting. I don't even know why I'm thinking I'll miss them! Maybe I should go for the Keira Knightley look – she's gorgeous, isn't she."

"Nothing compared to you."

I looked up at him. "What do you think?"

"I knew you'd ask," he grinned. "I could sense you, wondering whether to or not."

205

"Well?"

He drew in a deep breath. "I just want you alive, Brianna, whatever it takes. And besides, their real purpose has long passed. They've seen their day." He touched my chin gently. "You said you wanted a change. Do it."

I sat up next to him. "Why don't we strike a deal? I'll have the surgery and no reconstruction afterwards. I'll find the courage to accept my physical changes. You find the courage to record an album. Deal?"

He smiled that heart-melting smile he does so well. "Deal."

It was later in the afternoon, when the three of us were relaxing in the garden after our walk, that I voiced the next thing on my mind.

"Patrick, how would you feel if we moved?"

He didn't even open his eyes. "Fine."

"I mean, permanently leave this house. Never come back."

He looked at me. "I know what you mean, Mum. And yes, fine."

"You wouldn't feel sad?" I pressed.

"No. I suppose it would be a bit emotional, because it's where I grew up, but that doesn't mean you have to make it into a shrine or anything, a museum of childhood. Won't you miss it, though? The village, the neighbours?"

"No, not now. Nobody speaks to me anymore, nobody's been round to see how I am. Not even Ron, and I used to work for him." It had hurt, I can't deny it.

"But Mum, these things are tricky, aren't they? Nobody knows what to say."

"They could say, '*I hear you're not well*'. '*I hear your husband left*'. But to completely blank me, is harsh."

Patrick gave me an awkward smile, glancing at Niall. He had his eyes closed, leaning back in his chair.

"I just feel I can't move on. I can't settle," I said.

"That's kind of a contradiction," Niall chipped in, proving he had been listening.

"I know. What I mean is, I find too many things about this place annoy me. Irrationally so. And I don't want to hate the house; it's not the house's fault."

"You can't move now though, Brianna, not while your treatment is ongoing."

"I have to, Niall. It's not helping me heal. I'm not at peace here. I can't forget about Geoff and focus on me – as you said I should – when I'm living, daily, in a home I built with him. He's here, all the time."

Niall sat up. "So where would you go?"

"I'm not sure. Somewhere like the holiday cottage."

"That would cost a fortune."

"I know. That's why I said, '*somewhere like*'." I turned to Patrick. "Don't mention this to the others, just yet."

"I won't." His phone buzzed by his feet. He read his message, a sudden smile erupting. "I'm just going inside to make a call."

"Okay," I said, watching him hurry into the kitchen. There was no mistaking that smile. Somebody special, I'd say. Not that he's ever mentioned anyone.

I took the chance to speak to Niall. "Will you come with me? Wherever I move to?" My words came out in a tentative rush.

"Yes," he said, very definitely. He nodded. I nodded back. That was the extent of our meaningful, life changing conversation.

We celebrated my last chemo session with a beach party, despite the late October chill. Kitty and Sean came home for the weekend. Julia surpassed herself with the picnic.

"I've gone, high-tea-meets-street-food," she explained, pleased with the groans of delight her spread was greeted with.

We spent the afternoon at the hut, Sean and Patrick bravely dipping in and out of the sea, playing catch with a huge beachball and generally chilling, with food and drink. I say, *we*; I sat in my comfy chair, wrapped up, watching the fun. But I ate the food. Did I vomit? Yes. Did we cheer? Yes. And we ended the day by designing a count-down chart to B-day – Boob Day. It sounds mad, I know, but it's something to celebrate. When you're in a critical situation like this, you either crumble, or you face it head on. Challenge it and embrace that challenge. That's what I decided to do. Cancer is a challenge. I know it'll never go away completely – not the type I have – but I'll do everything to stop it from taking me. As long as I have two fingers to salute it, I will.

"Are you sure you're going to be okay?" Niall asked again. He was off to the supermarket in Wareham and Patrick was tagging along.

"I'll be fine. I feel so much better already and it's only Monday. I could get used to this," I joked.

The car had barely left, when there was a knock at the door. Not sure who it was, I quickly donned my turban. Geoff was on the doorstep, a huge bouquet in hand.

"For you, to celebrate the end of your chemo," he announced, offering me the flowers. All my favourites were in there: roses, freesias, carnations and snapdragons.

"You can't be here, Geoff, not after what you did," I said. I wished I'd left the turban off. I think my bald head may have shocked him or at the very least, wiped that ingratiating smile off his face.

"But it's just you here, isn't it?" he stepped into the hall.

"Did you wait til they'd gone?" I stared at him, feeling unnerved. "Did you sign the papers?"

He frowned and shook his head.

"You need to sign them, Geoff."

"I just want to talk. Can we sit and do that?"

"About?" I cleared my throat, which was ridiculously dry all of a sudden. He studied my face, sensing the mounting trepidation. He never used to scare me but after our last encounter, I don't trust him.

"Bree, please; I'm not angry. I just want to talk."

I led the way through to the kitchen. Pip got up from her sunny spot and stood by my feet, watching Geoff, as I made coffee. We sat down on opposite sides of the table. He looked tired, sad.

"Are you not happy, Geoff?"

He shrugged.

"What is it? Work?"

"She's not you. I miss you."

I closed my eyes for a second, cursing myself for walking right into it. Note to self: Geoff doesn't deserve my sympathy.

"You mean, she's not a domestic goddess?" I made sure my voice was edged with sarcasm.

"She's not a domestic anything."

"Ah. But she must be good at something."

He gave me a withering smile, then stared at my turban as if he'd only just noticed it.

"Why haven't you signed the papers, Geoff?"

He didn't answer for a while. Instead, he feigned interest in the view of the garden, pointing out and commenting on the new, wooden bird table, Curtis had bought for me.

"Geoff, why are you here?"

"This isn't real, Bree. You're obsessed with anything Irish and he's taking advantage of that."

"No, he's not," I replied flatly.

"Wake up! Look at you – you're fifty, for God's sake, and he's what – twenty-five!"

"Forty."

"You see my point?"

"No."

"What would he want with a woman your age? In your condition. Surely, he'd be more interested in Kitty, and if he goes for her, I'll kill him."

I gave him the dirtiest look I could muster. I wasn't even going to rise to the comment about Kitty but couldn't let the other one go.

"My condition?"

"You know."

"No."

"Your assets, Bree. You're about to lose them. Then what?"

"How do you know that?" I knew the answer before he uttered it. *Kitty*. Why does she insist on keeping in touch with him, even after he assaulted Niall and Patrick?

"So, is this what you came to say? To throw insults?"

He sighed. "No. I'm sorry."

I watched him twiddling his mug, regretting what he'd said.

"How old is Francesca?" I asked.

"Twenty-nine." He looked up. "Why?"

"Twenty-nine? So, nineteen when you met her?" I felt sick. It had never occurred to me before. "You were forty-two, Geoff! Probably the same age as her dad!"

"She acts older than she is," he defended meekly. I could tell I'd hit a nerve. I couldn't stop staring at him, I was so appalled.

"She wants to move away."

"Good," I said. "Do it."

"I can't. We don't have any money."

"How? How can you not have any money? Sell that ridiculous house, then. That'll put over a million in the bank."

"What if we sell *this* house?" he said quickly. I was astounded. "It's silly you being here, all on your own. The kids are gone, so you don't need the room."

"It's not ours to sell, remember?"

"I'll talk to Mother about it. We can sort something out."

I don't know how, but he managed to persuade me; *sell the house and go halves.* It's as if he'd heard my conversation with Niall about moving on. It just grated that it would be Geoff's doing and Jessica's money.

As soon as he'd gone, I took the bouquet of flowers to the back of the garden and buried it deep in my compost pile. I didn't want Niall to see it, or even know that Geoff had been here.

# Chapter Fourteen

I hated myself for lying to Niall. They came back from Wareham in high spirits but anxious to know if I'd been okay by myself. I could feel myself blushing when I said I'd just been resting in the garden.

"Mum, would you mind if I go away for a few days?"

"Of course not, Patrick." I patted the chair next to mine. "Where are you going? And is this anything to do with the texts you've been receiving?"

He stared at me.

"It's okay, I haven't read them, I just saw the look on your face, that's all."

He instantly looked relieved. "I didn't think you would. I thought maybe you're just psychic." He waited until Niall came to join us. "I met a girl in my first year. We were an item for two years and then she went abroad for her third year. And now she's back."

"What's her name?"

"Saskia. She's from London."

"So, you're going to London?"

"No, we're meeting up in Exeter. It's our place, you know. Special."

I smiled. I wanted to cry.

"And are you still an item, then?"

He nodded. "Yes. Long distance for a year has been tough but it's what she needed to do. And I was happy to wait. She'd love to meet you, when you're up to it."

I looked at him for a long time, at his earnest face, his contented smile.

"Why didn't you tell me about her before?"

"I'm sorry. I didn't want Dad to know I was happy. I thought he'd try and ruin it for me. I don't trust him."

"Does she know he broke your nose?"

He nodded. "She does. Needless to say, she doesn't want to meet *him.*"

Patrick was packed and ready to leave, within half an hour. I've never seen him move so fast. We waved as his car disappeared down the lane. Niall put his arm around me as we walked back to the house.

"What do you fancy doing today?" he asked. "I was thinking a drive out somewhere, for a walk."

"You knew, didn't you?"

"Knew what?"

"About Saskia; about him going to see her."

He gave me an awkward smile. "Only just before you. He ran it by me this morning, to see if I'd be alright with him leaving us to it for a bit. I said I wasn't going anywhere, so it's fine by me." He saw my dejected face. "Hey, don't be like that. He's trying to do the right thing by everybody, you know, and that's not easy."

"But why am I always the last to know everything? I thought he and I were close, I thought he'd want to tell me everything that's going on in his life. He's had a girlfriend for three years and I'm only just hearing about it now!"

"And he told you why," Niall said quietly.

"And that makes me feel even worse. I'm not Geoff! I hate him so much for what he's done. I've missed out because of him. I've lost three years with Patrick because of him. I'm losing Kitty because of him."

Niall put his hands firmly on my arms. "Right, hush now. Let it go, Brianna. Patrick's told you now about Saskia, and it

213

sounds like you'll meet her very soon. Kitty is torn – understandably so – and is struggling to deal with it. You need to let them fight their own battles, live their own lives, and just be there for them when they're ready to share things with you. You can't live their lives for them. You can't expect them to put you first, forever. That's not how it works. They grow up and move on, and you have to let them."

I stared at him, wide eyed with frustration. "Why do you always have to be so level-headed and reasonable, Niall? I hate that you're always right."

He couldn't help but grin. I did sound like a whinging child, not a parent of three adults.

"It's a tough job but I'll manage," he winked. "Now, do we take a picnic or have lunch here, first?"


We ended up taking a picnic to Worbarrow. Niall wanted to see if he could catch a few shots of the deer. He also wanted to explore Tyneham, the forgotten village, on the edge of the car park. I've explored it a dozen times when the children were younger, and nowadays – as its unofficial name suggests – almost forget it's there. But it's new to Niall. I told him a brief history of it, en route.

"It was a coastal, farming village, like so many in this part of Dorset, until it was evacuated – overnight – in nineteen-forty-three, to allow the troops to practice, in preparation for being shipped over to Europe to fight. And then after the war, the MOD commandeered it and the villagers were never allowed to return."

I've always loved the story of Tyneham. It's sad yet romantic. Nostalgic. The kids had such fun exploring, imagining what life was like back then. We played games in the ruined cottages and re-enacted Victorian lessons in the perfectly preserved school house. Although, I don't think any of us ever really tried to imagine what it must've been like, to suddenly up sticks and leave the safety of your home – and the home of your forefathers – in such a national time of uncertainty. I was doing so now, with Niall. Like me, he finds history fascinating and loves to theorise.

After a happy hour exploring and watching Niall at work, we headed for Worbarrow Bay. On cue, the deer appeared, silently moving through the trees and stopping in full view of Niall and his camera. One even looked directly at him, studying him at length, while steadily chewing leaves.

Sitting by the water's edge, watching Pip dart back and forth, I suddenly realised this was the first time I'd been here without children. I leant my head on Niall's shoulder. He sensed my maudlin mood.

"Don't be so hard on yourself. It's okay to feel sad; you're going through hell right now. And showing weakness, doesn't make you a bad mother. Letting them go, doesn't make you a bad mother. And they don't expect you to stop living your life, just because they're not here with you."

"How do you always do that?"

"Do what?"

"Answer my questions before I've even asked them."

He shrugged. "Because I hear you thinking."

"Okay then," I challenged, "What am I thinking, now?"

He looked at me for a moment, then tutted and shook his head. "You're so depraved. What would your mother say!"

I hit his arm, laughing. "Ha! I was thinking, I fancy a burger right now."

215

He nudged me with his shoulder. "That's not what you were thinking at all, but nice idea. Do you want to eat out, or shall we make our own at home?"

"Make our own. I'm still not confident enough to go out for a meal yet. Do you mind?"

"Do I mind an evening in, alone with you? Let me think about that for a minute." He pointed his camera at me, telling me to smile. "Beautiful." He gave me that smile I'm sure he doesn't give anybody else. At least, I hope he doesn't. "I think I'd love nothing more than burgers at home with you, tonight."


"I bet you, I can," Niall said, flicking through my old box of records.

"Honestly, these are very old. I've had them for years." I watched him scanning each title, at speed. He sighed.

"CDs, then. Are they all here?" He ran a finger along the shelves of my CD tower. "Yes!" he hissed triumphantly. "I knew it! I have this one, too." He held up an album by Fionn Regan.

"No way! That's so random," I laughed in surprise. "That's one of my favourite albums."

"Mine too. I told you, didn't I? I knew we'd have at least one the same." He studied the track list. "Which one's your favourite?"

"*For a Nightingale*," I said, without hesitation. Grinning, he grabbed his guitar from the other sofa and started strumming as he sang. I sat watching him, hugging a cushion, like a teenage fangirl.

"How do you do that? You can sing any song I ask for and you do it so effortlessly."

"It's in my blood, I suppose. I've always had an ear for music."

"Even more reason for you to write that album, then," I reminded him. He nodded and carried on playing.

We took our usual walk around the village as it was getting dark, then Niall packed me off to bed with that paternal peck. Admittedly, I was beyond tired, but I wished he'd drop the carer role for once. I desperately needed a hug. A long, reassuring hug. As I drifted off to sleep, I could hear him downstairs, clearing away in the kitchen.

I managed a bigger breakfast the next morning and it didn't stick in my throat. Niall watched me eat, pleased.

"You look so much better. I bet your body is rejoicing as all that toxin is working its way out of your system."

"It is. I feel like I could eat anything, all day long, and not feel ill."

"Long may it last," he cheered. "Are we risking a second cup of coffee, yet?"

I pulled a face. "Maybe I'll stick to just the one for now, thanks."

He nodded, clearing our plates from the table and then pouring a glass of orange juice for me.

"Niall, how do you feel about tattoos on women?"

"Umm, I don't. I mean, it doesn't bother me either way. I have tattoos."

"I know." He has a traditional Celtic cross on his right forearm; and on his left shoulder and bicep, a more unusual tattoo of a dragon, with its body made up of Celtic knots.

"Why do you ask?"

I fetched my laptop from the side. "I was looking at this." I quickly loaded the page to show him. "It's a tattoo somebody had done after their mastectomy." It was an incredible work of art. Very floral, very feminine. She'd had a band of flowers, vines and butterflies, tattooed across her chest. Red and yellow roses, orange Californian poppies and blue forget-me-nots, all weaving through vibrant, green ivy. Purple and pink butterflies, of varying sizes, were dotted throughout the blooms, and taking flight up towards her shoulders. The whole effect was that of a floral bralette.

Niall gave a low whistle. "Wow, that's some work, there."

"I'd have pink dog roses rather than those yellow ones. They're my favourite thing in the garden. You've seen them growing through the hedge, haven't you? And I'd have blue butterflies."

"Adonis Blue?"

"Yes. It would remind me of our first day up on the hill together. Do you like it?" I watched his face for his honest reaction.

"Yeah. Bear in mind though, you don't actually like needles. This is going to take a lot of needle work and it'll be painful." He studied the picture again. "But it's beautiful. If that's what you want to do, go for it."

"Yes?"

"Yes." He took my face in both his hands, looking deep into my eyes. "You know that I'll love you whatever you look like, don't you?"

"Will you?"

"Of course I will." It was hard not to be hypnotised by those eyes.

"Why won't you sleep with me, Niall?"

I hadn't meant to say it out loud. But there it was, out *and* loud. Should I apologise? Or just wait and see what he says? I opted to wait. He smiled and sighed deeply, letting go of my face.

"I've told you why."

"I know, but you're not going back to her."

"It's not because of her. It's because of Geoff."

I blinked, surprised. "Geoff? He's not coming back!"

"But you see, Brianna, that's the thing. You say, '*he's not coming back*'. Not, '*I don't want him back*'."

"But I don't want him back! I hate him!"

"Vehemently. Too vehemently."

"What does that mean?" I really didn't understand his point.

"You protest too much. It's too raw, still. You're hurt, your heart's been broken, your pride's been wounded. I'm not convinced you know *how* you feel." He raised questioning eyebrows. "And he keeps messing with your head. Jesus, Brianna, it's been a hell of a couple of months – how can you possibly think clearly or rationally. How can you possibly know how you truly feel?"

"But I do know. He makes my skin crawl. Yesterday, he said you were more interested in Kitty than me. Just because *she* was Kitty's age when he started sleeping with her. That's what he's like; a pervy, old man, trying to be young. And he thinks every other man is the same as him. Why on earth would I want him back?"

Niall stared at me in silence, registering what I'd said.

"Yesterday? You saw him yesterday? Why didn't you tell me?"

I faltered. Damn my motor mouth. "I don't know."

He sat back. "You can't do this, Brianna. You say you want me here with you. You want me to move all my stuff in. You want me in your bed. You say you want to make a life with me. And yet, you don't tell me that your husband's been to see you. We agreed: he wouldn't be allowed here after he assaulted me and Patrick. How can I trust you?" He leant forward, eyes searching mine. "Has he been in your bed since I moved in?"

"No!" I practically screamed. This wasn't going the way I'd planned at all.

"Are you sure?" He looked away briefly, his shoulders dropping. "I'm sorry, Brianna, but can you see – you've just proved my point. I am *so* in love with you. I've never been in love before. There's been infatuation, there's been lust, but nothing like how I feel about you. Whereas you have. You have a family, a home. You've had a happy life. I come along, lay myself bare, confessing my all to you. Weeks later, your husband is gone, and you turn to me. And I'm here for you. But deep down, I know I'm the rebound." His eyes pleaded with me. "You're hurting, you're angry, you're scared. You're told you're dying. I get how confusing that all is. And I've been waiting. Waiting til you're sure you know what you want. And I don't think you do. Otherwise, why would you hide this from me?

We stared at each other in silence. I'm amazed I hadn't cried. I desperately wanted to. My mouth had gone dry. I licked my lips, trying to speak.

"Are you going to leave?"

He recoiled his head, frowning. "No! Why on earth would I? You need me here. Look, I loved you even though I knew you were happily married. I didn't plan it. I tried not to fall for you, but you just did that to me. I can't *not* love you."

I suddenly realised that we were having an argument that wasn't anything like an argument. Geoff would have been out the door by now, slamming furniture on his way, if I'd let it get that far, but Niall was sitting with me, trying to reason things out, rationally. Passionately, yes, but not aggressively. This was new to me.

"I *do* love you, Niall. And it's completely different to Geoff – how I felt about him. But he keeps confusing me. He keeps telling me you're not real, you're just using me."

"*Using* you?"

"I know! It's the other way round, isn't it. I'm using you."

"Are you?"

"It feels like it. You've been so good to me, you've been wonderful. I think I may have taken it for granted that you'll be here for me." I tried to cover my shame with a smile. "The thing is, I told you I want a fresh start somewhere, with you. And then he came round to say he wants to sell the house."

"But it's not his to sell."

"I know. But I couldn't tell you because you'd think it was all his idea – me, wanting to move – so I..." I paused for breath; I could feel myself gabbling. "I'm sorry. I'm scared that I'm not enough for you. That I'm broken. Incomplete. Ugly. And I'm scared that you'll see it – any day now – and leave. I'd like to be independent, strong, brave – all those things – but I'm not. I'm weak, scared and used to being told what to do. I want this new life, this new love, this new *me*. I can see it. I can see her, but I'm just scared to really go for it. It's life changing."

"Cancer usually is. Divorce usually is."

"And I got double whammy."

"Yes, you certainly did that." He reached for my hand. "I'm sorry for what I said. I didn't think for a minute that you'd been with him again. That was uncalled for. Forgive me?"

"That's okay. You were angry." I put my hand over his.

"No! No, I'm not angry – why would I be? I'm scared – like you. I'm scared of losing you. I'm frustrated at our situation. I want to move on too, you know, with you. I wish things were different. I wish we were both free to make our own choices. No ties. So, not angry, Brianna." He shook his head. "And as for you being broken and ugly," he tipped my chin up to look at him, "You grow more beautiful with each passing day." He stood up and pulled me to my feet, wrapped his arms around me and held me tightly.

"I'm sorry," we both said at the same time.

"Jinx!" Niall laughed softly. "I have something to show you. It's not ready yet but I think you need to see it." He led me into the front room, sat me down and grabbed his laptop from its case. He opened a file of photos.

"What's this?"

"This is our memory book."

The first picture was of me in Kitty's old baseball cap, on the day Niall shaved my head.

"My cancer journey?"

His hand hovered over the mouse pad. "Yes, but I know you don't like that term, hence, *memory book.*" He clicked on the slideshow. Julia and I dozing in our beach chairs. All of us cheering and jumping in the air during our beach party. Niall and me at Worbarrow. Me kissing Pip. Sean and Kitty kissing me. Me in the garden. A close-up of me with my face

222

in the buddleia. Shot after shot of me, on a walk, in the kitchen, sleeping on the sofa, smiling at the camera. It was like that scene in *Love Actually,* when Keira Knightley realises that Andrew Lincoln has been taking candid photos of her – obsessively so.

"It's not only to remind us of this time, but it's also to show you how loved you are, by all of us. It's to remind you just how incredibly strong you are. And beautiful. Your pure beauty radiates, Brianna. We all see it. Except you. It's time you see it, too." He watched me as I tried so hard not to cry at the snapshots unfolding in front of me. I look nothing like I imagine I do. I actually *do* look good with no hair. Especially with those earrings Julia gave me. I smiled an '*I'm trying not to cry*', kind of smile.

"Thank you, it's perfect. Memories are much better than a journey." I put my arms out for a hug. He obliged but broke away far too soon.

"Brianna, I don't know what else to say to you to make you realise, I'm not going anywhere. Except this." He got down on one knee - *he got down on one knee!* – looking heartbreakingly vulnerable. He looked me dead in the eye, though.

"Look, I'm not convinced by the whole marriage thing – it seems to be a bit of a sham – but I do know that I want to spend the rest of my life with you. For better or worse. You know how I feel about you."

"I feel the same," I said, nodding.

"Do you?"

"Yes. Probably since that first day, when you blanked me at work."

He laughed. "I was such an idiot!" He quickly regained his composure, taking my hand. "So, without a marriage proposal, how would you feel about me moving out of Sean's room sometime soon, and us spending the rest of our lives together?"

"I'd love that. But what about you and your principals? Your divorce isn't through and neither's mine."

"I think, on reflection, that principals are sometimes very overrated."

"Absolutely. I agree." We stared at each other, neither one wanting to say what we were thinking.

Niall broke the silence. "How about tonight?"

I smiled, trying not to grin like a Cheshire cat. "Do we have to wait until tonight? I really think I need a mid-morning nap. Don't you?"

"I do," he said, quickly getting to his feet. "I really do."

# Chapter Fifteen

I opened my eyes, moving my head carefully from Niall's chest. He was fast asleep. I grinned, aching to laugh out loud. He looked so peaceful. And his hair looked great on my paisley pillow.

I slid silently out of bed. His hand grabbed my arm, making me jump.

"Where are you going?" he growled.

"My phone's ringing. I left it downstairs."

"No, leave it. What did I tell you? We're going to spend every minute together, naked, and never leave this bed." He pulled me back onto the bed.

"Or field," I laughed.

"The field is next week. This week, it's this bed." He was about to kiss me, when his phone rang. He fumbled about under his jeans on the floor, where the phone had been dropped.

"Hey, Julia. Oh, sorry, her phone is downstairs. No, no, she's fine. It's my fault. She had to take me to bed … put me to bed, I mean. Oh, okay, yeah, she's here." He handed me the phone, laughing at my horrified expression.

"Hi, Julia."

"Are you in the shower?"

"No."

"Are you naked?"

"Maybe."

There was a brief, stunned silence. "Right. Fine. Good. Then why are you answering the phone? Put it on silent. Get back to it. Bye!"

I handed Niall his phone back. "Why did you say that to her?"

"Why did *I*? What was that about the shower? Did you tell her?"

I pulled a face. "Maybe. It's Julia; she has a way of finding out everything."

"Right," he tried not to smile at my guilty face. "Well, I've just saved her the bother then, haven't I. Now, where were we?"

We had a late lunch, which Niall brought upstairs. I felt so decadent, lounging across the bed with nothing more than a thin IKEA blanket draped across my bare shoulders. Niall was propped up against the pillows, in his boxers, watching me, a contented smile on his face.

"Penny for them."

I shook my head. "I don't want to ruin the mood."

His face dropped. "Why? What's wrong?"

"You think I'm going to die, don't you?"

"No! Why would you say that?" He quickly moved down the bed, lying on his stomach opposite me, our noses touching. I tried to ignore his concerned stare.

"Brianna?"

"Because you said – before – that we would only do this, if you thought I was dying."

He laughed with relief, shaking his head. "Yeah, well, I was an idiot. Again. I was so busy trying to prove to you that despite how much I want you, I'm not one of those bastards like your husband, who sleeps with women when he's still married to somebody else."

"So...? What made you change your mind?"

"Something you said about missing out because of him. It hit me – that's what we're doing. Missing out on us, because of me not wanting to be like him."

"You're nothing like him."

"And then I thought, we all die. What if I die tomorrow in a car crash and I'd been putting this on hold because, in some crazy way, I thought it would prove to you how much I love you. By not loving you."

"And all I've been wanting you to do is hold me, and love me, like this." I sighed, much deeper than I meant to. He frowned.

"There's something else, isn't there?"

"I'm scared, Niall. Scared about the surgery and what happens afterwards. What if it doesn't work? All that pain and sickness, for nothing."

"Hey," he ran a finger down the side of my face. "I won't let you die."

"Don't make promises you can't keep."

"I didn't promise," he said quickly, "I said, I won't let it happen. There's a difference."

"Is there?" I laughed lightly at his defiant nod. He rolled onto his back, patting his chest for me to lay my head there.

"I've noticed something of late. You use the word *scared*, a lot. I mean, a lot a lot."

"That's because I am scared," I said.

"But if you keep reinforcing that feeling, it will consume you. You need to be brave, positive, unafraid. Determined."

"I think I am being all of those. I'm trying to be. But I can't help being scared, too."

"I know. I just think we should ban the word. Let's be something else entirely."

227

"Like what?"

He thought about it for a moment.

"Let's be adventurers. As of today."

"Okay." I twisted my head to look at him. "What kind of adventure do we start with? Rock climbing? On the cliffs out by Worth Matravers?"

"Ooh, we absolutely should do that! But I was thinking, to start, we go house hunting. Let's do this properly. You said you need to move, so let's do it. If there's nothing available straight away, let's pack up and rent the holiday cottage again."

"You said that would be too expensive."

"I say a lot of things without thinking," he sighed. "I have money – not much – but I have commissions lined up, wedding shoots, and sales from the gallery in Dorchester. And besides, you told me once, you came from nothing. We can do this – together – from nothing."

I wasn't convinced it would be as easy as he seemed to think but he was so eager, so fired up to do the right thing, that I didn't want to dampen it. Instead, I nodded and set about planning how to pack everything up, ready to move, as soon as possible. Besides, there's nothing I wanted more than to move on with him. Away from all this.

As if on cue, Jessica arrived half an hour later. We heard the knock, and both froze.

"Let's ignore it," I whispered. Niall nodded, then grimaced. Pip had run downstairs and was barking at the door. We hurriedly dressed, giggling like teenagers caught on the hop.

"Sorry, I was upstairs resting, and Niall was outside," I explained, welcoming her in. "Tea?"

She got straight to the point, following me into the kitchen, greeting Niall when he emerged from upstairs. Actually, she gave him a lovely smile. Unexpected.

"Geoff came to see me last night. He says you want to sell – is that right?"

"No. Yes. What I mean is, *he* said he wants to sell. I reminded him, it's not ours to sell. But yes, I do want to move. I can't live here anymore."

"It's your home, Bree."

"I know, but it was my home with Geoff. He's tarnished it for me."

She looked at me for some time, head cocked, assessing. Debating. I stacked the tea tray and motioned to the garden.

"Bree, if this is *your* decision, then that's fine. But if Geoff has bullied you into this ..."

"No, he hasn't. I knew, right from day one, that I didn't want to stay here but it's been convenient and necessary during the chemo. Now that *that* bit is over, I really want to move before the next stage. The surgery."

"That soon?"

I nodded. "Yes. I have to."

"And will Niall," she turned to peer into the kitchen at him, "be moving with you?"

I faltered. "I ... I think so, yes."

"I hope so, Bree. You deserve some happiness."

"I thought I was happy with Geoff," I said quietly. She didn't respond. We drank in silence. Done, she put her cup on the table and drew in a decisive breath.

"I know you'll protest but I've done it anyway; I've changed my will. I'm putting the house on the market, and you will get half. You'd get that anyway, in a divorce. And the other half will go into a trust fund for the children."

"And Geoff?"

"Will get none of it."

My mouth dropped open in shock. "But he's your only child!"

"And I've ruined him. And consequently, your marriage. So, I'm putting my foot down. It's about time he grew up and took responsibility for his actions."

"I don't know what to say."

"Don't say anything. I've seen my solicitor this morning and sorted it all out. I just needed to hear it from you, that it was what you want, not what Geoff wants. But I'm thinking now, if you want to move in a hurry; once the house has been valued – that'll be imminent, by the way – I can give you your share ahead of a sale. So you can move and get settled, before the surgery." She smiled, a sad kind of smile. "Do you know where you'll be moving to?"

I shook my head. "I'm thinking of just renting a holiday cottage over by Studland beach but I'm not sure yet."

"Ah. Now, I know somebody who has property over there. Let me see what I can find for you." She hesitated. "If you don't mind, that is."

"Of course I don't mind. Thank you, Mother."

She smiled at my use of *Mother*. "Don't be a stranger, Bree. I know this is awful and he has behaved appallingly, but you will always be my family. Don't forget that." She stood up and put her arms out, signalling the end of her visit. I hugged her. She kissed my cheek, then hugged me again.

Niall, who had been hovering in the kitchen, jumped up from his chair and showed her out. I heard her talking to him. Well, it sounded more like a short list of commands than a cheery chat.

"Everything alright?" he asked when he came back, with a dutiful Pip by his side.

"Yes," I nodded. "What did she say to you?"

"Oh, she wants me to make sure you're resting, make sure you're eating, make sure you're not getting too stressed. And to make sure I make you happy. In her words, *'treat her well and do everything my son didn't. She deserves to be loved'.*"

"She said that? Are you pulling my leg?"

"Those were her exact words. What did she say to you?"

"She wants to give me money now, for my share of the house. And she wants to find us somewhere to live, in Studland."

"Wow!"

"Yes."

"She really hates her son, doesn't she!"

"I think she does."

I didn't say it, but I worried about it. Geoff would not take this lying down. Not at all.

"Right then," Niall clapped his hands together. "So, Jessica has taken charge of our first adventure. What shall we do instead? Rock climbing? Or go back to bed?"

I laughed, then looked at his face. "You're serious, aren't you?"

He shrugged, holding his hands up in defence. "When it comes to loving you, I'm always serious."

"Niall, that would make a great lyric but please, don't use it as a chat-up line. Cheesy, springs to mind," I teased. "Besides, we really need to take Pip for a walk."

He nodded. "Absolutely. If we run, we can be back home in five minutes."

I laughed again. "You're taking this whole, *naked for a week* thing, too far, you know." I touched his arm. "But thank you, I love it. I love you. You're exactly what I need in my life."

"Good job, too. Because I'm staying put."

"And you'll write that album?"

"And I'll write that album. Just for you."


I phoned Kitty. It had been playing on my mind since the day before. I needed to ask her why she thought it was necessary to tell Geoff about my surgery.

"I'm sorry, Mum, but he has a right to know, doesn't he? It wasn't a secret or anything. He's worried about you."

"That's not the impression I got."

"Of course he worries about you. It's all he thinks about. He told me. He's made a colossal mistake and he knows it. He desperately wants you back. He wants to make a fresh start. But he's worried that you'll start a relationship with Niall. I told him you wouldn't do that."

"Why did you say that?"

"Well, you wouldn't, would you."

"I have, Kitty." There was an audible gasp. "I'm in love with Niall."

"No! Mum, you need to get back together with Dad!"

"Darling, you need to understand; Dad moved on. I've moved on." I could hear her weeping, but I had to explain it

232

to her. "As far as Dad and I are concerned, there is no happy ending. He knows that. But you keep offering him hope. You have to stop doing that." I paused. "Kitty, as a young woman, I thought you of all people, would understand this. Dad has cheated on me for so long. How can you think that's okay? It's not."

"People make mistakes, Mum, especially men. They do stupid things, even when they really love the person they're hurting."

"So, you're saying I should forgive him?"

"Yes."

A thought dawned on me. "Are you speaking from experience?"

Silence.

"Kitty?"

"Mum, you can't throw away all those years because of one mistake."

"This isn't you talking; this is your dad. He said exactly that to me. And I hope I'm wrong, but if you've met somebody and they've cheated on you … please do not forgive them! That's crazy, Kitty!"

"If you love somebody, you give them another chance."

I sighed. "I've filed for divorce. I'm sorry Kitty, but it is all over for us."

She started to cry more openly and then hung up. I stared at my phone. Do I call her back? Do I leave it a while? I tried to call back, but it went to answerphone.

Two minutes later, I got a text from Patrick. *'Spoke to Kitty. Love you Mum. Be happy xxx'*

That was closely followed by a gif on messenger from Sean, of a cat reaching up for a hug. *'Sending hugs'*. Simple and straight to the point.

"I worry about Kitty. I don't understand why she's being like this."

"She'll come round," Niall said, "But it's obviously going to take longer than we thought. We find it hard to understand her because we've never been in her shoes. My parents are still married – as are yours – so we have no experience of this, of how she must be feeling. Give her time. I know I've said it before but that's all you can do."


I instantly recognised the sound of Geoff's car pulling up outside. We were curled up on the sofa, watching *The Adjustment Bureau*. Neither of us had seen it before but it came highly recommended from Curtis. We were at a really tense part, when Geoff pulled up and banged on the door.

"Don't open it!"

Niall hesitated. He banged the door again.

"I'll just tell him to leave," he said. I jumped up and followed him into the hall. Niall opened the door just a little way. Geoff immediately pushed it wide open, glaring at him.

"You're screwing my wife," he snarled, "I'm going to kill you!"

Niall slammed the door shut and bolted it. Geoff was swearing and banging, demanding to be let in.

"Go away!" I screamed. "I've got nothing to say to you."

It went quiet. Too quiet. We stood by the door, listening. Waiting. There was an almighty crash in the front room. We ran through, to find glass and soil everywhere, and a stone planter in the middle of the floor. How he managed to throw it, I'll never know; it weighs a ton.

Niall swore under his breath. The television was face down. It had taken the full impact of the planter and hit the floor with such a force, shattering the screen.

"Mind your feet," Niall warned.

"I'm phoning the police!" I turned to grab my phone from the coffee table, when I saw Geoff launch a second planter, directly at Niall's crouched figure. I screamed and pulled him out of the way as it cannonballed in through the adjacent window, sending another shower of glass and soil across the room. Geoff was screaming and swearing at the top of his voice, most of it incoherent. I heard *whore,* and *pikey,* and *I'll kill you.* Then he started to kick at the jagged edges of glass, trying to climb through the window.

At that point, a previously terrified Pip, launched into action, baring her teeth, snapping and snarling at Geoff as he straddled the window frame. He aimed a kick at her, narrowly missing her. He let out a sharp yelp of pain as a spear of glass caught his thigh. He fell backwards onto the lawn. I grabbed Pip and ran from the room. Niall followed, phoning the police.

Geoff abandoned the window, opting to try and shoulder-barge the heavy, solid oak front door, instead. He was like an enraged bull. Unstoppable. Unrelenting.

I banged on the door. "The police are on their way! You'll go to prison for this, you maniac!"

Miraculously, he stopped and moments later, his car roared off down the road, horn blaring. I held my breath, waiting for the sound of a crash, a screech of brakes, or the scream of a pedestrian. But nothing.

The police arrived. They took statements. We took photos of the damage. They did too. A call went out for Geoff's arrest.

I was outside, showing the officer where Geoff had been standing and where the pots were taken from. Somebody called out. It was our neighbour, Ron.

"Is everything alright, Bree?" He stared at my bald head, not able to disguise his horror. He put his arms around me. "Bree, what's happening, my dear?" His hands trembled. In fact, his whole body was trembling. Janice was close behind him, wide eyed, as she surveyed the flashing lights and damage done.

Once the police had left and the locksmith was on his way to board up the windows, we went round to Ron and Janice's, on the promise of hot coffee and cake. Pip sat on my lap, still shaken by the events.

"I'm so sorry, Bree. I had no idea you were ill, or that Geoff had left. We've been away, visiting Carole and the grandchildren," Ron said. Their daughter, Carole, moved to Devon some years ago. A GP, like her dad, she has her own practice now, in a small village, not far from Tiverton.

"Well, everything has happened so fast. I didn't even notice you were away, so we're as bad as each other," I smiled.

"Did you know I took early retirement from the practice?"

"No! When?"

"Seven months ago. I tried to plod on after the Parkinson's diagnosis, but then we decided to take time out for us, and the family."

"I'm so sorry, Ron. I didn't know." Parkinson's. That explains the trembling.

236

"That's understandable. It's easy to lose touch, even if we're neighbours. How's the job at Athelhampton?"

"I love it! Obviously, I've not been there for two months during the chemo, but yes, a great place to work."

Two months. I hadn't even given them a thought in two months. I'd had cards and flowers, and text messages, when I first told them about the cancer, but even though I'd promised to keep in touch, I hadn't. Too much going on and not enough hours in the day.

"We really should go and visit the family at work," I said to Niall, once we were back home.

The house smelt very peculiar, of damp bricks and equally damp wood. Pip didn't like it any more than I did.

"Will we be safe here tonight?" I hated the thought of Geoff out there, boiling over with pent-up rage. There had been no call from the police to say he'd been apprehended.

"Do you want to go to Julia's? I can phone and see if they'll put us up for the night."

"Yes, please. I can't settle here." I stared at the horrible wooden boards, where my beautiful windows once were. "This is Kitty's doing."

Niall looked surprised. "Why do you say that?"

"I told her about us today, didn't I; then Geoff comes round this evening, shouting the odds. I don't think it's a coincidence, do you?"

Just then, my phone rang. The police had Geoff in custody. He would be kept there overnight. Relieved, we opted not to bother Julia and Curtis. I just needed to sleep, and first thing in the morning, pack up and leave.

"I don't care where we go, just as long as nobody knows. I'm not telling Kitty," I said.

# Chapter Sixteen

I didn't think I'd sleep, all things considered, but I did. I'm not sure I can say the same for Niall. I was aware of the light from his mobile, and him scrolling through websites, for quite some time. He held me tightly all night though, not letting go, until I woke up just after five.

We wasted no time, packing cases with essentials – again – and emptying the fridge and cupboards of food into crates. I stood in the front room, staring wildly at all my belongings; years of treasured possessions and hoarded tatt, none of which I wanted to part with but none of which I could take with me. It was crushing, demoralising, panic-inducing. How had it come to this? How had it switched so dramatically from a placid, ordered life, to one filled with fear, doubt and chaos; one where I am running away from a husband I no longer recognise. One where I am losing the daughter I thought would be my closest ally for life.

"Hey," Niall soothed, finding me perched on the edge of the sofa, tears streaming down my face. "Come on; leave this for a moment. I've made coffee."

"I can't stop. I need to pack."

"No, you need to listen to me. I've sorted things. I spoke to Imogen, and we've got the holiday cottage – the same one – for two weeks. I've been trying to organise storage, but time isn't on our side. So for now, take what we need, then we can come back and pack up, or get somebody to come in and do it for us. Your kids will have to decide what they want to keep, or we just pack it all up for them, too. Stick it all in storage."

"But … not furniture, surely?"

"Yes. And once it's out of here, we can decide what to do with it all."

I grabbed the framed family photos, dotted around the room, and my book, *Anam Cara*. I hovered by the record box.

"Brianna, it'll all be packed safely; trust me."

"Okay, then just take these for now," I nodded, passing him what I'd gathered together. I cast an eye around the room, imprinting it into my memory, saying a silent farewell to the room I had loved for so many years.

And then, from out of nowhere, a surge of rage swept through me, extinguishing any sadness. I snatched up my phone and called Kitty.

"I'm busy, Mum," she said abruptly and hung up. I called again. No reply. Incensed, I sent her photos of the carnage left by Geoff. I only had to wait thirty seconds before she phoned me back.

"Mum, what's happened?"

"Your dad happened. Why the hell did you tell him about Niall?"

"I…"

"It was you. Wasn't it?"

"Yes." Her voice was small and scared.

"Well, thanks to you, we are leaving today. I can't stay here any longer. He is insane. And dangerous."

"But Mum …"

"Kitty, I don't want to hear it."

"Where are you going?"

"I can't tell you. I'm sorry."

And with that, I hung up. Niall observed me from the doorway.

239

"Was that wise? Or fair?"

"Yes, to both. I've had enough of trying to make it easy for them to deal with, and get nothing but grief from Kitty in return. She needs to know what he's done. What *she's* done."

He nodded slowly, ushering me into the kitchen, where mugs of coffee and a half packet of biscuits awaited us. I sat down heavily, watching Niall carefully pack the photos and book into one of the Sainsburys shopping bags.

"You think I was wrong, don't you?" I challenged.

"I do, yes. Look, she's just a kid, Brianna, who's had her life turned upside down."

I snorted with frustration, glaring out at the garden. He sighed.

"I know, I know – you've had your life turned upside down too, but you're living through it. Kitty is a bystander, helplessly watching it all unravel. Her parents' marriage, her safe haven, her steady life. All gone," he clicked his fingers, "In an instant. On top of that, she's had to deal with knowing that you could die."

I switched the focus of my icy glare, from the garden, onto him. "Precisely! And how does she respond? By creating havoc! By being deceitful. By refusing to see that what her dad has done, is so, so, wrong. She thinks this will all blow over and we'll be back to happy families, just as soon as I roll over and play doormat for him." I waited for him to say something. He didn't. "She's done this to you too, Niall. Why aren't you angry with her? Don't tell me you weren't scared last night."

"Of course I was scared. But being angry with Kitty achieves nothing. My focus is to get you somewhere safe,

240

away from here. That's all I'm concerned with right now. Kitty can wait. Kitty can have time to reflect. But you really can't be shouting at her down the phone; that's not fair. To either of you. Don't let Geoff destroy any more than he already has."

I was about to retort, still not able to calm my rage, when the phone rang. It was Jessica. She sounded furtive, as if making the call just out of earshot of someone. Jeremy, most likely.

"Bree, is everything okay there?"

"Have you heard? I was going to phone you, but we've been a bit busy this morning."

"Yes, I've heard. We've had a long night and an even longer morning, at the police station. Geoff is home now."

"*What?*" My voice went ten octaves too high. "How?"

"I've dropped the charges."

"*You've* dropped the charges?"

"Yes."

"But he did so much damage."

"To my property, yes, but not to you."

"Not for want of trying! If he'd got in, he would've killed us."

"But he didn't," she said evenly. "You're alright, thankfully."

"Physically, yes, but mentally, not at all! He terrified us."

"I'm sorry, Bree." There was silence.

"This is Jeremy, isn't it?" I said intuitively.

"You mean, *Father*."

"This is his doing."

"Geoff is his son. He can't stand by and let him go to prison or spend another night in custody. We can't allow

241

that. I have to drop the charges. It's a family matter, Bree. Geoff was upset."

"Upset!"

"But I haven't changed my mind about the house. Jeremy doesn't know about that arrangement."

"But Geoff's expecting that money from the house. If he doesn't get that, I'm worried he'll come gunning for you."

"I'm sure it'll be fine, Bree." She almost sounded like she believed it herself. Almost.

"How can you be so sure? You should see the damage here – what he's capable of in a temper. And he values money much more than he values a wife. Or a mother. He will come for you, and then he'll come for me."

"Then leave," she said quickly. "I'll give you all the money from the sale."

"No, no, I don't want that. You can't do that."

"I can. To make up for being a coward."  There was a crack in her voice that made my stomach lurch. She's scared, too. I could sense it.

"You're not a coward. You're just preserving your marriage."

"Bree …"

"It's okay; I don't blame you. But he is unhinged, Jessica."

"*Mother,*" she corrected.

"I can't do this! Stop trying to keep this all family orientated. Geoff has destroyed that! I'm divorcing him; we aren't a family anymore. Stop hanging on to it."

"But if I let go, what then? You're the mother of my grandchildren. You're the daughter I never had."

"Really? I didn't see that." I flinched after I'd said it. I knew I'd gone too far. I heard her gasp.

242

"Bree, that's an awful thing to say."

"But you made it so difficult for me. You all did. You all stood by Matthew. You're standing by Geoff. What happened to women's solidarity?"

"That's so American." It hadn't taken long for her to regain her composure.

"No, it's not! It's worldwide. Look, what I'm saying is, be careful. Your son is unpredictable and violent. And right now, he's feeling trapped. Anything could happen." I heard a door slam and a voice call out.

"Take care, Bree. Thank you for phoning," she said in a high voice.

"But you phoned me. Is everything okay? Is he there?"

"Okay, dear. Yes, I'll send Father your love. Bye, now." The line went dead.

I stared at Niall.

"What's happened? You've gone white as a sheet."

"He's there, with his parents. I heard him. We need to leave."


We drove in convoy to Studland. I hadn't driven in weeks and felt very uneasy behind the wheel, but we took it slowly, and gradually my confidence grew. Niall had already phoned Julia, giving her a brief outline of what had occurred. She was there to greet us, hugging us both tightly. For once, she didn't utter a word about Geoff.

"Just like old times," she said brightly, helping unload the cars.

"I'm sorry, Julia. Just when you thought it was safe to go back to work. Curtis doesn't mind that you're here instead, does he?" I asked.

"Of course not. He'll be over this afternoon; he's going to try and get off early."

I nodded, bending down to pick up a box. The world spun round. Niall rushed forwards and caught me as I swayed. What a dramatic moment to feel faint. Dramatic or pathetic, I can't decide. Either way, he scooped me up in those strong arms of his and carried me over to the sofa.

"I could get used to this," I smiled weakly.

"I noticed," he smiled back. "Now, will you please just rest and let us unpack and sort things."

"Oh, but ..."

"Brianna, forget *perfect*, okay? We'll do our best and you'll just have to accept that. If it's not all in the right place, then deal with it later. Enough, now."

I didn't argue.


"The thing is, I wanted to leave – I'd planned to – but when it came down to it, I felt robbed of making that choice. We were running instead of leaving when we're ready to, and it made me so angry. A primal kind of rage. Yet again, it was something that was out of my control. I'm sorry, Niall. I shouldn't have shouted at you; it was wrong of me. And I shouldn't have phoned Kitty and shouted at her. I didn't handle it very well, did I."

"That's totally understandable, though. I think you keep underestimating how much this is affecting you. I knew it would catch up with you."

We were lying in bed, talking quietly. Curtis and Julia were in the next room. It had been a surreal kind of evening again; that feeling of a new beginning yet returning to somewhere we felt so at home. We'd had a throw-together meal of whatever had been in the fridge, followed by a late walk on the beach, and coffee in the hut.  But before any of that, once I'd had a rest, Julia took me to task.

"I completely get why you're so annoyed and frustrated with Kitty – I am too – but you can't take it out on her over the phone. She phoned me in such a state. Think, Bree. This is so unlike you!"

"The whole thing is unlike me. It's all new. I've never had confrontation or upsets, or any slight deviation from the norm, Julia. I can't cope with much more."

But she was right.

I phoned Kitty. We quickly cleared the air, both apologising, both forgiving. I broached the subject again of what she had alluded to and yes, I'd been right. She *had* met someone, and yes, he *had* cheated on her and yes, she had forgiven him and taken him back.

"But why, Kitty? How can you trust him after that?"

"I have to."

My heart sank. "Are you pregnant?" I breathed.

"No! No, I'm not pregnant but we did … you know…" she cleared her throat, embarrassed. "I didn't want you to be ashamed of me."

"Ashamed? Why would I be?"

"Because I slept with him."

"And?"

"And you and Dad …"

My brain raced on ahead, trying to read between the lines of her very hesitant confession.

"Oh, my goodness, Kitty – Dad wasn't my first."

"Wasn't he?"

"No. I met Dad when I was twenty-six."

"So, he was your second, then?"

I faltered. "Let's not worry about numbers just now. What you need to realise is that you don't have to stay with a cheater, just because you've slept with them."

She was quiet for a moment. "I'm sorry, Mum. I thought he was the one."

"Don't apologise. It's part of growing up, of finding what you want in life. It's nothing to be ashamed of."

She was quiet for a long while. "Dad scares me."

"He scares me, too."


Kitty played on my mind for a long time afterwards. I thought I'd raised them all to be quite liberal, to know their own minds and not be afraid to branch out, grow up. We had the sex talk when they were old enough and I'd always stressed – regularly – that I was there if they ever needed to talk or ask for advice. So for Kitty to be feeling so guilty and ashamed, was very upsetting. It had never occurred to me that she'd think like that; that she'd compare herself to her parents. If truth be told, I thought she'd lost her virginity back in sixth form. She had a few boyfriends, one in particular that she spent most of her days with, and she seemed different: more mature, worldly wise. Turns out, I was just kidding myself. At the time, I was more worried about drugs. There had been a spate of raids on parties, locally, where drugs had been seized, but thankfully none of mine were at any of them. I wonder, do we ever stop worrying about them? Is there a handbook out there with a cut-off age for letting go?

Curtis had taken the rest of the week off work, claiming a family emergency and calling in a favour from his partner. We hadn't asked him to but appreciated it hugely. Safety in numbers.

Nobody mentioned Geoff and equally, Julia and Curtis didn't mention mine and Niall's shift in relationship. I thought Julia would be dying to ask questions – prise every little detail out – but no, she was uncharacteristically mute on the subject. It was as if he and I had always been a couple, in their eyes.

While we had, on the surface, forgotten Geoff, he hadn't forgotten us. Jessica phoned to ask where I was; I'd already let her know I wouldn't be at the house to greet the valuers when they came. She accepted my polite refusal to divulge our whereabouts. She seemed quite relieved, I think; she certainly didn't insist on knowing. But fifteen minutes later, Kitty forwarded a text from Geoff.

*'Tell Mum I will knock on every door in Dorset until I find her. I just want to say sorry. That's all.'*

I quietly showed Niall the text. He quietly deleted it. Just that one, simple action, felt so freeing. Not daunting or scary. Liberating. I'm beginning to enjoy being liberated.

I took it one step further and deleted my Facebook account. I hadn't looked at it for weeks. I hadn't wanted to see all the Hillingdon family faces, or all the friends that were more Geoff's than mine, with all their inane posts. I wanted to disappear from their lives and not feel beholden to them for existing in mine. Instagram and Twitter went the same way, regardless that I'd barely touched either account since setting them up. Geoff had already been deleted from my phone and his number blocked.

On a roll, I made a brief call to Linda at Athelhampton House, arranging to visit them the next morning.

I stood in front of the mirror, holding up dresses and blouses, one after the other, discarding each one with an agonised grunt.

"Why did I think this was a good idea?" I uttered for the umpteenth time.

"How about that one with the pink flowers?" Niall suggested, sitting on the bed, patiently watching.

"No, that'll clash with the turban I'm wearing."

"You're wearing a turban?"

"Yes. Why? Do you think a sunhat would be better?"

He shrugged. "I would say, wear nothing on your head."

I stared at him, about to cry. "I can't do that!"

"Brianna, you have been. You've been to the beach with nothing on your head. You're not wearing anything now."

"But that's …" I sat down heavily on the bed, next to him. "That's because I'm here, with you. You're all used to it now."

"And they haven't seen you for two months. They'll quickly get used to it, too. I'm sure they're expecting it anyway. Everybody knows what chemo does. Don't hide it."

I took a deep breath in and out, nodding to reaffirm my decision.

"Okay. But what do I wear? All of my clothes scream of the old Bree. I don't want to be her anymore."

"I know. And once you've had the surgery, we'll go on a shopping spree. You'll need a new wardrobe by then." He studied my face, then cast an eye over my overstuffed wardrobe. "Why don't you go all out. Wear your best frock."

248

I love the way he says *frock.* He makes it sound so chic, so continental. I had a thought.

"Ooh, we should go to Paris, to shop!"

"Should we?" he laughed.

"Yes, we should," I smiled demurely, turning back to the discarded dresses. I picked out a grey and peach polka dot wrap dress, with a frilled edge plunging into a low v. The belt wrapped snugly under my boobs and tied in a bow on the side, giving me a great cleavage. It had been an impulse buy (as were most of my dresses, to be fair) and I'd only worn it once, to a garden party at Curtis's work. Geoff hadn't been there; he'd been called in to his office to deal with an emergency. I doubt very much now, that it had been an emergency. Unless you can call an afternoon session with your mistress, an emergency.

"This one." I said. "I won't be able to wear it again so this can be its second and final outing."

"Good choice," he smiled. "And a hat?"

"No hat. Maybe a hat. Maybe … No, no hat."

"Has anyone ever pointed out how indecisive you are?" he teased.

"I'm not sure," I laughed.


Athelhampton glowed in the morning sun, welcoming us back. I had an overwhelming urge to weep; I hadn't realised how much I'd missed it. I really love this place.

My nerves were swiftly quashed by the unabashed welcome we both received. There were tears of joy, of shock, of sadness and relief.

"I can't believe how well you look," Annabelle said, for the third time. "I had visions of you emaciated and pale, with no energy."

"Well, the energy comes and goes, and I have lost a bit of weight but on the whole, I'm doing okay."

"And you had no idea you were so ill?" Linda asked.

"No. I felt fine. It was a total shock. The only time I felt ill was once I started the chemo. It's the cure that makes you feel so ill, not the cancer, ironically."

Nobody mentioned the fact that Niall had been holding my hand when we walked in, although I noticed the curious glances. Annabelle was the one brave enough to voice their question.

"So, you two have kept in touch, then?"

"More than that. Niall is the reason I'm looking so well. He's taking such good care of me."

"Oh," a murmur rippled among them. In for a penny.

"The fact is, so much has happened, you wouldn't believe. We're living together now."

Stunned silence. Even Annabelle was stumped. Maybe I should've dressed it up a bit more than I did. All eyes turned to Niall. He cleared his throat, smiling awkwardly.

"What Brianna means is, Geoff left, and I moved in to look after her. Along with Patrick."

"Patrick's home?" Linda looked surprised.

"He is," I nodded.

"So, you're not actually *living* living together?"

I shot a look at Niall. He gave me a subtle wink. "Yes, we are. He's just trying to save my blushes. Long story short; Geoff was having an affair. He left. Niall came to look after me, and we fell in love. I mean, who wouldn't?"

It worked. It broke the ice and spurred Annabelle back into life.

"I think we all fell in love with Niall," she laughed. "Good on you, Bree." She gave me the biggest hug. "I never liked Geoff," she whispered in my ear. "Something about him just didn't sit well."

Minutes later, Martyn and his wife, and more of the staff, joined us in the office. Jim was carrying a tray of glasses and Martyn an ice bucket, with a couple of bottles nestled in it.

"You didn't give us much warning, Bree," he scolded, "So the champers hasn't been chilling long but I thought we could all do with a glass. Here's to you!"

We left at midday, laden with flowers from the gardens and boxes of chocolates. I felt quite lightheaded from the champagne and giddy from the welcome we'd received.

"Well, you certainly made sure that they'll be talking about you for weeks to come," Niall exclaimed. "I didn't expect you to come out and say all that."

"I know," I smiled. "But they're my friends and I wanted to show you off."

He squeezed my hand. "Thank you. And I was right: nobody batted an eyelid at your lack of hair."

"I know! Why was that?"

"Because it really suits you. You look beautiful."

"You don't have to keep saying that."

"Oh, but I do. I won't let a day go by without telling you how I feel about you." He gave me that look again, the one that makes my stomach flip.

"Thank you," I said softly. "And I'm sorry about your plans for a week locked away in the bedroom. And then naked in a field."

He nudged me with his elbow. "You're not going to let me forget about that field, are you?"

"Never. Nobody has ever made a suggestion like that to me before! I'll remind you of it when we're old and grey."

"You probably will!"

"That was Imogen," Niall said, rejoining us at the dining table. "She's given me the number for somebody who has a property to let, just down the road. It's a long term let rather than a holiday one. And it's fully furnished. Three bedrooms, so room for the twins when they come home."

"Fully furnished?" Julia asked, looking at me. "Is that what you want? What about everything in the house?"

"I don't want any of it, anymore. A clean slate. That's what I want."

My car was the first thing to be sold. I'd only had the ad up online for two days before we had a buyer. Yes, I did feel a twinge of sadness, but I ignored it. It had to be done.

I gave the Aga to Annabelle. She'd always admired it and I desperately wanted it to go to a good home. I had visions of it, centre stage in her farmhouse kitchen — she has a proper farmhouse, just on the outskirts of Dorchester — with her four cats curled up by it, on a winters evening. I also gave her the antique, solid oak console table from the hall. They were the first two things I'd bought for the house, and they meant a lot to me. Not enough to keep but enough to make sure they were passed on to an equally loving home, where they'd be appreciated for many years to come.

Other bits of furniture went, in dribs and drabs. Patrick had returned after the weekend, and he and Niall spent two days packing up everything we were going to keep, and logging everything we were going to sell. The *keep* pile was very small. My old records, a few CDs and DVDs, photo albums and some books. Childhood treasures, toys, first shoes. All of Kitty and Sean's belongings that had been left behind when they went to uni. It was actually quite a pitiful amount, from a fair-sized family. Not much to show for all those years.

"I don't want to keep any of it but it's making me feel so wretched that there isn't much to keep. This is so hard, Julia."

"I know," she rubbed my arm, comforting me. "I've been through this, and I can safely say, it does pass. Honestly. Soon enough, you'll be in your new place, filling it with new things. The past is just that: the past. You have memories, Bree. Just pick which ones you want to keep in your head. That's enough."

She and I sorted through my clothes. I'd decided to do it in advance of surgery, get it out of the way. Initially, I was going to bag it all up and give it to charity but so many outfits had hardly been worn, so many bags had hardly been used, and I knew they were the kind of thing that would sell well online. I'd never had to worry about money before; not since I'd married Geoff. It's a new concept and one I kept foremost in my mind, trying to be practical.

Julia offered to take charge of the selling. All I had to do was say goodbye to each item. I started out doing just that; picking out a dress, running a hand across it, smiling, reminiscing, holding it up to me. But I soon got tired of that, and within fifteen minutes, I just bunched the hangers all together in the wardrobe, turned to Julia and said, "Sell the lot."

It was making me nervous that we hadn't heard anything from Geoff. None of us had. I kept waiting for the door to knock, his car to pull up outside, or my phone to beep with a message from him, via Kitty. I was so on edge, waiting, and any little sound would make me jump. It wasn't doing me any good, I knew that. I had a permanent knot in my stomach and a vein throbbed by my temple. I could actually see it pulsating, in the mirror. I knew Niall had seen it too, but he didn't say anything. On top of that, the countdown clock was ticking, and B-Day was looming fast.

The three of us had been to the beach with Pip – our usual walk, twice a day – coming back past the cottage we were waiting to move into. The previous tenants were in their final week and then some repairs were needed before we could move. If all went to plan, we'd be in, twelve days before surgery. Enough time to settle. It helped having something else to focus on. I just wished I could get rid of this ever-increasing anxiety. Peter had recommended yoga and prescribed some mild antidepressants. I hated taking them, but they did seem to be helping.

We all saw Geoff's car at the same time, parked outside our cottage. Patrick swore under his breath, pulling Pip in on her lead. Niall tightened his grip of my hand.

"Keep walking," he instructed quietly. My legs turned to lead, and I walked as if I'd forgotten how to. We passed the car – none of us breathing – and let ourselves into the cottage, all leaning against the closed door, waiting for the knock. It didn't come.

"He's just sat there," Patrick said, covertly peering through the window. "Not moving."

I waited for my phone to ring. A text notification. Anything. Nothing happened.

He was there for nearly two hours.

"Has he moved at all? Is he alive?" Horrible images flashed through my head.

"He's alive, yes. He's just eaten something," Patrick reported back. "Should I go out and ask him to leave?"

"No," Niall replied. "Leave him be. He's playing a game; let's not rise to it."

Sure enough, after another twenty minutes, he left. I sat by the window, watching the road. Waiting.

"I can't live like this. I can't."

And then the floodgates opened. I hadn't cried like that since the night I told Geoff and then Niall, that I had cancer. All the fear, the anger, the frustration, came pouring out, in gigantic waves of tears and mucus. I cried so much, I made myself sick. Niall and Patrick sat on either side of me, encouraging me to let it all out. Pip sat by my feet, watching. If she could talk, I'm sure she would've agreed with them. Better out than in.

# Chapter Seventeen

By the time Julia and Curtis arrived the following Sunday for lunch, Niall, Patrick, Sean and I had talked over our plans, again and again. I hadn't included Kitty – I hated not doing so but I couldn't trust her not to talk to Geoff.

"We've changed our moving plans," I announced, as we sat down to eat.

"How come?" Julia wondered, looking round at the three of us.

"We need to move away from here, from Geoff. It's the only way I can get peace."

Julia stared at me, not liking what I was telling her. "So, you mean, away away, as in, far away?"

I nodded.

"Where?" Curtis asked.

"Dublin," Niall replied. Julia's eyes flew open wide. Curtis smiled, nodding approval.

"Ah, you'll love it there, Bree!"

"You've been?" Niall asked him.

"Yes, we honeymooned there, for a month. It's a beautiful, fascinating city." He reached for Julia's hand. "We loved every minute."

"Niall has family there, so we'll be looked after," I said.

"I don't want you to go," Julia said quietly.

"I know. I don't want to leave you, but I can't stay here, living each day in fear of Geoff turning up."

"Get a court order on him, then! Don't let him push you away."

"I'm not. He's giving me the push that I need, to move on."

"Without me," she said, eyes pleading me to change my mind. Niall watched us. He turned to Curtis.

"Come with us! I know you can't just up sticks like we can, but if you ever think you could move, do it."

"I'd love that," Curtis said. "I've often talked about early retirement. Imagine that, Julia; retiring and having an extended second honeymoon."

She gave him a wan smile. "The trouble is, you've been talking about early retirement for so long now, it's no longer early."

They stared intently at each other, Curtis's mind going into overdrive. A knowing smile spread across Julia's face.

"Let's do it! I'll set the ball in motion, hand over the reins, sell the house. Yes?" he waited for Julia to respond.

"Yes!" she laughed. Curtis hi-fived Niall, then Patrick. It always makes me laugh when he does that with the boys. It should look out of place and awkward, but it doesn't.

Julia hugged me, giving an exaggerated sigh of relief. I cried, naturally. I hadn't in my wildest dreams considered that they would drop everything to come with us. The fact that they were, filled me with such a joy and sense of peace that I couldn't contain. Hence the tears.

"So, what are the plans?  I'm assuming you'll wait until after the surgery? And are the twins moving with you? Are *you*?" she asked Patrick.

"Sean wants to move over as soon as he's finished uni. He's very excited about it; he's already been looking at job openings for an Economics graduate. As for Kitty," I shrugged lightly, "I haven't told her, yet. I feel bad but I know she'll tell Geoff. I'll have to wait to tell her, until we've got everything sorted."

Julia gave me a long, hard look, weighing up what I'd told her. "I'm not sure what the fall out will be from that, but I can understand why you've done it. And you, Patrick?"

"Yes, I'm moving with them but only until next September. I'm determined to finish my fourth year and then maybe we'll move over too, at a later date."

"And when do we get to meet the lovely Saskia?"

"Next weekend."

"Just before my surgery," I added.


Saskia was exactly what I'd expected: lovely, from head to toe. Just such a natural, down to earth, little bit shy but very friendly, kind of person. And she adores Patrick, that's plain to see. Shorter than him, with a darker shade of his blonde hair, they look so good together. I couldn't stop smiling for the entire visit – which lasted for three days – so my face ached a little by then, as you can imagine.

We all gathered for the weekend, partly to meet Saskia and partly to mark the imminence of B-Day. The cottage was certainly very cosy with all of us in it. Kitty and Sean camped out in the living room, without any fuss. It was very much an up-beat kind of gathering; nobody mentioned cancer or surgery, Dublin or Geoff. We just had fun introducing Saskia to the beach and the surrounding walks, and spent one evening over in Poole at Julia and Curtis's house. Julia put on an amazing spread as always, and Curtis was delighted when his polite offer of showing Saskia his telescope, was met with genuine enthusiasm.

"I can't believe you have an observatory!" she exclaimed. "I did Astrology as one of my options for GCSE's. I would've killed for a proper telescope."

The observatory, on the third floor of their immaculate nineteen-twenties house overlooking the bay, had always been the children's favourite room when they were younger. They weren't so fussed about looking at stars, more at being nosy and using the telescope to spy on Curtis's neighbours or watch the boats out on the water. Patrick had a fleeting interest in Astrology and spent a few months studying books and charts alongside Curtis, but it was a phase, and like all phases, it quickly passed.

December arrived. The countdown had finally ended. Patrick propped a chocolate advent calendar next to the countdown one.

"Get rid of one calendar and start the other," he smiled. "This one's more of a celebration calendar."

I'd said I wanted to spend my last day before surgery, with Niall and Patrick, going for a long walk along the clifftop, but Patrick tactfully declined.

"Spend your time together, just the two of you," he said to me quietly. "I hate being a third wheel, anyway."

And so began a morning of *lasts.* You know, the game everybody plays on New Year's Eve: *this is the last drink I'm having all year,* or, *this is the last time I kiss you until next year.* That kind of thing. I had my last shower, smothered my head in moisturiser and pasted a sticky mask all over my face, lured in by the promise of a soothing experience, leaving me refreshed and glowing. I'm not convinced it worked.

I stared in the mirror at my boobs. My mighty, heavy, unwittingly toxic, boobs. Panic gripped at my throat. I'm not sure I'm doing the right thing, discarding them completely. I

259

can't imagine me without boobs. I was eight when they started to grow. Eight! That's forty-two years of my life, with boobs. And now we're going to be separated.

I pressed them as flat as I could, assessing, trying to imagine what I'll look like without them.

"*Hideous!*"

What if Niall hates it? Hates their absence. They're so much a part of me. They make me curvy, sexy, everything I want to be.

"Is that what I still want, though?" I stared accusingly at my reflection. "Curvy, sexy – do I really want to be that person?"

Who am I kidding? Of course I do! Who doesn't want to be?

I scraped off the mask, splashed my face with cold water and scowled at the '*glow*'. Slapped cheek, more like. Nothing goes right when I'm stressed.

I went downstairs to the kitchen, a towel wrapped tightly around me.

"I've just been kidding myself. I think I'll hate being boobless. Won't you miss them, too?" I announced. "Oh, sorry, Patrick! I didn't see you there."

"That's alright. I'll just be in the living room and … leave you to it. I'm sensing this is a chat I can't really help with." He grinned at me, trying valiantly to prove he wasn't embarrassed but in fact, every inch of him was cringing.

Niall put his arms around me, pulling an awkward face to mirror mine. Poor Patrick.

"Okay, well, you can always opt for reconstruction later. Don't fret about it, now. Not the day before."

"That'll be painful, won't it?"

"I believe so. As will a massive tattoo. Either option involves some element of pain."

"What do I do?" I wailed dramatically.

"Drink your coffee – last one for today – then make sure you have everything packed. And then we'll go for that walk. It may be the last time for a while."

Niall was in such a positive mood. Almost too positive. I know it's for my benefit and I appreciated it but part of me wanted him to be fretting, just a little, so I didn't feel like I was fretting alone. But that's not his style. He's not dramatic – apparently, I am, according to him – he's just very calm and practical about most things thrown at him. Underneath however, I think it's a different story. A well-hidden one.

He still hasn't talked much about the rift with his dad, only that he considers his mid-twenties to early thirties to be his teenage angst years. A late developer. I can identify with that. I drifted a little, not knowing what I wanted to do with my life. Hence my epic move across the Atlantic. If I'd stayed put, maybe I would've become frustrated with life. Disillusioned. It's strange but I never felt like I belonged in Brooklyn, even though that was the only place I knew. My family was there, part of our history was there and yet, my soul longed for the unknown isle of Ireland. I'd heard so many stories and so many romanticised accounts of our ancestors lives there, that I wanted to be a part of it – of them. As they say, *the grass is always greener on the other side*. But is it, in fact? I'll soon find out, once we've moved there.

Part of Niall's current positivity, stems from his meet-up with Lizzie two days ago, going so well. Better than he'd hoped. He'd come away with any worries about moving to

Dublin and leaving Layla behind, put to rest. Lizzie has moved back to her parents' house, with Layla. Her parents dote on the pair of them. *Smother*, Niall says, but I think all things considered, smother isn't such a bad thing just now. She's dating the guy she slept with, and they seem happy. She's happy to keep Niall in contact with Layla, and Niall is happy with the care she's receiving, living with her grandparents.

Now all we need to do, is tell Kitty about moving.

We'd arranged to have an early dinner at Julia and Curtis's. My hospital admission was booked for seven in the evening. That way, I'd be prepped and ready for surgery first thing. Niall, Patrick and Pip, would stay with them until I was ready to come home. I'd been told two days but expect three, depending on how everything goes. Either way, it meant they were all close by for visits.

I was doing absolutely fine – *absolutely* fine – until the moment I watched Niall walk down the corridor and off the ward. Then I cried. I stuck my head in the stiff, white pillow and wept. They've seen it all before, the nurses, and astutely left me to it for a good five minutes, by which time, I'd regained my composure and had started to sort out my belongings.

'*Bring things to cheer you,*' they'd said. So, I brought a framed photo of all of us on the beach, when we celebrated the end of chemo, and another of my parents. Propped up next to the frames, a little pink teddy, with *Mummy* embroidered on the red heart it was holding. An old Mother's Day gift from them, and one that's always been on my bedside chest.

I put my laptop and headphones in the bedside cupboard for later. I'd got a list of films lined up to watch and several playlists on Spotify. They'd asked if I wanted a particular song played when I went down to theatre, before I go under. I thought about it for quite a while. It's that age old thing, when somebody puts you on the spot and asks, *what's your favourite film?* Or song, or book. I can't think. My mind goes blank. Panic blindness.

Julia reminded me. *I'm So Excited,* by The Pointer Sisters. Odd choice for the occasion, I know, but it was the opening song from my favourite film in the mid-eighties, called *Deceptions,* starring the very handsome Barry Bostwick and equally beautiful Stephanie Powers. It's not a great film, not a masterpiece, or even a very clever plot, but for some reason, I love it. It's my guilty pleasure film, and the thing that first brought Julia and me together. We were chatting in the hotel reception, and I happened to mention the film – I think actually, she asked me what my favourite film was, and for once, I remembered. Turns out, it was her favourite film, too. We became best friends from that moment on, and the song became our 'going out' anthem. Those were the days, getting ready for a night out, laughing and getting tipsy, without a care in the world. Dressed to impress, with my ample cleavage leading the way.

I slowly came to, aware of Niall's presence. I'd been drifting in and out of sleep all afternoon, not wanting to fully wake up. My stomach was lurching, so I'd kept my eyes shut, in a bid to keep the nausea at bay.

He gently stroked my cheek. "How are you feeling?"

I licked my dry lips and took a sip from the offered cup and straw. "I'm not sure yet."

I felt woozy from the anaesthetic, as to be expected, and an ache in my chest, but nothing screaming out at me. I'd expected to be in so much pain.

That came soon enough, once the initial pain relief had worn off. Two days later, back in the comfort of the cottage, propped up with plump pillows and loosely covered with an airy, lightweight duvet, Niall asked the same question. I winced, shifting position slightly.

"Like I've been stamped on by an elephant, split open, then stitched back together again with a thousand bee stings." See: not dramatic at all.

He raised his eyebrows at my description. "So, not ready for the tattoo parlour just yet?"

"If you come anywhere near me with anything remotely resembling a needle, I may just stick it in your eye!"

He laughed lightly. He looked so tired. He'd insisted on sleeping in a chair by my bedside, rather than on the sofa in the living room. Sean was home; he and Patrick had both offered to sleep in the living room so that Niall could have Patrick's bed, but Niall would have none of it and the boys could see their efforts, although well intended, were futile. Niall hadn't left my side for more than a few minutes at a time. He even sat there watching me sleep.

"You look done in, Niall. Why don't you lie down for a bit? Have a hug."

He shook his head. "I'm fine. I'd hate to catch one of your drains if I fell asleep. Once they're out, then we can hug as much as you like. I'm fine on the chair; it's surprisingly comfy."

I laughed abruptly. "You're so bad at lying! But thank you. For being by my side, I mean." I stared down at my flat, bandaged chest. I hadn't bothered with a nightie; it just irritated my skin. Even the lightest of fabric felt like a lead weight. I had four drains in situ: two in my chest and one under each arm. They were only temporary; another few days and they'd come out, along with the bandages coming off. Each tube had a little bulbous bottle attached, which needed emptying regularly. So grim. Niall did it without hesitation. I can't say enough, what a hero he's been.

Before we left the hospital, I was given a sheet of arm exercises to do, and some cute, knitted covers for the bottles. They had long straps to hook over my shoulders, so that I could be more mobile. It was all very practical but all I could think about was my Nana doing her knitting, with bobbins of coloured wool hanging from the main bulk of it. I had become a Fairisle jumper.

"What was I thinking, Niall? I thought I'd breeze through it, come out boobless and petite – a beauty. Not this hideous lump of drains and patchwork quilting."

"You don't look hideous."

"I feel it."

He looked at me for a long time, sensing that no amount of flattery would make me feel better right now.

"Would a chocolate biscuit help?"

"Always," I nodded.

"Shall I help you to get outside? Sit in the garden for a bit?"

I shook my head. "Not right now. I feel like even a slight breeze on my skin, would feel worse than being punched."

"Fine. How about sitting in the living room. Just to get you out of bed for a bit. You don't need to get dressed, if you don't want to."

Sean came up the stairs, two at a time, and stuck his head round the door, summoning Niall out onto the landing. I heard whispered voices; Sean's indignant, Niall's reasoning.

Niall came back into the bedroom. "Geoff is outside. He has flowers – I'm assuming, for you."

"Don't let him in," I said flatly.

"I'm just going to talk to him. If nothing else, to tell him not to keep doing this; appearing on the doorstep or sitting by the gate in his car."

"Niall …"

"I know. I'll be cautious, okay. It needs to be sorted."

I strapped the bottles across my shoulders and eased myself out of bed, walking gingerly over to the window. His car was parked by the gate, but he was nowhere to be seen. Niall had let him in.

Standing on the landing, I could just about make out voices downstairs; Niall's deep, reassuring tone and Geoff's slightly higher pitched, equally calm, tone. It seemed to be going well. How frustrating that I couldn't actually hear *what* they were saying, though.

Niall came up the stairs, smiling at my guilty face.

"He wants to see you."

"No!"

Niall held his hands up. "I know how you feel but just give him five minutes – that's all he wants. Five minutes, to apologise. We need to sort this, Brianna. He seems very calm, very serious."

"But …"

"You look fine. I'll help you put a shawl on or a loose top. Do you want him to come up here, or will you come downstairs?"

"I'll come down. He is *not* coming into our bedroom."

"Fair enough. I'll stay with you, if you want."

I put on a loose top and draped a blanket scarf across my shoulders to hide the drains, silently cursing Geoff for making me suffer the discomfort of clothes.

Geoff stood up when I entered the room, eyes wide, staring intently at my face so as not to look at my chest, but it was obvious he was aching to. He offered me the flowers.

"Hello, Bree. I'm so, so sorry for what happened. I was completely out of order, I know that."

I sat down, refusing to accept the flowers. He floundered, hovering, until Niall accepted them and murmured that he'd put them in water. He looked to me first, silently checking if I was okay to be left with Geoff for a moment. I smiled briefly and nodded.

Geoff sat opposite me. "How are you? Did it all go well?"

I nodded. I couldn't look at him. I just couldn't.

"Bree, I know I have no right to be here, but I can't carry on without apologising. I hate myself for what I did. Not just that night, but all of it. I think I had some kind of break down. I really wasn't in control, wasn't able to think clearly. I already knew you and … Niall … were together, but hearing it from Kitty, just crucified me."

"We weren't together before that though, Geoff. I know you thought we were, but we were just friends, supporting each other. That's all."

"So, if I hadn't …"

"Don't! Don't build your hopes up and make it something it's not." I was about to explain Niall's admirable morals and how I'd been desperate for us to be together, but I stopped short. Why on earth should I explain myself to him? How does he do this to me, every time? Turns everything around to be about him and how he's feeling. Am I just primed to put him first and always be apologising for having feelings myself, or my own opinion?

There was such a long silence that I had to look up. He was visibly disturbed by my appearance. There was a sadness in his eyes which made my chest hurt. He looked about five. He's good at doing that; looking lost and vulnerable, making it impossible to hate him.

"I'm so sorry," he uttered. "I couldn't believe what I'd done. The police thought I was drunk at first, and they were ... not jokey exactly, but chastising, thinking I was not compos mentis. But when they discovered I was completely sober, they changed their tune. They were contemptuous, and rightly so. I could've really hurt one of you."

"Yes."

"Thank God, I didn't."

"That's what your mother said, too."

"She was horrified. Naturally." He paused. "It's been hard to live it down, let it go. She's very angry with me."

"Geoff, you're fifty-two! You're talking like you're fifteen." I stopped short at his surprised expression. I wanted to say so much more but was cautious of fanning the flame. Yes, he looks broken now but that can change at the flick of a switch.

"I thought about ending it all, you know," he said at length. "I came that close. I drove up to West Bay, up by our spot. Remember how we used to park up there on the cliffs, when we were first dating? I stood on the edge there, staring out at the black sea, thinking, *what is the point in carrying on?*"

"Not because of me, surely?" I couldn't hide the shock I felt at such an image. Of course I remembered the spot he was talking about. We used to go there all the time, away from the prying eyes of his parents. It was romantic, exciting. A lifetime ago.

"Yes," he replied. "I hate how happy you are without me. I can't cope without you. I can't be happy. I wanted to prove a point to you, show you how devastated I am without you. Then a lone seagull screamed above my head, in the dead of night. It made me jump, snapped me out of it. And then I realised, if I jump now and die, how will I know if you've got the point I'm making? And why make the point, if I don't gain anything from it."

"Geoff ..."

"I know. There is nothing to gain. I get that, now. I hate how together you are, even though you're so ill. You bounced back too quickly after I left." He gave me a sad smile. "I thought I made you happy."

"You did. But Niall makes me happier."

"I can see that."

I swallowed hard. He meant it; I could tell. "Thank you. That took a lot of effort to say, didn't it."

"It did." He smiled. His smile faded. "She's pregnant, Bree."

"What?" I sat up, stunned. "Was it planned?"

"Not by me!"

"What are you going to do?"

He shrugged. "Spend a ton of money on baby stuff, apparently. She told Mother. She seems pleased."

"That's good."

"Hmmm," he frowned. "Is it?"

I thought for a moment. "Does she know how you felt about having kids? That the reason you started an affair with her, was to get away from us?"

He shook his head.

"Maybe you should've told her. Irrelevant now, sorry," I apologised quickly. I couldn't help thinking that Francesca had just signed her own death-of-relationship certificate. Clearly, the baby was her way of ensuring Geoff saw the light and moved on with her. How wrong she was.

"Don't be a chicken this time, Geoff. She must love you; she waited long enough for you. Don't do the same to her."

"I don't think I've changed, Bree. I'm too set in my ways." He almost smirked. It twisted my stomach. Just that one look, spoke volumes.

"Does that mean you're already seeing someone else?"

"No, but …"

"But it's crossed your mind?"

He nodded.

"Geoff!" I suddenly felt like his mother, scolding and disapproving. A leap from the wronged, devoted wife.

"Look, never mind about that. I came to cheer you up after your op, but you seem cheerful enough." He stood up. "I'm sorry, Bree. For everything. I was an idiot." He looked intently at me, waiting for a spark, a glimmer of submission. I held my own. "We could've started again, you know; got over it and carried on, if it weren't for him."

"No, Geoff," I said firmly, "I would never have forgiven you and carried on. Never. Luckily for me, I met someone who would never expect that of me."

He nodded, shuffled on the spot, not sure whether to try going for a hug. I just smiled.

"Bye, Geoff. Thank you for coming round."

As if on cue – I'd seen him hovering by the door, in fact – Niall appeared, to show him out. They shook hands. Geoff didn't ask after Patrick or Sean, although he must've seen that they were there. Or maybe he didn't. Maybe he was too wrapped up in what he'd come to say, that he hadn't noticed anything else.

We watched his car disappear down the lane, from the safety of our window. Sean eyed me.

"We're still moving to Dublin, right?"

"Absolutely, we are!" I smiled, a surge of happiness and relief coursing through me. "I'm going to phone Kitty right now and tell her our plans.

# Chapter Eighteen

And so began the healing process, both physically and mentally. That last meeting with Geoff, released me from him. I finally saw him for what he was; not the romantic notion I'd always clung to, been drawn to, dominated by, but rather, a spoilt, confused and immature man, ruled by the need to be in control. I'm sure he loved me – probably still does – but not in the same way that I loved him, or that I needed him to love me. Unconditionally. Selflessly. Openly.

I don't want to fall into the trap of comparing, because that could come across as point scoring. Having said that, I can't help but compare. Niall is so easy going, so giving, so ready to indulge me. Not materialistically, but physically, mentally. We spend every minute we can together. We've done so much together in such a short space of time, cementing that feeling of always having known each other. We go exploring, delighting in finding new paths to wander down, new stretches of coastline to clamber along.  We curl up and read on the sofa by the fire; him one end, me the other, and our feet touching in the middle. I hadn't read a book in years. Niall was shocked by that. He said he couldn't imagine not reading. I'd forgotten the joy it brings. And we talk, constantly. About everything and anything. Serious or random, we discuss it at length. We laugh. A lot. We sing. We dance on the little patch of lawn at the back of our rented cottage. We sit out til late, listening to the crickets make their own kind of music. We gaze up at the stars and thank our lucky ones that we had found each other.

The drains came out and the bandages came off. Kitty was home for that. She and I stood, hand in hand, studying the scars in my full-length mirror. It wasn't as horrific as I'd expected. I was healing remarkably quickly, and neatly, too. I couldn't envisage a tattoo there, though.

"Maybe some pretty camisoles?" Kitty suggested. "Lacy, or floral. Something feminine and soft, underneath your clothes. That'll make you feel better, I'm sure. And less painful, or permanent, than a tattoo."

We went shopping. Correction: we *aimed* to go shopping. My confidence waivered in the very first store, so we opted for an online shopping spree. It wasn't just my confidence, to be honest, it was also the close proximity of people. I feel so protective of my chest, of my whole body. I panic if I think people are too close. Oh, I'm fine with family, but not with strangers. I'm told it will take a while.

The online orders arrived. It was so much fun, trying on all different kinds of clothes, styles I would never have dreamed of before. Kitty and Julia both embraced the changes I was trying to make. We had a few disasters along the way. Skater dresses do not suit me, nor do leggings – animal print, or otherwise. The lack of boobs and cleavage has made me rethink my whole style. Shift dresses work, and anything with a dropped waist. The temptation to binge on comfy, baggy clothes was huge but that would make it easier to hide away in my own comfort zone. Not the idea at all. The idea was to embrace life and do what I have always loved doing most - dressing up and going places.

Niall and I drew up a list, entitled, *Must Visit Before We Leave*. Places neither of us had ever been but always wanted to, or places we'd loved and wanted to share with each

273

other. We also found a few places we'd never heard of, so quickly added them to our list, too.

The talk revolved mainly around the move to Dublin. Kitty loved the idea. A little too brightly, I think, but at least she was onboard with it. I'm not sure she'll join us permanently, but I know she'll visit often.

"The question is," Julia started the conversation as we sat around the table, full from another lovely Sunday lunch. "Do we want to live together, commune style, or do we want to live independently but near each other?"

"Oh, together," Curtis said without hesitation. Julia eyed him.

"Are you sure? I mean, you're pretty set in your ways and you like things in order."

"I think Bree is pretty ordered," he countered. "She's an excellent housewife."

Nobody spoke. He swiftly gauged from the stunned silence, that he'd said the wrong thing. He apologised, unreservedly.

"I know what you mean, Curtis, it's fine. I just don't want to be that housewife anymore. I think it would be lovely to share a house but equally…"

"Lovely to have your own space," Julia finished for me.

Curtis smiled. "I see. Give the lovebirds some room, you mean?"

"Well, actually, I was thinking of us, too. This is our second honeymoon, as you keep saying," she said, patting his hand.

"Besides, I like quirky and cute, whereas your style is more traditional," I added. Curtis nodded but I could see Julia and I had just crushed his dream of a comfortable home in Dublin city, with the two ladies looking after the men.

Patrick was making plans too for the coming year. He and Saskia set about looking for somewhere to live in Exeter, while he finishes his Masters. Then, who knows? The world is theirs to make of it what they want. I said as much to him.

"It's all very well making long term plans but what this past year has taught me, is that life can turn upside down in the blink of an eye. Just follow your heart, go with your gut. Do what *you* want to do, not what you think others expect of you. Don't live your life trying to please everybody else."

"I know what you're saying, Mum. And for the record, I think it's great that you're finally doing what you set out to do, all those years ago. I'm only sorry it's taken you this long."

"I don't want you to think I regret any of my life, because I don't – well, apart from your dad cheating – but I wish I'd done more. I should've taken you all to Dublin and Cork, on holidays, done my pilgrim a long time ago. Not put it off for as long as I have. But there's no point regretting things; that doesn't achieve anything. Just be happy, Patrick. That's all I want for you. Do what makes you happy."

Jessica paid a visit, bearing gifts of cake and flowers. After Geoff had found where we were living, I saw no reason to keep her in the dark any longer. She gave me a tentative hug, glancing briefly at my chest. She didn't really ask about the surgery – not that she didn't want to know, just that she didn't know how to ask. I should've helped her, but I'm done with that. Besides, she had more pressing news.

"I think we have a potential buyer for the house. They're very keen."

"So soon?"

"Yes, well, it's a desirable location and an even more desirable property. Who would've guessed?"

Certainly not you, I thought, feigning polite surprise.

"I still think you should give Geoff his half, or maybe give it to Francesca," I ventured.

"Why?"

"Because she has a baby on the way. I feel for her."

Jessica gave me a stony look. "Admirable as that is, no. I don't agree. You either take the full amount, or if you still insist on just half, then I'll put the other half into a trust fund for the children."

"And will you do something for the new baby?"

"I'm sure I will, yes. But I don't understand you, Bree; she destroyed your marriage. Why do you even care?"

"Yes, she did but she was thoughtless, that's all. Geoff, however, was devious, conniving. *He* destroyed our marriage. She just happened to be his accomplice. I think she'll regret it when she realises the same thing will happen to her."

"Oh, I'm sure Geoff has learnt his lesson by now. Besides, there's a baby on the way."

I stayed shtum. Why rock the boat when I already know it won't achieve anything.

We'd given ourselves until my two-month check-up, to pack up, find a new home and move. And we'd agreed that if we hadn't found somewhere permanent by then – the chances were incredibly thin – we would move anyway and rent temporarily until we did. Niall had wanted to rent rather than buy, but I needed a base – for the children as much as for us – that was ours. I fully intended to utilise my share of the proceeds from the sale.

"Nothing grand, nothing pretentious. Just a home that screams to be loved, that's big enough for us, and visiting children. Yours and mine. That's all I want," I told Niall. "And with the rest of the money, I want us to find a gallery, a shop, in Dublin, for you."

"A gallery?"

"Yes. I can just picture it; you off on a shoot and me behind the counter, manning the shop. Pip sitting guard, by my side."

He smiled at the image. "I thought the idea was for you to rest and for us to have time for each other."

"I'm done with resting, Niall! I will take it easy, I promise, but we can't ignore your talents. Running a gallery will be fun. And if I pitch in, it gives you more time for music, too." I had a thought. "I bet Curtis and Julia would want to help run it, too. Can you imagine Curtis, sweet-talking the clientele – they'd be falling over themselves to buy your work!"

"It sounds perfect," he nodded. "But it's your money, Brianna."

"Exactly. And I say, let's get a gallery. How's the album coming along?"

He chuckled. "About as far as it had got yesterday when you asked. It's going well, thank you."

"Sing to me," I demanded happily, taking his offered hand as he led me into the garden, snatching up his guitar from the chair. Pip trotted along behind us, tail wagging. She loves his voice as much as I do.

277

Despite our plans, I was itching to get back to work, to finish the website project I'd started with Niall. Martyn agreed it would be best for me to work from home, away from any bugs, and to my own timetable that allowed me to rest when I needed to. I don't think I could've had a more understanding and accommodating boss. I did go back into the office though, just to show my face and catch up with everything. And to tell my team about our moving plans.

They stared, dumbstruck. They'd just about got used to the idea that my perfect marriage was over, just about come to terms with my illness and just about recovered from the shock of my new body image. This latest segment of news, seemed to be just too much for them to take in. They couldn't quite believe that Niall had so innocently come into my life and turned it around in such a dramatic way. But they were happy for me – as they told me repeatedly, reassuring themselves of the fact more than me. Annabelle was particularly pleased for me and didn't hesitate taking credit for it all.

"Just think, if I hadn't insisted on proving a point to Darren that I could just as easily prune the apple tree myself, rather than wait forever for him to get around to it, then I wouldn't have fallen out of the tree, been off sick with concussion, and you wouldn't have taken my place working with Niall. He would've passed you by completely. You can thank me later. Ooh, you can thank me by inviting me to stay at your new place in Dublin."

I laughed at her eager face. "Absolutely! As soon as we're settled, you will be our first guest."

Niall got back to work too, more able to focus once I was on the mend. He hated leaving me though, so we worked out a rota which enabled me to accompany him on location shoots. The fresh air did me good, and to be honest, I could happily sit and watch him work all day long, despite the chilly weather. Pip was, without doubt, in her element, too.

Christmas came and went. I had such mixed feelings about it. It was always a time for the children. I'd instilled a love of Christmas in them, right from the onset, and we always went to town, celebrating the season. But it felt very flat this year. It wasn't our place to decorate, and besides, I'd thrown away the decorations and was loathe to buy more just before we move. My heart just wasn't in it.

The twins came home, equally flat. Kitty went to visit Geoff, found out about the baby, and came back feeling even more dejected.

"Maybe we should just cancel the whole thing. Let's just forget it this year," she said.

Julia wouldn't hear of it. She announced she was making the most of their last Christmas in their house, and invited – no, insisted – we all spend it with them. Which we did, and thoroughly enjoyed it. It was the perfect pick-me-up and because it was at their home, which is so different from our old home, the children enjoyed it more. I think the champagne that Curtis plied everybody with, may have had something to do with it.

And before you know it, we were at the beginning of February, and my two-month, post-surgery check-up. The weather was grim, giving me a chance to show off my new winter wardrobe. I had plenty of hats. My hair hadn't shown any signs of growing back yet, stare as I might at my scalp in the mirror. I didn't have that itchy feeling that so many

279

describe. Nothing. I'd already decided that when it did grow, I'd keep it short – fuzzy hedgehog short. I've got used to no hair. And maintenance is obviously zero, so that's not a bad thing. Niall has taken so many photos of me and dotted them about the place, as a permanent reminder of how good I look – his words, not mine – although I have to agree, I *do* look good. Better than I ever imagined I would.

I toyed with the idea of a fake bra – I even tried one out – and granted, it made dresses hang a little better, but it felt exactly that: fake. So, I did what I'd promised myself I would; I came to terms with my new body shape, my new look. I think I've embraced it. I'm certainly enjoying wearing new styles; more knitwear than ever before. Nothing baggy, not like that. Just comforting. Still feminine, still pretty, just no cleavage. And on Niall's gig days, I dress a little bit more like a rock chic, and I carry it off. How cool is that? It's strange, but I feel so much more confident now that I can't hide behind my cloud of hair or impressive boobs. I feel like the inner me has been well and truly thrust into the limelight, and I've dealt with it. I won.

I felt quite nervous about seeing my consultant again. I'd been in regular contact with my assigned breast cancer nurse and been checked over to see how everything was healing, but going back to see Peter was more emotional than expected.

After the initial greetings and him expressing how well I looked, he got straight to the point. I knew, before he even spoke. I knew.

"I'm sorry, Brianna." He peered over his glasses at me. "The results of the MRI you had yesterday, are not good."

"I thought it was working," I stuttered. I could hear Niall next to me, breathing heavily in and out through his nose. I knew he was fighting the urge to cry out. I just felt numb.

"So did I, but I'm afraid it spread further, most likely before your procedure."

"Is it in my bones?"

"Your lung."

"I thought so. I ache there."

"And you have a cough?"

I nodded. Niall reached for my hand, squeezing it tightly. Peter addressed us both.

"I'm afraid, this is the scenario we initially predicted."

I nodded again. "Yes."

"There is one more course of action but ... I have to tell you, it is very much, last chance saloon. It would mean more surgery and more treatment. I'm not convinced it will work but I think we should try."

"More chemo?"

"In a tablet, though. Not as invasive."

I nodded. I couldn't stop nodding. The nodding was somehow tamping down the panic.

"Can I travel?"

"Travel?" Both Peter and Niall spoke in unison. I turned to Niall. I was going to say, '*I'd rather die in your arms, in the Irish rain, than in a sterile, hospital ward,*' but I couldn't bring myself to. He was coming undone. I could see it in his eyes. Instead, I spoke to Peter.

"We were about to move to Ireland. I was on my way there, many years ago. That's where I should be now."

He didn't need to know but I needed to tell him. He gave me a curious look, not quite sure if I was serious or not.

"We really can't advise this. Not at all."

I could feel Niall's hand start to shake, uncontrollably. His breathing quickened. I needed to get him out of that room. Peter sensed it. He handed me sheets of paper.

"I've printed off some information. I know this has come as a shock for you. I suggest you go home and read it, talk it through, and I'll phone you tomorrow at eleven, to discuss our next course of action."

We got as far as the corridor outside, before we fell into each other, clinging together, trying valiantly not to weep. Somehow, we got to the car in the multistorey. We sat and stared, unseeing, at the concrete wall in front of us. Numb.

"Take me home," I whispered. He nodded. Neither of us spoke. Thank God, Patrick was away in London, visiting Saskia, and I'd told the twins not to rush home to be by my side after this appointment. *'It's just a formality, really, a check-up, that's all.'* I'd known, deep down, that it would be more than that.

Julia sent a text, asking how it went. I texted back, *'Fine. I'll tell you all about it tomorrow. Going home to sleep. I feel done in today.'* I knew she'd accept that. It wasn't unusual for me to feel so tired.

We sat on the sofa, staring out of the window, Pip by Niall's side, me, clutching Niall's hand.

"I don't accept this. I don't feel like you're going to die."

"I do."

"Do you?" He stared at me. "Really?"

"I'm just so … done with it. I'm so tired."

"Yes, but surely that's just recovery?" He gave me a searching look. "How long have you been feeling pain?"

"A while."

"Why didn't you tell me?"

"Because I didn't want it to be real." I hated the look on his face; like he'd been betrayed. "The thing is, when they first told me – my God, that was a lifetime ago – after the initial shock, I saw it as a challenge. It was exciting! I know that sounds weird, but it was. I'd left Geoff, you'd moved in, with all your positivity. You made me believe I could conquer the world. It was like a new beginning. I almost forgot I was ill. And despite all the downsides of the treatment, the upside has been the past five months, with you here. So, I didn't want it to end, but it's taken its toll. On all of us."

"That doesn't matter. We're all in this together. We can still fight it."

"I don't want to."

Niall stared at me in horror. "Brianna, you have to! You must."

"But it's just delaying the inevitable, isn't it?"

"That's not fair. I can't accept you dying. I can't accept you just giving up, when there's still a chance."

"I'm not just giving up! It's got me. It's won." I watched him take his hand from mine, my heart sinking. He stood up. "Where are you going?"

"To make coffee."

"Niall..."

"I need to be doing something, Brianna. I can't sit and listen to this. I can't."

I followed him into the kitchen, slipping my arms around his waist as he filled the kettle at the sink.

"Stay with me, Niall."

He turned to hold me. "Always." His eyes told me what he didn't voice. *Don't give up.*

283

The silence, as we drank our coffee in the garden, was alien and painful. Even the sparrows in the surrounding hedge, had stopped their incessant chatter. They knew.

"Shall we have dinner out, tonight?" I ventured. It was the last thing I wanted to do but I needed to get a conversation going again.

"I'd rather not," he shook his head. "But if that's what you want to do, then that's what we'll do."

I sighed, frustrated. "No, it's not, but I don't want to sit here in silence, all evening."

He hung his head.

"Niall, talk to me! Shout at me, if you must. Just say something."

"Okay." He put his mug down slowly, deliberately. "I understand that you're done with surgery and chemo. I understand that you've accepted your fate. But what *you* don't seem to understand, is that when you're gone, I'm still here. Your children are still here. Julia and Curtis are still here. And I can't see a way forward for me, without you. I don't *want* a way forward, without you. So, forgive me but right now, I'm angry. Angry with cancer, angry with fate, angry with you. I know I shouldn't be but I am. Just … just give me some time, please, to get my head round this."

I nodded. I felt a tiny spark of resentment but that was quickly put out by the overriding feeling of guilt. I'd been so busy being buoyant and enjoying a new way of living, that I'd forgotten those initial feelings of panic at how they would cope without me. Initially of course, it had been about Geoff, and we all know how that went. I hadn't considered Niall and how he would deal with it. He's been so strong throughout – my rock – the one looking out for me, but who will be there for him?

We sat on the step of the beach hut, leaning against each other, cradling steaming mugs of hot chocolate. Kitty had given us a selection box of Whittard's hot chocolates for Christmas, and we were slowly working our way through them. The sun had set an hour or more previously, leaving the faintest glow along the far edge of the water, like a washed out, yellow highlighter pen.

Draining his cup, Niall stood up, apologising, saying he needed to stretch his legs, alone. I watched him walk to the farthest point of the beach, his image slowly disappearing into the dark. Pip whimpered after him but stayed by my side, her ears cocked and eyes hanging onto the last glimpse of him.

We hadn't spoken much. My brain was whirring with everything I needed to sort, yet again, but I knew I couldn't discuss any of it with him. Not yet. Then again, time wasn't on our side, so, when? How do I handle this and be sensitive to everybody's needs, not just my own? Where is that much-needed manual on how to die, stress-free? Maybe there *is* one; I should really check on Google.

The stillness was broken by the anguished wail of a wounded animal, in the distance. Pip jumped up, barking. There it was again. The hair on the back of my neck stood on end. My arms too. My instinct was to run towards the sound. I knew it wasn't an animal; rather, a wounded soul. A desperate, broken soul.

I found him, crouched in the sand between two branches of the fallen trees, his head buried between his knees. His

285

laboured breathing slowed when he sensed me there. Pip sniffed at him, nudging him to respond.

I squatted next to him. "I'm sorry, Niall. Sorry for giving you false hope. I always knew this would be the outcome. I just thought – hoped – I'd buy us a bit more time with the mastectomy."

He sniffed repeatedly, regulating his breathing before straightening up to look at me. I'd never seen such raw pain.

"Why did I meet you so late, Brianna? It's not fair. It's just so unfair," he choked, wiping his nose with his hand.

"I know, I know," I nodded.

"I feel like I've just found my purpose in life, and it's being snatched away from me, and there's nothing I can do."

I murmured, "I know," again.

"But *you* can. *You* can do something. You can grab whatever chance they give you, however small, and fight it, with all your might. We're all here to help you do that."

"But …"

"Yes, I know it's putting off the inevitable but maybe it isn't. Maybe you take that chance, and it works. But you'll never know if you don't even try."

I sat down heavily in the sand. He took my hand in both of his, watching me, waiting for a reply. I couldn't speak. Not because my throat was dry, or tears were choking me, but because I was suddenly struck dumb by fear. This is actually the end of the line. I've done the shock, the grieving, the heroic rebellion, the valiant recovery, the new lease of life. Was that really all in vain? Am I being defeatist because of fear?

Niall watched every flicker, read every thought, saw the fear I was battling with.

"We know what to expect now, with chemo and surgery. We know how it affects you, we know how to deal with it, how to care for you. Please, Brianna, let us continue that fight. Don't take that final chance away from us. Not now, not when we've come this far."

"I'm scared, Niall."

"Of course you are. I'm scared, too. But it's worth it, surely?"

"Will you take me to Dublin?"

His shoulders dropped. "You heard what Peter said. Dublin was just a pipe dream. You can't possibly travel, not now."

I thought about it for a long time. We shifted position in the cold sand, so we were half-lying, propped up by the branches. The water lapped gently along the shore, white foam illuminated by the moonlight.

"If I do have more surgery and treatment, you have to let me plan everything for the inevitable."

"How do you mean?"

"I need to sort out in my head, what will happen after I'm gone. And I know you don't want to hear it, but I have to talk it through with you."

"Okay."

"And don't argue, please. Just accept what I want to say."

"Okay," he reiterated.

I took a deep breath. "When I'm gone, move to Dublin. Curtis and Julia want to go, so do it. Make peace with your dad. Spend time with your brothers. And take Sean with you. Give him a good start in adult life. Look after Kitty. And Patrick. Get them away from Geoff – he's toxic."

"Of course I'll take Sean, but I can't be a father to him. I'm just not equipped to do that."

"That's not what he needs. He'd hate that, anyway. He needs a mentor, a friend. An adult friend. He's so vulnerable and I think he'll spiral, without the right care."

Niall nodded, tightening his grip of my hand. He knew there was more coming.

"Take my ashes with you, please. Scatter them somewhere in Dublin, as near to where my grandparents came from as possible. It's where I belong, I know it is. Or better still, scatter half in Dublin and half in Cork. That way, I've well and truly come home."

Voicing my thoughts made it feel less daunting and more comforting. I'm sure I won't feel this positive when the time comes. Right now, I feel like a romantic heroine in a novel, dying from the plague. Not far off, I suppose. Cancer is a plague. One I'd never really considered before. You always think, *'wouldn't it be dreadful'* – usually just before your regular smear test, when your head is full of horror stories relayed in the leaflets they always have at the doctor's surgery. But you never think it will actually happen to you. I didn't.

A thought struck me. "Needless to say, Pip stays with you. Love her always. Spoil her rotten. Oh, and always keep my biscuit tin full. That way, you'll never forget me."

He gave a sad laugh. "I'll never forget you. Ever." He pulled me close. "Don't leave me."

## *Ten months later*

The grey sky over Duke Street, in Dublin city, was heavy
with the promise of snow. Late afternoon shoppers, wrapped
up against the elements, hurried along the bustling street, in
a bid to finish their Christmas shopping. Warm fires and cosy
sofas back home beckoned, as the retail day was winding to
a close.

Further along the street, near the corner of the ever-
popular Grafton Street, and a stone's throw from the historic
pub, The Duke, a brightly lit shop was coming to life. The
smell of freshly brewed coffee and warm pastry, beckoned
shoppers in.

'Feenan's Gallery' had opened its doors six months
previously, to great acclaim. Tonight, was their Christmas
Late Night Bonanza, as the flyers touted, where everything
was half price; not just to celebrate Christmas, but also to
promote the launch of a debut album.

The shop, one of the older buildings along Duke Street, was
tastefully decorated for the season. A tree, covered in
garlands and fairy lights, stood in the far corner. Strings of
twinkling lights, entwined with swags of thick tinsel, hung
between the portraits on the walls. Maybe someone had
overdone the tinsel a bit, but the overall effect was eye
catching, without being obtrusive. Christmas songs could be
heard above the general hubbub, from a CD player on the
main counter.

Photographs of all sizes, some framed, some mounted and
some, boxed canvas, filled the whitewashed walls.
Landscapes of the Dublin coast, of the river by night, of

289

*bridges and landmarks, mingled with close-ups of plants, birds and butterflies. A striking portrait of Pip, posing by the water's edge, hung above the counter, taking pride of place.*

*Curtis, in a tweed jacket and festive bowtie, shook hands with customers and chatted amiably, while offering warm mince pies, and indicating to the trays of mulled wine and coffee on a long trestle table. Julia's laughter rang out across the room, as she too wooed the clientele.*

*Niall leant against the counter, a pile of CDs by his side, and one in his hand. He smiled for the reporter, busy taking photographs.*

*"Just hold it up, a little bit higher. Perfect."*

*The artwork for the album cover was striking; a tattoo design of a Celtic trinity knot, interwoven with vines of pink dog roses, and dotted with blue butterflies. In the top right corner, a pink ribbon, to symbolise breast cancer awareness.*

*The reporter put down his camera and held a phone to his mouth, to record the interview.*

*"So, what was the inspiration behind your debut album, 'Anam Cara'?"*

*"Ah," Niall gave a wistful smile, "I was living in England, when I fell in love with an incredible woman – Irish, by the way. I met her just as she was diagnosed with terminal cancer." He paused, looking out across the shop. "This was her idea, this gallery. And the album. She inspired me. She encouraged me to crack on with it. Music was my first passion, you see, long before photography." He laughed lightly. "I say, encouraged – she badgered me, daily, to make the album. Even though she was so ill, she never stopped pushing me to follow my dreams."*

*Niall watched Sean gingerly lift a framed landscape from the wall, talking animatedly to the woman eagerly watching him. A sale had been made. Sean glanced over at Niall, who gave him a thumbs up.*

*"That's her – Brianna – on the back of the album," Niall told the reporter, turning the CD case over. A black and white image smiled out at him.*

*"She's beautiful," he said, "like a Sinead O'Connor."*

*"She'd love that, thank you," Niall acknowledged, studying the photo for the umpteenth time.*

*The reporter watched him. "I'm so sorry for your loss."*

*Snapped out of his reverie, Niall looked surprised. "Oh no, you misunderstand. She's still with us." He pointed to the far side of the room, near the tree, where a wheelchair was parked next to a small, round table of food. "She's over there. Eating biscuits."*

*"Oh!" the reporter couldn't hide his relief.*

*"She's just had more surgery, hence the wheelchair. We hope it's temporary because she hates it! It makes her so miserable. She's an outdoor person, happiest scrabbling across a moor, or on the beach in the rock pools, with our dog, Pip. We have a cottage by the sea, just a short drive down the road from here."*

*"So, you're back in Ireland to stay?"*

*"We are."*

*"And is Brianna – I'm sorry to ask – still terminal?"*

*Niall gave a determined incline of his head. "Well, to quote James Bond, never say never. We're doing fine. We take one day at a time and just keep praying. She's brave. And stubborn. And she's back with her ancestors, which was always her dream. She finds her strength in that." He smiled, watching her take another biscuit from the plate, offering half to Pip, who sat patiently on her lap. "Personally, I think she'll outlive us all."*

***

*THE END*

## Acknowledgements

A massive thank you, as always, to my incredible family, Team Griffiths: Simon, Carina, Dino, Anton, Lou, Damon, Heidi & Ollie.
Not forgetting my three furry amigas, Phoebe, Polly & Ren, who supply me with constant cuddles and plenty of zen moments.

A mountain of love and thanks to my sister-in-law, Jackie, for all the invaluable info, messages & chats, and for being the initial inspiration for *Anam Cara*. She was diagnosed with Stage 4 breast cancer in 2013 and given a 10% chance of survival. She refused to let it beat her. She's still refusing.

Thanks to the residents of Corfe Castle and Studland, on the Isle of Purbeck, for always being so welcoming. Our children spent their childhood rampaging the castle ruins, dressed as soldiers or pirates; exploring the common, squealing in the playpark (they still do, whenever they come home for a visit) and endless, glorious days enjoying Studland beach.

As ever, thanks to Spotify for supplying me with an epic choice of music.
Thanks to Ed Sheeran for keeping me company on this one.

To my friends & family, Facebook family & lovely readers across the globe – you're all awesome, and you keep me smiling. Thank you.

Kristabel was only seven when she was transported to England, to escape the tyranny that tore Europe apart and stamped out her family. It's not until seventy-eight years later when she befriends her seven-year-old neighbour, that she dares to look back on her life and open the door to the past she has always kept shut.

*The Box* is a touching story about coming to terms with grief, confronting mistakes made, and growing old.

When the father of her eighteen-year-old daughter walked back into her life, Alice knew she was in trouble. She had kept their child a secret after he disappeared with her best friend, leaving her in the lurch and broken hearted. But now he seemed intent on picking up where they left off.

The consequences were far greater than she could have possibly imagined; exposing dark secrets, harboured grudges and a web of deceit that ensured life would never be the same again.

*Cobbled Streets & Teenage Dreams* is a tale of forbidden love, lies and loss, spanning three generations. It follows the painful journey of four women as they come to terms with the past in order to confront the present.

Printed in Great Britain
by Amazon